Cover of
DARKNESS

OTHER BOOKS AND BOOKS ON CASSETTE
BY SIÂN ANN BESSEY:

Forgotten Notes

Cover of DARKNESS

A Novel

SIAN ANN BESSEY

Covenant Communications, Inc.

Covenant®

Cover image © 2002 PhotoDisc, Inc.

Cover design copyrighted 2002 by Covenant Communications, Inc.

Published by Covenant Communications, Inc.
American Fork, Utah

Printed in the United States of America
First Printing: March 2002

08 07 06 05 04 03 02 01   10 9 8 7 6 5 4 3 2 1

ISBN 1-57734-985-7

Library of Congress Cataloging-in-Publication Data

Bessey, Sian Ann, 1963-
    Cover of darkness/by Sian Ann Bessey.
      p. cm.
    ISBN 1-57734-985-7
    I. Women travelers--Fiction. 2. Women teachers--Fiction. 3. Wales--Fiction. I. Title.
PS3552.E79495 C68 2002
813'.6--dc21   2001058407
                                              CIP

To my children,
Jonathan, Laura, Matthew, Anna, and Elizabeth
and
To the thousands of innocent men, women, and children
whose mortal lives have been cut short by
the actions of terrorists throughout the world.

Acknowledgments

I would like to thank my husband, Kent, for his meticulous editing of the first draft of my manuscript. His keen eye for detail and command of language contributed greatly to this novel. Thanks also to my friend, David Pulsipher, who gave of his time and talents to generate the maps included in this book.

My sincere gratitude to all those at Covenant who have worked so hard on my behalf—particularly Shauna Nelson for her unwavering support and encouragement; Angela Colvin for editing this novel; and Jessica Warner for designing such a stunning cover.

"Whether the wrath of the storm-tossed sea
Or demons or men or whatever it be, . . .
Peace, be still; peace, be still."
— MARY ANN BAKER

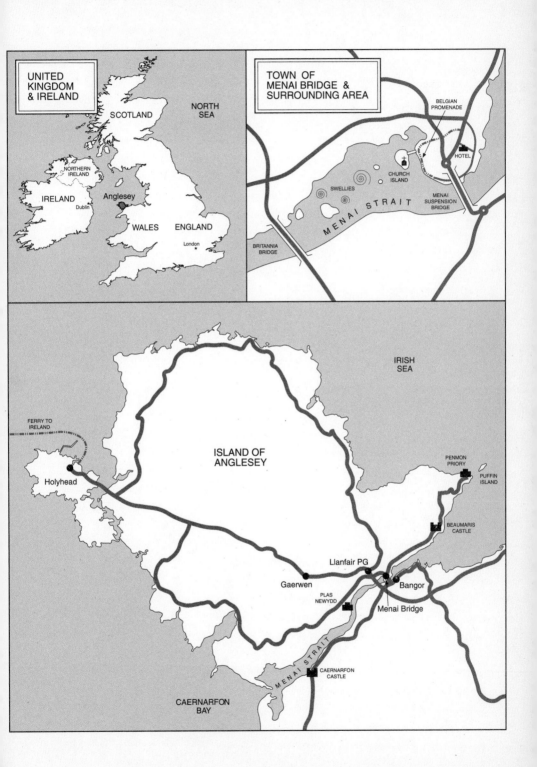

CHAPTER 1

"Now this is starting to feel like a real summer vacation," Fran sighed blissfully and leaned back in the wicker chair. The seat creaked noisily as Fran found a comfortable position and stretched out her long, tanned legs before her.

Megan spared an envious glance at the honey-brown, shapely legs and smiled over at her friend. "Oh come on! You can't possibly mean that all we've seen and done during the last ten days doesn't qualify as an amazing, exciting vacation?"

"Amazing and exciting, yes! Vacation, no!" Fran teased. "Megan, we've toured and admired every historic brick, mound, and marker between London and Edinburgh. Now that we've finally reached the sea, I, for one, am going to break out of the history-starved American tourist mold, and spend the whole day on the beach!"

"But, Fran," Megan countered with feeling, "don't you know what there is to see here?" She pulled a well-worn guidebook out of her purse and opened it to a dog-eared page. "Within a ten-mile radius of this hotel there are a couple of stately homes, half a dozen castles, an ancient priory, iron-age burial mounds, a nineteenth-century jail complete with gallows— "

"Mmm . . . now that's inviting," Fran murmured, lowering her sun hat over her eyes and appearing even more firmly entrenched in her chair.

Megan ignored her. ". . . not to mention the first major suspension bridge in the world, a tenth-century church on its own small island, remains of a druid stone circle . . ." Megan sensed movement out of the corner of her eye and paused. She looked over at her friend's relaxed form and caught the slight motion of her shoulders.

"Fran Brown, you're laughing at me!" Megan accused.

Fran pulled off her sun hat and let her mirth bubble forth. "Oh Megan, if only we could bottle up all your enthusiasm for anything old and divvy it up among those high school students you teach back home—oh, what joy history classes would be!"

Despite her best efforts, Megan couldn't maintain her starchy composure in the face of Fran's giggles, and her laughter soon joined her friend's.

"Oh Fran, I'm sorry," Megan said. "Have I really been an obsessive, compulsive tour guide?"

Fran waved her hand dismissively. "Megan, you know as well as I do that I'd be lost without you. If it weren't for your shepherding, I'd never have made it out of the Tate Gallery in London. I'd still be there a week after entering, trying to soak up artistic vibes, and would've forgotten everything else on our carefully planned agenda."

"But is that really what you'd rather be doing?" Megan pressed.

"Of course not!" Fran replied. "I have six rolls of film in my hotel room, full of photos most artists only dream about: landscapes, architecture, human interest, nature at its most beautiful. I know I'll never be a Michelangelo, but I can't wait to capture some of what we've experienced this week on canvas when we get home. That'll bring me more satisfaction than two months of gazing at all the masters' paintings in London."

"Well, I guess you've earned a day lying in the sun after ten days of marching to the beat of my drum," Megan conceded with a smile. She knew that her propensity for order and organization was a perfect foil for Fran's haphazard approach to life, but Fran's ability to pause and see beauty in everything around her had taught Megan to recognize the importance of slowing down and appreciating each moment. For the first time that day, she focused on the magnificent vista and allowed the quiet serenity of the morning to wash over her.

She wasn't sure how much time elapsed before the uncomfortable feeling that she was being watched began—but it was not long. Despite her best efforts to ignore the sensation, it persisted, and hesitatingly Megan turned to scan the patio where they sat.

There were half a dozen round tables set with white linen tablecloths, napkins, and silverware. Four white wicker chairs were placed around each table, but few were occupied. Megan's glance brushed over a young couple who had eyes only for each other, and a family of young children all engrossed in eating breakfast, then paused briefly on the waitress who was leading a dark-haired man to a table. The waitress was intent on her duties, and her customer's face remained hidden from sight as he was seated and given a menu.

Megan watched while they exchanged a few words. Then the waitress moved away, opening to Megan's view a man whose astounding good looks were diminished only by his frigid expression. He appeared tense as he swiftly surveyed his surroundings. And without warning, his eyes met Megan's.

Startled, and not wishing to be caught staring herself, Megan quickly turned away. But as she faced the beautiful scenery once more, she chided herself for not automatically exchanging a friendly smile or greeting. Surely that would have dispelled the prickling discomfort engendered by the brief encounter.

A little perturbed, she took a deep breath and released it slowly. Fran glanced at her, and misinterpreting Megan's exhalation said, "Pretty amazing, huh?"

Megan smiled at her friend. It was true. Beyond the small cement patio, a green lawn rolled down a gentle slope to end at a low brick wall. From Fran and Megan's vantage point, the wall resembled the lower portion of a frame, and the picture above was breathtaking. A blue sky looked down upon the majestic Snowdonia mountain range. The craggy granite peaks in the distance pierced the azure above, as though asserting their dominance over the scene. The gray of the mountain tops deepened into a rich green as the austere rocks of the upper elevations gave way, first to hardy shrubs, and then to the verdant rolling foothills. Clusters of homes sat along the base of the hills, shrouded in part by dense foliage provided by intermittent groves of trees. A pewter ribbon cut through the scene, and an occasional flash of moving color and reflected light indicated far-off cars traveling swiftly along the coastal road. Just below the thoroughfare, the foliage gave way to the turquoise waves of the Menai Strait.

Megan knew a little about this stretch of water, thanks to the reading she'd done before her trip. A narrow strip of the Irish Sea that passed between the island of Anglesey and the coast of North Wales, the Menai Strait epitomized the dichotomy of the ocean. On warm summer days, the glistening blue waves and exhilarating sea breezes made it a sailor's paradise. Yachtsmen from all over Britain were drawn to its beauty and tranquillity. But when storms moved in from the Irish Sea, the merciless gray depths, cruel whirlpools and eddies challenged even the most experienced seaman, and had claimed more than a fair share of human life.

The strait was narrow enough in a couple of places to allow for two bridges that linked the island to the mainland. Megan and Fran had driven across the Britannia Bridge—a rail and road link, and the most-used connection—the night before. But by far the more spectacular bridge was the Menai Suspension Bridge; and it was this edifice, in the forefront of the magnificent view before them, that drew the girls' attention as they sat on the patio of the Anchor Hotel in the small town of the same name, Menai Bridge.

"I'd like to sketch that," Fran mused, breaking the silence.

"The view?" asked Megan

"No, the bridge," Fran clarified. "Just look at the lines, Megan. It's perfect and yet it was built ages ago—long before all the equipment and computers we take for granted now. How did they do it?"

Megan reached for her guidebook again. "The Menai Suspension Bridge," she read, "was built by Thomas Telford in 1826. One of the design requirements for the bridge was that it needed to have 100 feet of clearance under the main span to allow for the passage of the tall sailing ships that plied the strait. This was done by designing a suspension bridge, with 16 massive chains holding up a 579-foot length of road surface between the two towers.

"The stonework was finished in 1824; then began the monumental task of raising the chains that would hold up the central span. Tunnels were driven into solid rock on either shore to anchor the chains. Then the first section of the chain was secured on the mainland side, drawn up to the top of the eastern tower and left to hang down to the water level. Another chain was drawn up to the top of the tower on the Anglesey side. About 150 men used block and tackle to heave the chains up to complete the span . . . "

A shadow crossed the page, and Megan looked up. It was the young waitress who had served their breakfast.

"Can I get you anything else?" she asked in her lilting Welsh accent, while deftly stacking the dirty dishes from the table onto her arm.

"No, that was great, thank you." Megan smiled at her and she returned the smile. "We're just enjoying the view from your patio. Do you need us to vacate the table for some of your other guests?"

"No, no, you're fine!" the waitress hurried to reassure Megan. "We've got quite a full house today, but not many people are up this early."

"Are you often this busy?" Fran asked.

"Oh, yes miss," the waitress replied. "In the summertime people come from all over—England, France, and Germany most often, but we've got other Americans this week too. A couple of gentlemen. They're not together, you understand. One of them's been here a day or two. The other arrived after you did, last night. Funny isn't it, that we'd have four Americans at once?"

Megan and Fran looked suitably surprised, and so the waitress, encouraged by her audience's interest, continued by lowering her head and voice conspiratorially and indicating one of the nearby tables.

"That's Mr. Marks. He's one of the American gentlemen. I haven't seen the other one this morning. Got in a bit late last night, so he probably won't be up for a while yet."

Megan prevented herself from immediately turning around to look at Mr. Marks, as the action would have drawn attention to the fact that he was the subject of their discussion. Fran however, who was facing him already, gave him a surreptitious glance followed by a humor-filled wink at Megan.

The sound of male voices drew their attention to the French windows leading from the hotel dining room onto the patio. The waitress looked up. "That'll be the young men from Germany. Here to climb, they are. I'd best see about getting them a table. You stay on as long as you'd like," she added, smoothing her skirt down with her free hand, and then quickly weaving her way between the tables and toward the doors.

Megan and Fran watched her greet the waiting young men. The previous quiet was replaced by exuberant voices in guttural tones, the sound of heavy hiking boots, and chair legs scraping on cement.

"Shall we go?" Fran asked. Megan nodded and picked up her guidebook and purse. She followed Fran around the edge of the patio, past a few flowering rose bushes heady with perfume, and toward the open dining room doors. She stopped once to look back. There was nothing left behind on their table, and the young men were busily placing an order for breakfast in heavily accented English.

On impulse, she glanced at the table occupied by Mr. Marks, only to find that he was the same man she'd seen earlier. Once again, his eyes were upon her—and his look was not fleeting, nor friendly. His intense scrutiny did not waver when their eyes locked, and Megan felt her color rise as he showed no sign of acknowledging her whatsoever. With barely masked disquiet, she mustered a weak smile before turning away and hurriedly entering the dining room.

After the bright sunlight of the patio her eyes had to adjust to the dark interior. The deep crimson carpet and wood-paneled walls seemed to soak up what little natural light entered through the open French windows. A few decorative lights augmented the sunlight with an orange glow, highlighting the polished sheen of the wood paneling. Wooden chairs and tables were scattered throughout this room too, and a handful of people who had chosen to dine inside rather than out on the patio were seated with breakfast plates before them. Grateful to be out of Mr. Marks's sight, Megan quickened her pace to catch up with Fran and they passed through the dining room, blissfully unaware of the other glances, both curious and admiring, that followed them.

To the casual observer, the two girls appeared very different from each other. Fran Brown was tall and willowy with long dark hair, brown eyes, and olive complexion, while Megan Harmer was small in height and bone structure, and her naturally wavy golden-red hair was cut short and curled softly to frame her elfin face and large green eyes. Much to Megan's chagrin, she had the pale peaches-and-cream skin often associated with red hair, and she enviously watched her friend's tan deepen each summer, while *her* limbs went through a three-stage cycle: white, red, peel, white.

There were easily noticeable differences in their personalities as well, but from the early days of their acquaintance, Megan and Fran seemed to have instinctively used their differences to strengthen their friendship rather than diminish it. However, it was actually their similarities that had originally drawn them together as teachers at the high school in Jackson Hole, Wyoming—deep-seated similarities that transcended personality traits and preferences. They both had an abiding love for the humanities, teaching, and the gospel of Jesus Christ.

Megan had joined the Jackson Hole High School faculty a couple of years earlier, fresh out of college. She had grown up in Provo, Utah, and upon graduating from high school, had gone on to attend Brigham Young University, located in the same city. Although she had visited the Jackson Hole area on family skiing excursions in her youth, moving there to teach was, for all intents and purposes, her first foray into life away from family members, long-standing friends, and familiar places.

She had anticipated the move with relish, knowing that she was old enough to be making her own way in the world, and equally aware that the love of a close-knit family would always be there as a safety net, should the need arise. She had begun that school year excited to have a teaching position and anxious to do well. And if student response was any gauge, she was an excellent teacher, despite the disadvantage of having to teach material that most young people considered dry and boring—American and European history.

However, Megan's success in the classroom had only slightly tempered the unexpected loneliness that set in once the initial frenzy of her first few weeks in Jackson Hole had subsided. Instinctively she had reached out for a friend at both work and at church, and was doubly blessed to find one person who fulfilled both requirements: the high school art teacher.

Francesca Brown had taught art at the high school for two years when Megan joined the faculty. Unlike Megan, Fran was a local and, as far as Megan could tell, she knew everyone and every place of any interest in the area. Her father operated a white-water rafting company in Jackson Hole, while her mother, well known in the area as a local artisan, provided many of the gift shops in Jackson Hole with intricately worked jewelry. It was Mrs. Brown who had insisted upon naming her daughter Francesca. She claimed that it gave romantic, artistic flair to an unimaginative last name. However, as soon as she was old enough to make her wishes known, her daughter insisted—equally adamantly—that her name be shortened to Fran.

Fran had displayed her independent spirit at other pivotal times in her young life. With her parents' reluctant approval, she had joined The Church of Jesus Christ of Latter-day Saints at the age of fifteen, thanks to the example of a few LDS youth at her school. She had left Jackson Hole after high school to attend a prominent art school in New York; but upon completing her course there, she had been drawn home by the beauty of the Tetons, and had taken a position teaching art at the high school. Although her talent inspired many of her young students, and she loved to see their skills develop, it was her time outdoors with her canvas that brought her the greatest joy. She was a gifted artist and her work had been very positively received at the galleries in town, and so her primary reason for joining Megan on this tour of the United Kingdom was to garner material and inspiration for future work. She was scheduled to take the next year off teaching, and planned to use that sabbatical leave to focus on painting.

Megan had dreamed of visiting Britain for years, and when Fran expressed a similar interest, she decided that the time for procrastination was over. She booked them flights in and out of London with a three-week interim, then poured over every atlas, guidebook, history and art textbook she could lay her hands on to ensure that they made the most of every minute in a land so rich with heritage. They had both agreed to pause their whirlwind tour for a few days on the Island of Anglesey. Fran insisted that she needed time to absorb the atmosphere and soak in the scenery, and Megan realized that she could easily fill a month visiting all the places of historical interest in that small corner of North Wales.

The hotel they had chosen was ideally suited, which was a good thing as it was also the only one in the small town. Built of gray, granite slabs well over a century earlier, the hotel stood on the main road into the town. The heavy, navy blue front door with an impressive shining brass knocker opened right onto the sidewalk, a few short yards from the passing traffic. But that didn't disturb any patron's sleep because the bedrooms were all located at the back of the hotel, looking out onto an incomparable view of the Menai Strait and the Snowdonia mountain range.

A narrow lane passed by one side of the hotel, and it was down this road that Megan had driven their small rental car the night before to park in a graveled area behind the building. From her bedroom window Megan could see their car alongside three others. She could also see the small patio that they had just vacated. A larger contingency of guests now filled the tables outside. The German boys were still there, and from this distance it appeared as though they were making great headway through an enormous stack of buttered toast that had been placed in the middle of their table.

A small family now sat at the table she and Fran had occupied. The parents were obviously trying to coax some cereal down their two young offspring—but with little success. Both children wore splashy swimming suits and had not yet relinquished their holds upon red and blue plastic shovels and pails. Megan guessed that the youngsters were anxious to be on their way to the beach and would only worry about breakfast when hunger pangs hit them in an hour or so.

There was no sign of Mr. Marks. His table was now occupied by a man with thinning gray hair and glasses who was completely immersed in his newspaper. Megan watched as the older man turned a page of his paper, apparently oblivious to the movement and noise of others in the vicinity. Then, turning away from the window, she expelled a long breath and ruefully acknowledged to herself that the earlier silent encounters on the patio had unsettled her. Not for the first time, Megan wondered why, and for how long, she'd been under Mr. Marks's surveillance.

She had little time for analysis, however, as a brief knock at the door announced Fran's arrival from her room next door. Fran entered carrying a bulging canvas holdall bag with her sketch pad sticking out prominently at the top.

"You won't mind if I don't come with you on your excursion today, will you?" Fran asked, although it seemed to Megan, since her friend was standing there with her bag all packed for the beach, that the question was somewhat perfunctory. She was right.

Before waiting for a reply, Fran plopped down on the bed, tucked her legs beneath her and asked expectantly, "Have you decided where you're going to go?"

Megan smiled. She couldn't feel bad in the face of such genuine interest. Besides, she knew that Fran would make the most of her day by the sea, which was just as important as how Megan spent her time.

"I think I've narrowed it down to either Plas Newydd, a mansion that dates back 500 years, or Penmon Priory and Dovecote."

She reached for a local map that was lying open on the bedside table. "They're only about ten miles apart, so maybe I could visit both of them," Megan added, as she studied the map thoughtfully.

Fran joined her at the table. "Maybe," she concurred, "but remember, you'll be without your trusty navigator."

Megan looked over at her and laughed. "Hey, that's right! I might make it to my destination without having to turn around for a change."

"Actually, I plan those little detours so we can see the real British countryside—you know, off the beaten track," Fran said.

Megan snorted. "Off the beaten track and paved road! You're just too busy snapping photographs to watch for road signs. Come on you faker, let's head out together."

Gathering up her purse, map, and trusty guidebook, Megan gave her room a quick glance to make sure that she wasn't forgetting anything obvious.

"What are you going to do about lunch?" she asked Fran, as they stepped into the hall.

"Oh, I don't know. I'll probably be close enough to the hotel to come back if I really want to, or else I'll walk through the town and see if I can find a bakery."

"That's a good idea," Megan said. "Maybe I'll stop at a bakery en route too."

They had reached the head of the stairs that led down into the main foyer when Megan heard voices below, and immediately recognized one as American. Fran, who was slightly ahead of her, peered down through the slats in the banister railing, then turned around and whispered, "Mr. Marks." Megan's heart sank, but she nodded and followed her friend down the stairs.

Tall, strongly built, and casually dressed, he was talking to the hotel proprietor. As though suddenly aware of eyes upon him, he turned and faced the two women as they descended the stairs. Not here on business, Megan guessed, judging by the jeans, khaki short-sleeved shirt, and tennis shoes. His hair and eyes were dark, and the look he gave them was penetrating.

"Ah, ladies!" Mr. Jones, the hotel proprietor, greeted them enthusiastically. "Are you finding everything you need?"

"Yes, thank you, Mr. Jones," Fran responded with a smile.

"Very good," he beamed. His short, portly figure and tendency to puff as he spoke reminded Megan of a small steam engine; even his bald head shone as though it were polished brass. He seemed to be a jovial man and anxious to accommodate his guests in any way.

"Let me introduce you to another guest from your side of the big pond." He chuckled at his own wit, and Megan found herself smiling at the fact that Mr. Jones really thought his comment funny, rather than that there was any great humor in it. "Miss Brown, Miss Harmer, this is Mr. Joseph Marks."

Mr. Marks shook Megan's hand. His grasp was firm, and she looked up to see his eyes upon her again. She was struck with the uncomfortable feeling that he was in some way mentally weighing her worth, and couldn't help but wonder what conclusions he had drawn.

"Nice to meet you." His deep voice gave no indication that he had seen them before. "Where are you from?" he asked.

"Wyoming presently, Utah originally," Megan replied, automatically following his lead. "Fran's born and bred in Wyoming." She smiled and gestured to her friend.

Mr. Marks shook Fran's hand, and she asked "Where are you from, Mr. Marks?"

"Boston," he said, "but I work with someone from Utah."

Before they could exchange further conversation, a clatter of feet and the babble of voices announced the entrance of the young men from Germany. They raised their hands in general greeting as they cut through the foyer on their way to their respective rooms. Mr. Jones called out a morning salutation to which a couple of the young men responded with nods and greetings in German and English.

As they disappeared up the stairs, Joseph Marks turned to the man beside him, "You've got quite an international clientele, Mr. Jones."

"Yes, indeed," Mr. Jones puffed proudly. "I often tell the wife it would be right useful if we spoke a few other languages. We get people from all over stopping here."

"Really? What brings so many to Anglesey d'you think?" he probed.

"Well, the scenery I imagine," Mr. Jones replied, "but we get all sorts. There's the outdoor enthusiasts, the families going to the beach, those that come up to sail—'course, they only stop off here a night or two. Once they're situated they usually sleep in their boats. Can't imagine being comfortable like that though, can you? Even some of those big fancy boats with their stabilizers, or what have you. I mean the strait's not like a calm pond. Bobbing up and down all night—sounds terrible to me, but then I've never been a boater myself."

"So people berth their yachts and boats nearby do they?" Marks asked.

"Some do. There's a few private landing areas along the coast within a mile or so of the bridge. There's a big jetty at Beaumaris, four or five miles down the road here. Some bring their boats in with them—from down south, Portsmouth area mostly."

"D'you ever see any coming in from Ireland?" he persisted.

The American was either obsessed with sailing, Megan decided, or needed some lessons in social skills. Poor Mr. Jones was all but getting a grilling, and she and Fran hadn't been part of the conversation since the Germans had come and gone. Fran's thoughts were obviously running along the same lines, for she seized the pause between Joseph Marks's question and Mr. Jones's answer to break in.

"It was nice to meet you, Mr. Marks. Perhaps we'll see you again."

Megan added her good-byes, and they both made a hasty retreat to the front door before either of the men really had a chance to say anything.

Closing the door behind them, Megan looked over at Fran who rolled her eyes expressively, groaned, and said, "Come on, let's go!"

Megan laughed and followed her friend down the lane. They reached the small rental car within minutes.

"I'll keep on going down this lane. It can't be far to the sea from here, so I'll let you know what I find," Fran said. She dug her sun hat out of the big canvas bag, smashed it onto her head, and gave Megan a cheerful wave.

"Alright. See you later," Megan called as she opened the car door.

Once in the driver's seat, she spent a few minutes carefully scrutinizing her local map before setting off through the small town. She was heading for Penmon, one of the northeasternmost tips of the island.

CHAPTER 2

The road to Penmon took her along the coast. The land dropped off to her right in a gentle decline that ended at the sea. Most of the time large trees and the rooftops of houses obscured her view of the Menai Strait and the mainland beyond, but every once in a while there was a break in the foliage or in the concatenation of buildings that allowed her a glimpse of blue. She couldn't afford the luxury of looking that way often, however. The highway meandered back and forth in a zigzag fashion, and Megan found herself driving with her left hand on the gear stick and her left leg tense over the clutch as she shifted up and down gears following the curves and slope of the road. She was grateful, on a road like this, that she'd already had over a week's practice driving with the steering wheel on the right-hand side of the car and the gear stick on the left.

Although the narrow roads still gave her cause for concern, Megan had passed the stage of hyperventilating when meeting an oncoming vehicle. She was gaining confidence in her ability to judge the width of cars—her own and those that passed by—and was quickly learning from the drivers around her. As far as she could tell, British drivers hugged their side of the road, moved along at a good clip, and if they needed to pass anything, they simply aimed their car for the narrow opening, closed their eyes and put their foot on the gas. So far she had never seen an accident, although she'd witnessed a few near misses. She offered up a silent prayer that this record wouldn't be blemished today.

After a few miles the trees began to thin, the road dipped down, and bright sunlight, unfiltered by leaves or branches, scorched the asphalt ahead. Megan slowed the car as she passed the sign announcing her entrance into the town of Beaumaris, and suddenly the sea was before her. Separated from the road by a narrow sidewalk and low granite wall, a pebble-strewn beach led down to the water. White caps curled their way up the sand, licked the pebbles, then retreated quickly, only to re-form and come again. A few people walked the beach; some were alone, some had dogs, and a few were being towed by eager children anxious to begin their exploration of the tide's morning treasures.

Farther up the beach Megan could see a wooden pier stretching out into the water. A large white building sat to one side of the pier with *Blue Peter Lifeboat* emblazoned across the wall in red letters so large they could be read from the road. It served as a somber reminder to the tourists milling about Beaumaris that the sea demanded great respect from those who visited it.

That this was a hive of tourism there could be no doubt. Megan followed the main street that ran parallel to the ocean front and wove her way through the congested traffic. She passed Welsh craft shops on either side of the road, and small cafés with colorful awnings that beckoned to passersby. Clusters of people wearing sunglasses, with bags and cameras slung over their shoulders, walked the narrow sidewalks, dodging the ice-cream stands and postcard racks along the way.

Despite the high-density tourist traffic, Megan received no forewarning of what was to come around the last bend in the main street. For the locals it was so normal that no thought was given to it at all, but for Megan, the sight was stunning. She gave out a gasp, and instinctively put her foot on the brake, only to receive a castigating honk from the car immediately behind her. Contritely, she inched forward again, desperately hunting for a place to pull over. A tiny space on the corner of the street ahead was vacant—not a true parking spot, so she wouldn't be able to stop and get out, but enough of a gap that she could pull out of the moving traffic for a few minutes. She did so, wound down her window, and gazed at the structure before her.

Positioned at the corner of the road, overlooking the seething mass of twentieth-century humanity and the sea below, was a magnificent medieval castle, complete with moat and wooden footbridge entrance. As Megan looked on, a pair of elegant swans floating silently on the moat glided under the footbridge and around the corner of the enormous stone gatehouse, completely indifferent to the passing cars and sightseers. Megan reached for her purse and withdrew her small automatic camera. With the car window still down, she leaned through and took a photograph. Then she reached for her guidebook and quickly found the reference she sought: "Beaumaris Castle, begun in 1295, was the last and the largest of the castles to be built by King Edward I in Wales. Raised on an entirely new site, without earlier buildings to fetter its designer's creative genius, it is possibly the most sophisticated example of medieval military architecture in Britain."

Megan gave a sigh and looked over at the imposing structure again. Somehow she was going to have to make time to go inside that castle. She just couldn't come this close and ignore it. She glanced at her watch, then at the rearview mirror. Cars were still streaming by and she didn't think it was possible to move from her temporary parking spot in any other direction than with the flow of traffic. So, she would stick to her original plan and drive on to Penmon, but she determined to return with enough time to visit the castle. This decided, Megan put on her blinker, watched for the smallest of gaps in the traffic, and moved off.

The hustle and bustle of Beaumaris quickly gave way to the pastoral farming land that gave Anglesey its historic title: The Breadbasket of Wales. Once the producer of most of the wheat for Wales, the green fields that Megan drove past were scattered with sheep and cows. The road veered inland slightly, and she lost sight of the sea for several miles. Rolling green pastures were interspersed with arable fields; blackberry bushes were rampant, along with hawthorn, gorse and broom. Another distinct bend in the road, and Megan could tell she was heading back to the coast.

Unlike Beaumaris, Penmon was still largely undiscovered by tourists, and Megan found herself slowing before a sign that read "Penmon Priory and Dovecote," before she had even realized that she'd reached her destination. The sign pointed to a worn footpath leading away from the road across a grassy hillock. She pulled the car off the road onto a small rectangular area that, although unpaved, seemed to be functioning as a parking facility since its surface was sandy shale rather than grass. There appeared to be no one else in the vicinity, so Megan carefully gathered her belongings, locked the car, and set off on foot, following the arrow on the sign.

It was not, after all, a long walk. Once Megan crested the rise, she could see the ruins of the priory below and to the left of the narrow path. She walked slowly toward it, soaking in the tranquility of the isolated spot. It was no wonder, she thought, that this had been a monastic setting for over a thousand years. The juxtaposition of the peaceful, rolling verdant hills and the powerful, incessant crashing ocean waves served as a constant reminder of the beauty of creation and the majesty of the Creator.

She took her time to walk through the two-story remains, noting the areas set aside for a dormitory, a dining hall, and kitchen. Nearby, an impressive dovecote, built about 1600 by a local landowner, drew her attention. The massive domed roof had once housed over one thousand birds, each in its own small hollow in the walls. It was cool and shadowed inside, so it was with pleasure that Megan walked out into the sunshine again and rubbed the goose bumps off her arms. Another small sign indicated an even less-traveled path behind the dovecote. It led to a holy well.

The well was rectangular, surrounded by slabs of rock, and protected by a stone alcove. Megan moved closer and looked down. The water was clear and only a foot or so in depth. The bottom of the well was lined with rock and littered with coins. She smiled. So others had come here before her after all, and in typical fashion had equated the holy well with a wishing well. Not wanting to pass up any oppor-tunity, they had left their coins and wishes for the consideration of the long-gone Welsh saints. She decided against adding her own coin to the bottom of the well, but instead turned away from the ruins and toward the sea. She walked a few yards to the crest of the hill and looked out over the ocean.

From this northeasternmost point of Anglesey the Menai Strait opened up into the Irish Sea. Two tiny islands were just offshore. The farthest one, she knew from her reading, was uninhabited by man, but was the home of many species of sea birds, in particular, the rare puffin. People were strongly discouraged from visiting the island in case they, in some way, hindered the puffins' breeding. Compliance was apparently high, probably because word was out that the island was also teeming with rats.

The second small island was not far offshore, and its sole denizen was a tall lighthouse. The black-and-white-striped imposing structure stood sentinel, with its mesmeric light flashing warning to all vessels that passed by—a warning of rocks, whirlpools, shifting tides, and treacherous currents.

Despite these hazards, there were many boats out at sea. Megan stood on the rise and felt the sea breeze buffet her gently. She could taste the salt in the air, and as the gray and white seagulls wheeled overhead, rending the air with their raucous cries, she could imagine how it felt to be on board one of the tiny yachts far out on the water. Their colorful sails billowed, and as they tacked from side to side, they appeared like butterflies, flitting about in the sun.

The ground dropped off sharply at Megan's feet, but the shore below boasted no stretch of sand to lure beachgoers—only large boulders, rocks, and pebbles, smoothed by the battering of centuries of tides. Megan was drawn to the craggy isolation, and on impulse she looked around for a way down. There was no well-traversed path to be seen, but there was an area a little to her right that seemed negotiable, so using both hands and feet she scrambled down between the blocks of stone until she found a large, smooth boulder at the water's edge, on which she sat and rested.

She wasn't sure how long she quietly watched the fluttering sails in the distance, lulled by the rhythmic swishing of incoming waves followed by the gravelly grating of moving shale in the swirling water below her perch. Neither could she pinpoint a time when she first became aware of the sound of a motor above the pulsing of the ocean, but suddenly it was there. And just as suddenly, the boat it belonged to appeared motoring in between Puffin Island and the lighthouse.

It was a large cruiser, white with royal blue trim. The cabin sides were polished wood, and sunlight reflected off a metal handrail that wrapped around the entire boat, apart from a small gap where there was a narrow ladder positioned on the hull near the back of the boat. There was no sign of life on deck, and the cabin windows appeared to be tinted. Whether this was for protection from the sun's rays reflecting off the water, or for the privacy of the occupants, Megan had no way of knowing.

To her unknowledgeable eyes, it appeared to be an expensive craft and was cutting through the water as effortlessly as a knife through butter. Just as she wondered why any crew would bring such a large boat in so close to a rocky shore, she watched the prow veer away from the coast and move out to deeper water. Moments later it was out of sight around the wooded shoreline. Large, choppy waves sloshed inland in the wake of the boat's powerful turbines, spraying Megan and her boulder with cold, salty water. Reluctantly, Megan recognized that the peaceful serenity she had enjoyed was gone, and she could not call it back. It was time to move on, return to the car, and from there, join the throngs exploring Beaumaris Castle.

**

Crowds were still milling through the streets as Megan pulled into the town of Beaumaris again. She had to circle through the town twice before finding a parking spot not far from the pier, but she enjoyed the short walk from there to the castle. After paying her admission fee, she spent a pleasant hour wandering through the crumbling walls of the ancient edifice.

She forced herself up one of the towers, clinging to the thick rope on the way up and the cold stone on the way down. For as long as she could remember she had hated heights; and although she routinely talked herself into believing there was nothing to fear, quivering nerves and a churning stomach would quickly take over as soon as she put herself to the test. And walking the castle ramparts was truly a test. The broken walls and precipitous drop to the murky moat below did little to instill confidence in her, but as long as she stayed at least two feet from the edge and focused on the horizon rather than the vertiginous view below, Megan was able to at least appreciate the splendor of the castle's location and its magnificent towers.

The almost perfect symmetry and concentric floor plan of Beaumaris Castle, with its high inner ring of defense surrounded by a lower outer circuit of walls, displayed an amazing level of strength and military advantage. Before the age of the cannon, attackers would surely have been faced with an impregnable fortress. Although she was able to marvel at it, Megan was overwhelmingly grateful that she would never have to live in that era dominated by cold stone battlements and harsh living conditions. It was with relief that she left the shadowed walls and walked back out into modern life.

Megan meandered through the main street, stopping every once in a while to admire the assortment of handiwork in the windows of the Welsh craft shops that lined the road. She decided to buy a sandwich at a bakery, and she ate it as she walked. The lateness of the hour and the sea air had given her an appetite, and by the time she'd reached the pier the sandwich was long gone and she soon succumbed to a craving for an ice-cream cone. Feeling rather like a child again, with her sandals beside her and her legs swinging freely, she sat on the edge of the pier licking her ice cream, her toes barely brushing the cold water below. She leaned back against a pillar and watched the bobbing yachts, some clustered in mooring not far away, others just colorful specks in the distance. The air rang with the laughter of children who were exploring rock pools and scrambling away from waves that threatened to catch them before they could escape. Seagulls swooped low, looking for leftovers from picnic lunches. They seemed to have no fear of the noisy people on the beaches and made bold reconnoiters both by air and ground, searching for neglected morsels, which once seen, would be gobbled up before other birds could contest the winnings.

Megan watched one particularly impertinent bird fly off with a large crust of bread in its beak, two other seagulls screeching their displeasure in its wake. It flew high over the pier, circled widely, then sailed far out over the forest of masts at the boat dock. And it was then, as Megan watched the thieving bird fly out over the sea, that she noticed the cruiser again.

It was no longer moving, but still out in deep water. It was fairly well hidden from the pier by the creaking, swaying craft already berthed at the dock. But the yachts served only to partially obstruct the boat from view, not to camouflage it. It stood out from the other boats in the area, both in size and style. If the motor boat was a pleasure craft, then it was intended for far more than the short hourly jaunts made by most of the colorful yachts nearby.

"Impressive-looking boat, isn't it?" The voice made Megan jump. Startled, she swung around and shaded her eyes from the sun so that she could look up at the man standing behind her. He was in the process of lowering a pair of powerful-looking binoculars, but continued to stare out to sea toward the blue-and-white motor boat.

"I wonder where she's coming from? Doesn't look like she's got a berth here does it?" he continued.

For the first time Joseph Marks's gaze wavered, and he looked down at Megan with an eyebrow raised.

Megan wasn't sure if he was really expecting a reply, but she was illogically anxious not to appear too juvenile in front of this over-bearing man. Grateful that she had at least finished her ice-cream cone before his unexpected arrival, she got to her feet and brushed the sand off her pants. Ruefully, she realized that standing up did very little to lessen the difference in their heights, so she took a short step backward and looked up at him.

"I don't think the motor boat's owners are from this area. They don't know the water well," she answered.

Megan drew satisfaction from seeing the look of surprise flit across Joseph Marks's face, but it was short-lived. Almost immediately his expression returned to one of intense scrutiny—not of the boats in the distance, but of her.

"And what makes you say that?" His question was abrupt, but Megan sensed something else too—an urgency. It was almost as though the enigmatic man before her needed information badly and didn't have time for niceties. He just needed answers.

Megan looked up at him again. She guessed he stood a little over six feet tall, and his broad shoulders and muscular arms suggested that he was accustomed to physical work. His hands, however, did not exhibit the calluses usually associated with hard labor, and she found that she could not immediately pigeonhole him into any type of profession. His dark brown hair was cut short, but not short enough to disguise the natural wave, and his eyes, which were now boring into hers, were the color of chocolate drops.

The thought made her smile, and suddenly, despite his repeated and unnerving surveillance of her, Mr. Marks wasn't as intimidating.

"I saw the boat earlier today," she responded to his question, and instinctively knowing that he was going to want to hear more, she continued. "I was visiting Penmon, the northeastern tip of the island," she clarified, "when that motor boat entered the Menai Strait. I noticed it because it was so much closer to shore than any other boats out there, especially given its size. It was only after passing the lighthouse that it veered back into deeper water. It just struck me then that the person behind the wheel hadn't navigated these waters before."

A flicker of excitement flashed in the dark brown eyes. "It sounds like its movements were almost furtive," Joseph Marks suggested, putting the binoculars to his eyes again.

"Well, I suppose it could appear that way," Megan responded, a little perplexed, "but I guess I assumed the navigator knew the strait well enough to know of its reputation for treacherous water, but not well enough to avoid bad patches, so he stayed close to shore hoping to avoid the worst of the whirlpools and undercurrents."

"But then had to balance those things against a rocky coastline," Joseph Marks supplied.

Megan nodded, watching his face curiously. Why on earth was he so obsessed with the blue-and-white motor boat? She thought back to his conversation with Mr. Jones earlier that morning. It had been about boats then too. Was it this boat in particular that fascinated him, or boats in general?

"I think I'm going to walk down toward the boat dock for a closer look," he said thoughtfully, then looking back at Megan he surprised her by adding, "Want to come?"

Megan could think of a million other things she could do with her time, and walking down to the boat dock with this mysterious man wasn't in her plan for the day. But she found her curiosity getting the better of her. Unlike Joseph Marks, she had little interest in the blue-and-white motor boat, but she discovered that she *was* keenly interested in why it fascinated *him* so much.

Feeling as though she were stepping out of character, and therefore a little unsure of herself, she responded hesitantly, "Okay."

He smiled then, for the first time, and Megan knew her first impression had been right. Beneath his severe facade, Joseph Marks epitomized the phrase "tall, dark, and handsome." She picked up her purse and followed him off the pier and along the walkway that led to the boat dock.

"Where's your friend?" he asked as they steered around other pedestrians, dogs on leashes, and strollers.

"She's at the beach," Megan replied. Then as he looked expectantly toward the crowded shoreline to their right, she clarified, "Not here. She stayed near the hotel. She wanted to sketch the Menai Bridge and the view of the Snowdonia mountain range from there."

"She's an artist?" he asked with interest.

"Yes, and a really good one!" Megan warmed to the subject of her friend's skill. "She's already making a name for herself in the Jackson Hole area."

Joseph Marks smiled at her enthusiasm. "And what do you do in the Jackson Hole area?"

"I teach history at the high school," she replied.

"Boy, they sure don't make history teachers like they used to," he teased.

Megan felt herself color. "I don't know if I'm supposed to take that as a compliment or an insult," she said.

Joseph Marks laughed. "Let me tell you about my history teachers, and you take it from there! Miss Cowan was about a hundred years old, give or take a decade—and was a fire-breathing dragon. Dr. Harold Smythe was as tall and thin as a scarecrow. He'd peer at us over the top of his half-moon spectacles and mutter about the inexperience of youth. Then there was Dr. E. G. Benson, he never told us what the initials stood for, who was as round as Dr. Smythe was thin."

"Okay, I can see that I don't fit their physical descriptions," Megan conceded, "but you still haven't told me if they were good teachers."

Joseph Marks gave her an appraising look, then said with admiration, "Smart girl! They were some of the best teachers at the school. Are you always this perceptive, or have I caught you on a good day?"

Without hesitation Megan retorted, "Has anyone ever suggested you take a class on social skills, or have I caught you on a bad day?"

Joseph Marks threw back his head and laughed. "Touché, Miss Harmer! I deserved that."

"Yes, you did," she agreed without a qualm, "and it's Megan. If you call me Miss Harmer, I'll feel as old as poor Miss Cowan."

"Megan," he agreed with a smile, "and I'm Joe."

Megan looked over at him. Joe. Yes, Joe suited him she decided.

They had reached the jetty, and stepped onto it together. There was a small office building halfway down the walkway, so they headed toward it, admiring some of the yachts they passed as they walked. Megan noticed that Joe's comments didn't go much past the color, shape, and size of the craft. He certainly didn't use the technical jargon she would have expected from a boating enthusiast, but then she wondered if he were just toning his conversation down so as not to overwhelm her. If so, she thought with irritation, he was really doing his best to insult her intelligence.

"Think I'll see if anyone in here can answer some of my questions," Joe said as they reached the office. Megan looked over at the dismal gray cement building whose green door exhibited various degrees of fading and peeling. A few notices were pinned to a corkboard on the wall beside the door. Most were weathered and torn. A few of the more important ones had been laminated, but were still discolored and suffering the effects of salt, water, and sun.

"I'll wait outside," she said, then she pointed down the jetty. "I'll walk a bit farther, and meet you back here in a few minutes."

Joe nodded, then turned and opened the door of the office. As he disappeared inside, Megan continued her walk toward the end of the wooden walkway.

She hadn't gone far when she noticed a lone figure sitting at the end of the jetty, and it didn't take long before she also spied a fishing rod and tackle box. She approached quietly, but the creaking wood beneath her feet gave away her presence to the young man and he turned around at her approach.

"Hi," she said, and smiled.

"Hullo," he responded, but there was no answering smile.

"Had any luck?" Megan asked, looking over at the fishing rod expectantly.

"Nope," was the reply, and if anything his face looked even more sullen.

Did teenage boys all around the world speak in monosyllables? Megan wondered. She dealt with this all day, every day at school, so she wasn't put off. She knew from experience that if she could just find a subject that interested this youth, she would hold the key to unlocking his tongue. She looked down at the fishing tackle at her feet. It wasn't spread haphazardly over the wooden dock; instead, each item was compartmentalized in a box that opened up concertina-style beside him. Everything was laid out in an orderly fashion, and nothing appeared broken, rusty or worn. Megan was willing to bet that this was a serious fisherman, and banking on that assumption she made another attempt at conversation.

"What d'you usually catch here?"

"A whole lot more than seaweed," the youth responded with feeling, and then the floodgates opened. "An' I would've today too, if it wasn't for that idiot Paddy and his idiot boat with its idiot engines! Churnin' up the water like a ruddy great big mixer, it was. Any fish with half a brain would be long gone before that monster boat even got close to the dock.

"But I didn't have nothin' else to do, so I stayed—just hopin' some fish were still around, hidin' in the harbor; after all, they're not known for their smarts are they—fish I mean?"

Not waiting for a reply he continued. "But no! Not happy with scaring off half the fish around, that stupid Paddy lowers a rubber dinghy, paddles his way over here, and at the top of his lungs starts yellin' at me. 'Is there room to berth here? What's the name of the dock? Where's the next closest one?' I'm tellin' you, I took one look at him and knew fish weren't the only ones 'round here with half a brain!"

He stood up and started reeling in his fishing line. "Anyway, by the time he left, just a little while ago, he'd made enough noise to clear out everythin' but the seaweed and barnacles. So that's it. I'm off." He didn't look at Megan, but focused on the job at hand.

"What's a 'Paddy'?" she asked the back of his head.

He shot her a quick glance. "You're a Yank, aren't you?"

"I'm an American," Megan corrected.

He grunted and bent over to close the tackle box. "Ever been to Alaska?" he asked abruptly.

"No, I—" she didn't have time to respond.

"I want to go there one day," he interrupted, "to go salmon fishin'."

"My brother-in-law's done that," Megan said.

The teenager paused, and turned to face her again, this time with the spark of enthusiasm in his eyes that Megan had instinctively known was there.

"Did he catch much?"

"Enough that he had to pay extra to have it frozen, packaged, and flown home," Megan answered. "He sent me some too. It was the best salmon I've ever tasted."

"That's what I've heard," the boy said, his whole countenance animated now. "Man, I hope those fish are still runnin' by the time I make it out there."

Megan smiled. This time he returned her smile, and in much better humor added, "And there'd better not be any Paddies around when I go either!" He gave the big blue-and-white boat in the distance a scowl before turning back to Megan and clarifying, "A 'Paddy' is an Irishman."

"Is the boat from Ireland then?" Megan asked with evident interest.

"Imagine so," the boy replied. "The man that rowed over here had the strongest Irish accent I've heard in a long time, and besides, only an Irishman would come down the Menai Strait without any kind of nautical map. I mean really, how dense do you have to be? He's askin' me what this place is called with the castle right in front of him, large as life!"

Megan looked over her shoulder and had to agree that the ancient gray stone walls, less than a mile distant, were an imposing backdrop to the small harbor. However, she also remembered reading in one of the many books she had devoured before this trip that there was traditionally considerable animosity between the Irish and Welsh people; although nowadays, it was usually only made manifest during international rugby games. She had a feeling she was witnessing some of that prejudice in the young man before her.

"Well, there are quite a lot of castles in this area. Maybe he just wanted to be sure?" Megan tried to tactfully defend the Irishman's actions.

The boy gave a snort of derision. "He hadn't got a clue about anythin'! He asked how far it was to the Menai Bridge and Church

Island. And then, he asked if there was a dock on Church Island!" The teenager rolled his eyes. "For cryin' out loud! Church Island is just that—a church on an island. The only people there are dead in their graves, and they don't need a dock!" He gathered up all his fishing gear and moved away from the jetty's end.

Megan fell into step with him and he threw her a sly grin. "And just so you know, I did speak to him—even though he'd completely ruined a whole day's worth of fishin'."

"Good for you!" Megan encouraged.

"Yeah!" he responded, and his grin grew bigger. "I told him this was Liverpool, and the closest dock was Southampton!"

"You did . . . but . . ." Megan stared at him incredulously and he started to laugh. She couldn't help it, she started to laugh too. "Well," she finally said, "if he believes that then he really is an 'idiot Paddy'!"

"Absolutely right!" the boy agreed with alacrity, and when Megan stopped outside the forlorn office building, he gave her a salute with his fishing rod, then continued on until he was lost from her sight in the crowds at the end of the jetty.

***

Megan didn't have long to wait. Joe Marks stepped out of the office and blinked as the full force of the afternoon sun hit him. When he noticed Megan standing nearby, he moved toward her.

"Well," he glanced at his watch, "that was a complete waste of twenty minutes. That guy hadn't looked up from his newspaper long enough to even notice the motor cruiser in the harbor, let alone know anything about it."

Megan walked off the jetty alongside him. She sensed his frustration, but couldn't figure out what would cause it; so she remained silent for a while, giving him time to collect his thoughts. Finally she asked, "Why is that boat so important to you?"

Joe looked over at her with a start. It was as though he had momentarily forgotten she was there. "Sorry," he said. "This must all seem crazy to you." He paused again before continuing carefully. "I've been waiting for a boat to arrive from Ireland. I know it sounds far-fetched, but I don't know anything about the boat—what it looks like, who's on board, nothing. I just know that it will be here in the next day or so, and I've got to find it."

There was a tone of desperation in his voice, and Megan noticed that his fists were clenched tightly.

"Well, that blue-and-white motor boat is from Ireland," she informed him quietly, and promptly ran into him because he'd stopped so abruptly.

"What did you say?" his question was intense, insisting.

Megan looked up to face him. "I said," she repeated, "that boat is from Ireland."

"And just how do you know that?" His voice was almost a growl.

"While you were in the office I had a good conversation with a young man who was fishing off the jetty. He had quite a lot to say about the occupants of that boat. They didn't make a very good impression, I'm afraid."

Joe Marks took Megan by the arm. His grip was firm as he steered her over to the low stone wall and forced her to sit down. He stood immediately in front of her and said, "Alright, from the beginning, tell me everything!"

Megan gave him a long, steady look. "Would you mind telling me why this is such vital information?" she asked.

Joe's eyes flickered from Megan's face to the blue-and-white cruiser and back again. He took a deep breath. "I can't," he said.

"You can't," Megan repeated, her voice laden with disbelief.

He did not flinch at her tone. "I can only ask you to trust me," he said.

It made absolutely no sense. Joe had given Megan no real explanation for his actions—including his unwarranted and critical scrutiny of her earlier in the day—and yet she wanted to believe him. He had been unyielding, but she felt no menacing threat in his presence. She had to proceed under the assumption that her instincts wouldn't fail her. Her hesitation lasted only a few moments.

"From the beginning?" she said, and at Joe's slow nod she began her account.

When she'd finished, he asked her to repeat it. After the second time through, he stood silent, looking out to sea over her shoulder, and Megan knew that he was gazing at the boat. Then he looked down at her and gave a small shake of his head. "Whatever did I do right to run into you today?"

Megan gave him a small smile. "Compliment?" she asked tentatively.

He smiled. "Compliment," he concurred, "most definitely a compliment. But," and he paused momentarily, "just as you think my social skills are improving, I'm going to ruin it all. I have to run and make a pretty important phone call." He pulled an apologetic face. "Would you be really upset with me if I left you here to walk back to your car alone?"

Megan hopped off the wall and gave an exaggerated sigh. "Oh, I daresay I'll survive." Then she added with a glint of mischief in her eyes, "I know all about pulling students from failing grades to an 'A.' It takes a lot of patience and doesn't happen overnight."

She gave him a quick wave and left with Joseph Marks's laughter ringing in her ears.

CHAPTER 3

Megan could see Fran sitting at a patio table behind the hotel when she pulled her car into the small parking area. She appeared relaxed and happy and was talking to a man with sandy brown hair sitting at the same table. Megan got out of the car, and as she did so, noticed that she'd left a dusting of sand on the car seat. Impatiently, she brushed her hand over the seat, but the small grains just bounced around and fell right back onto the upholstery. Megan groaned and decided to give up until she had access to a vacuum cleaner.

She stood up and ran her hands down her T-shirt and pants. They had the same gritty feel to them as the car seat. She peered into the car's wing mirror and wrinkled up her nose. Her skin felt tight, and she knew what that meant. Despite a thick layer of sunblock this morning, her face was entering the red phase of its three-color summer cycle. Megan frowned at the liberal sprinkle of tiny freckles across the bridge of her nose and upper cheeks. The closest she'd get to a tan would be a head-to-toe covering of freckles, but it wasn't going to happen, and she knew she was in for yet another sunburn.

Even from that distance, Megan could see Fran's long, dark hair shining in the sunlight. Seeing her friend's graceful elegance, as she sat in the white wicker chair on the patio, made Megan even more keenly aware of her own windswept appearance, and she ran her hands through her hair. The damp, salty air had turned her short golden waves into unruly ringlets. She grimaced at the reflection in the wing mirror. No wonder Joseph Marks had commented on her appearance. Her diminutive form sitting on the pier, complete with freckles, ringlets, and an ice-cream cone, could easily cause a casual observer to place her in a twelve-year-old age bracket.

She glanced at her watch. If she hurried she'd just have enough time for a much-needed shower before dinner. She started up the lane, but had not gone far when she heard someone calling her name. It was Fran, who had just caught sight of her and was waving from the patio. Megan waved back, and with one last reluctant pat to her disheveled curls, she turned back and entered the hotel grounds through the small gate in the garden wall.

"Megan," Fran called, "how was your day?"

"Great," said Megan as she reached the table and its two occupants. "How was yours?"

"Wonderfully therapeutic," Fran replied. "I'm close to finishing a couple of sketches of the bridge. I'll show them to you later." Then, suddenly remembering that they were not alone, she turned to the man across the table from her. "Richard, this is my friend Megan Harmer. Megan, Richard Garrett."

Richard Garrett, who had politely stood up when Megan reached the table, now reached over and shook her hand.

"Glad to meet you, Megan," he said warmly.

So this was the other American, Megan realized as he spoke, and she eyed him with interest. He was not as big a man as Joseph Marks, but his hand clasp was firm, as though he was accustomed to getting what he wanted. There was an air of confidence and outward refinement about him, and Megan couldn't help but feel that he was far more worldly-wise than most people she knew. In contrast to Fran's deep tan, and even her own deepening pink coloring, Richard Garrett appeared pale. His skin was fair, and even his eyes were a light, washed-out blue. He didn't seem to be someone who spent a great deal of time outdoors; in fact, she thought it likely that he was behind a desk much of his life. Fran's next words confirmed this theory.

"Richard works for the Ford Motor Company. He's one of the big shots in Detroit."

"I'm not quite at the top of the totem pole yet," Richard demurred, but he looked pleased with the introduction nevertheless.

"Have you been trying to talk Fran into selling her battered old jeep at home, in favor of one of Ford's models?" Megan asked with a smile.

"No, we hadn't got that far in our conversation," Richard Garrett replied amicably, "but it sounds like an admirable subject." He turned to Fran. "So how old is your current vehicle?"

He sounded just like a car salesman and Megan laughed. "When she tells you the model year, just make sure she tells you if it's A.D. or B.C.!"

Fran pulled a face at her and Megan laughed again. "I'm going to run inside and clean up before dinner. It was nice to meet you, Richard." Megan gave a little wave and hurried off toward the hotel's open French windows before Fran had time to respond.

By the time Megan returned to the patio, feeling far more presentable, Fran was sitting alone at the table, with sketchbook in hand, her attention focused on an exceptionally beautiful rose that adorned a nearby bush. Megan stood behind her and silently watched the flower come to life under Fran's pencil. It was a miraculous process that never ceased to fascinate her.

Fran suddenly became aware that she had an audience and glanced over her shoulder.

"Megan," she cried, "how long have you been standing there?"

"Long enough to appreciate your genius, Miss Brown," Megan responded with a smile. "That's really very good." She pointed at the sketch of the rose.

"Thanks," Fran smiled her appreciation, "but let me show you what I worked on today, and then I want to hear all about your adventures."

She pulled a modest-sized portfolio out from behind her chair and opened it on the table. Then she handed a couple of sketches to Megan, quickly followed by three more. Megan looked at them carefully. The first few were rough sketches of the view across the Menai Strait. She could make out the transition from the rugged mountains to the rolling hills, and the dark shadowed areas created by the deep clefts gouged out of the stark granite. The tree line and smattering of houses were discernible, along with the broken shoreline and swirling water of the strait. There were even a few marks indicating yachts on the sea.

The next group were far more intricately worked and more narrow in scope. They displayed the skilled workmanship of the bridge builders: the hand-cut slabs of stone, the beautiful lines of the structure, and the impressive balance and proportion of the huge archways supporting the bridge from below.

"Fran, these are amazing," Megan said as she sifted through them again. "How ever did you get these perspectives on the bridge?"

"There's a narrow road down there," Fran replied with enthusiasm. "It runs under the bridge between the first and second pillar. You can stand right beneath the archway with the traffic rumbling above."

"Does it take long to get there?" Megan asked, genuinely interested.

"Not at all. Maybe ten minutes," Fran answered, "and if you think that's worth walking down there for, wait till you see this!" She handed Megan her final sketch, that of a small island. Situated slightly off center on the island was a tiny building with a steeply pitched roof, miniature bell tower, and arched windows. Surrounding the building were shaded gray slabs of stone—gravestones, not standing tall and upright, but leaning this way and that.

"Church Island," Megan whispered.

"You've heard of it?" Fran asked with surprise.

Megan nodded, still gazing at the sketch. "How far is it from the bridge?" she asked.

"Only about five minutes," Fran replied. "I was there at high tide, but when the tide's low you can cross over to it on a narrow causeway. By the time I left, the water had receded enough that part of the causeway was exposed."

"So you didn't go onto the island?" Megan asked.

"No, I wanted to sketch it from a distance, and then I knew if I waited for the causeway to clear, I wouldn't get back here until late." Fran saw the look of disbelief that Megan shot her and grinned. "Don't worry, I haven't gone through a dramatic change in character! I didn't have a watch and I hadn't a clue what the time was; I just knew that the lighting had changed, and if I kept working it would mess up what I'd already done. So I'd like to go back tomorrow to finish what I've started and do some more sketches on the actual island."

Megan nodded. "I'd like to go there too. D'you know when the tide will be low enough for us to cross the causeway tomorrow?"

"Early morning and evening, I think," Fran replied, "but if I'm to finish that one," she pointed to the sketch in Megan's hand, "I'll have to go down in the afternoon too."

"I sense another day on my lonesome coming up," Megan gave her friend a wry smile.

"Would you mind badly?" Fran asked with concern.

"No," Megan said slowly, then added with a sly grin, "but I don't want to hear any moaning and groaning when I get back and tell you all about the Rex Whistler Room at Plas Newydd, which supposedly houses Whistler's largest mural."

Fran moaned right then and there, and although Megan took girlish delight in her friend's pained expression, she was prevented from offering any superficial consolation by the appearance of a waitress at their table.

"Excuse me, miss," the girl spoke hesitantly, obviously reluctant to interrupt, "I've been asked by a gentleman at the bar to offer each of you a before-dinner drink. I'd be happy to bring them out to you here if you prefer that to going inside."

Fran and Megan looked at each other blankly, and then back at the waitress. Megan gathered her wits together first. "Oh, how nice," she said, "Uh, d'you happen to know the name of the gentleman at the bar?"

"No, miss," was the waitress's reply, "but I believe he's an American too. Light brown hair, blue eyes."

Fran and Megan exchanged glances again. Richard Garrett.

"Would you thank him for us?" Megan asked, and the waitress nodded obligingly.

"Shall I bring them here for you?" she asked.

"Uh, sure, if you don't mind," Megan said, giving Fran an inquiring look. "What are you going to have?"

Fran turned to the waitress. "I'll have a lemonade please."

"Make that two lemonades," Megan added.

Looking somewhat nonplussed, the waitress obediently wrote down their orders and set off briskly to fill them.

"A before-dinner drink!" whispered Fran across the table. "Have you ever had one of those before?"

"Of course not," Megan whispered back. "I've no idea what correct etiquette is. Got any ideas?"

"Not a clue," replied Fran, but she didn't seem unduly concerned about it either, so Megan decided to follow her lead—accept the drinks graciously and relax.

Two tall glasses of lemonade arrived shortly thereafter, and the women had just started to drink them when a long shadow fell across the table. Expecting to see Richard Garrett, Megan looked over to thank him personally. Fran had obviously had similar thoughts, for she was looking up at the tall, dark-haired man with surprise.

"Hi, you made it back okay." Joseph Marks spoke directly to Megan.

"Yes, thanks," she answered with a smile. "Did you find a phone?"

He nodded, and she was pleased to see his natural amenable countenance, instead of the inscrutable face she'd witnessed earlier. Within seconds of that thought, however, she saw a complete transformation occur before her eyes; it was as if an emotional shield appeared, once again rendering his face impervious to scrutiny. Turning to see what could have brought about so sudden and dramatic a change, she saw Richard Garrett approaching their table.

"Hi, ladies," he called as he drew near.

"Thank you for the drinks, Richard," said Fran.

"Yes, thank you," added Megan. She noticed Joseph Marks look down at their full glasses, but he didn't say anything. Richard Garrett, however, did.

"Lemonade? Didn't you want something a little stronger than that?" He was carrying a long-stemmed glass brimming with a shimmering red liquid. Megan had no idea what it was, but could smell the alcohol across the table.

"This is great," Fran reassured, raising her glass to her lips.

"Yes, really it is," added Megan quickly, and then eagerly trying to divert attention from their drinks she added, "And Richard, this is Joseph Marks, yet another American staying at the Anchor Hotel. Joe, this is Richard Garrett."

The two men extended a hand to each other, but watching them, Megan saw a wariness in Richard Garrett's eyes despite his outward social grace. Joseph Marks had completely reverted to his taciturn demeanor and offered not much more than a grunt at Richard Garrett's lukewarm "Nice to meet you." After a few banal pleasantries about the weather and hotel location passed in stilted awkwardness between the two men, Joseph Marks excused himself, and, using the necessity of replenishing his glass, Richard Garrett soon followed.

Fran watched Richard disappear into the hotel before confronting Megan. "Well, what was all that about?"

"I can't imagine. Wasn't it weird? It was like they were a couple of angry dogs circling around each other with their dander up." Megan was completely perplexed.

"Not the two men, you goose," clarified Fran. "No one can have a decent conversation with Joseph Marks. He's socially retarded. I meant, what was all that about you getting back here safely and him using a phone? And since when have you been calling him Joe?" Fran pressed.

"Oh, that," Megan gave a small smile. "I met him in Beaumaris this afternoon." Megan gave Fran a synopsis of her activities that day, and told of her short time with Joseph Marks. "So, he's not as completely socially inept as we thought," she finished. "At the very least he showed interest in my safe arrival back."

Fran looked unconvinced, but said, "For your sake I'll give him the benefit of the doubt, but I don't think he rates higher than a 'D' on my grade sheet."

Megan laughed. "Oh brother, we're pathetic. Here we are thousands of miles away from the high school and we're still giving people grades!"

Fran grinned. "You're right. Let's forget these incomprehensible men and get back to vacationing. I vote for a real Welsh meat-and-potatoes dinner and an early night."

"Sounds wonderful!" Megan said with approval, and rose to follow her friend into the dining room.

CHAPTER 4

Megan set off early the next morning for Plas Newydd. Fran had started even earlier for Church Island, anxious to spend time on the island while the causeway was still passable. They had arranged to meet later in the day. Megan hoped to return from her day trip early enough to cross over at evening's low tide.

She made good time on the road, and soon found herself driving through extensive gardens and woodlands along a graveled driveway leading to the mansion itself. Plas Newydd, she had read in her guidebook, was given to the National Trust by the Marquess of Anglesey and opened to the public for the first time in 1976. Although its name meant "new place" in English, Plas Newydd's history stretched back almost five hundred years. The present manor, however, dated from the late eighteenth century, when extensive alterations were undertaken.

Megan admired the Georgian Gothic style of the stable block as she followed the driveway that led into the main courtyard. The pointed archways, spires, and tracery made elegant housing for the horses of the manor. Arrows led to a roped-off parking area just to one side of the main entrance, where she stopped the car and looked around.

The lush greenery of the grounds was beautifully manicured and tended, and the mansion itself stood overseeing all below with stately elegance. The main building had three levels, and a good portion of it was covered in dark green and burgundy ivy. Many of the large windows were arched and pointed upward to the spires atop columns at the corners of the building. A narrow gravel path circumscribed the mansion with white wrought-iron benches placed every few yards, inviting visitors to stop and enjoy the serene beauty of the estate.

Megan moved forward to a small ticket booth and purchased a ticket for entrance into the manor and its gardens. Then, armed with a folded map that highlighted points of interest both inside and outside the buildings, she entered the stately home. The rooms were cool and echoed with footsteps and murmured voices. The recessed, small-paned windows could not compete with the darkness of the wood flooring and furniture, and so despite the strategically located lamps illuminating treasures from the past, the rooms remained shadowed, their corners tenebrous. The heavy brocade wall hangings, faded velvet curtains, and bulky, solid furniture contrasted with cobweblike lace doilies, fragile china pieces, and intricately worked mantle clocks.

Despite the absence of human residency, there was an aura of past opulence and stateliness to the uninhabited rooms that impressed even the most fastidious of visitors, and evoked awe and virtual reverence. Megan spent considerable time admiring Rex Whistler's enormous mural—a fifty-eight-foot canvas painted between 1936 and 1940 of an Italian coastal scene. She knew she would have to report on the work to Fran later. Then she moved outside into the sunshine and down the winding paths that led to the gardens.

The gardens were layered in three tiers before leveling off and rolling down to the shore. Stone steps led from one tier down to another. Ancient balconies covered with lichen and surrounded by large earthenware pots of gently nodding flowers and manicured bushes greeted Megan as she reached each level. Once she had reached the lowest point, she took a small path off to the left and wandered through a huge, riotous flower garden, delighting in the perfume, the sound of busy insects, and the myriad of hues. Each plant was painstakingly labeled with its Latin and common name. Megan recognized a few, but for the most part the plants were new to her.

Once through the flower garden, the pathway became edged on each side by a towering privet hedge, and she entered an old-fashioned maze. Mentioned in the guidebook as the whimsical folly of a long-gone Marquis of Anglesey, the path twisted and turned, often forking into two paths without warning, which left Megan hesitating as to which way to go. After a while, she decided to abandon all hope of maintaining any sense of direction, and just enjoyed the wonder of it all. She hoped that if she chose paths that were generally heading uphill, she would eventually come out near the buildings on the upper level again.

She delighted in the creativity of the gardeners. The privet hedge circumvented trees, and the grounds crew had worked like sculptors, cutting back the greenery to create little hollows, umbrella-like over-hangs, and twisted curlicues. Her favorite examples of horticultural art were the tiny alcoves that had been cut out of the hedge—just large enough to accommodate a small wooden bench. Megan tried sitting on one and found that by so doing, she became tucked completely out of sight of other passersby until they were virtually upon her.

Perhaps that was why she overheard the conversation that was obviously not meant for her ears, or for that matter, the ears of any other tourist who might wander by. It took place immediately behind her on the other side of the hedge—so she could not see the participants, nor they her. But as she was already buried halfway into the hedge, she could hear them clearly, and as she had been sitting quietly for some time, they were thankfully unaware of their unwit-ting audience.

Megan wasn't even sure why the voices drew her attention in the first place, unless it was the sinister tone that accompanied the conversation right from the start. The first man's voice was coarse and thickly accented.

"Govn'r, a word with you."

There was a pause before a second man spoke in a menacing whisper, "Move out of my way, you imbecile! You were told *never* to make personal contact with me."

The first man spoke up again, and the strong inflection in his voice left Megan in no doubt that he was Irish. "Them rules are fer when things go smooth. What we got 'ere is a real problem. And you need to know 'bout it, 'cos I'm not sittin' out there in that bloomin' luxury liner like a sittin' duck while you're out 'ere playing tourist. And on top o' that, if I don't bring Seamus back a ruddy great case of beer, he's leaving, and I'm not luggin' the goods onto that ruddy great ship by meself!"

The second man cursed viciously. "O'Connor swore I'd be working with professionals—not a couple of sniveling drunks that balk at following basic instructions."

"Jus' fer the record," the Irishman's voice was brimming with anger, "I wuz throwing bombs and shootin' at English pigs in uniform before you wuz even born. I know more about givin' and takin' orders and survivin' in a ruddy war zone than you'll know in a lifetime."

A couple of deliberate footsteps sounded, and when the second man's voice came again, it was closer and imbued with pure malice.

"The minute you start making the orders around here, I walk. And you know how much your life's worth if that happens!"

Megan shuddered as a miasma of evil seeped through the hedge, as real as any fog she'd ever experienced. The cold fingers of fear and darkness that had swirled around her soon after the conversation began were rapidly strengthening into a strangling terror. Her horror at being drawn into the evil surrounding her only intensified as she realized why it was so easy to follow the words of the second speaker. His accent was no accent to her. He was American.

"And just what is this great problem that you and your sidekick can't fix?" the American continued derisively.

The Irishman replied with unveiled resentment. "The goods got held up."

"What do you mean 'got held up'?" Megan heard the fury in the American's voice, quickly followed by a thud and a grunt, as he shoved the Irishman into the hedge. A flailing arm hit Megan squarely in the back, and she swallowed a scream before it left her mouth. The Irishman struggled to his feet, cursing in protest, and Megan felt panic well up within her—she had to get out of there.

"Don't you ever do that to me ag'in, you hear me? You won't be the first man I've killed!" The Irishman cleared his throat and spat. "There's no suspicions. Nothing like that. O'Connor called. Said there'd been a problem on the line and freight's backed up down Dagenham way. Just means we got to wait fer British Rail to fix the line."

At this point the Irishman gave the American a graphic description of his opinion of British Rail, using vitriolic profanities that caused Megan to instinctively cover her ears. She offered a fervent prayer, and when she finished the Irishman was speaking again. He seemed to be responding to a question. ". . . most likely tomorrow's all he'd say, but couldn't tell which one it'd be coming in on."

"What?" the American's voice was rising. "And just what does he expect us to do? Wait at the station for two days?"

The Irishman's voice was sullen. "I dunno 'bout that. But I'm thinkin' I'd rather be standing around on a train platform than sitting in that ruddy boat waitin' for the coast guard to come callin'."

"Have they made contact with you?"

"Not yet, they haven't. But we don't stop in one spot fer long. Heck, we stick out like a sore thumb with all those bloomin' sail boats everywhere. I don't like it."

"Well, that's *your* problem." The American obviously had no time or inclination for sympathy. "Just make sure you're anchored off the island when you need to be. And don't do anything asinine in the meantime."

"An' just what d'you mean by that?" It was the Irishman's turn to sound menacing.

"Shut up! You know what I mean. If that idiot O'Connor ever finds out what train I'm to meet, let me know through the *usual* channels—and don't ever follow me again!"

The American's message was clear, and so too were the clipped footsteps that followed. The interview was over. Nothing more was to be discussed.

There was a long pause followed by a guttural and vehement curse, then more footsteps moving off in the other direction. The silence that followed was profound, but brought no sense of peace to Megan. She sat as still as before, but emotionally reeling, her back still aching from the blow she'd received.

Looking down, Megan noticed that her hands were trembling. She balled them up into tight fists, stood up decisively, picked up her purse, and moved away from the bench. Her steps were slow at first as she focused on remaining calm, breathing evenly, and drawing no attention to herself; but as soon as she'd put a little distance between herself and the bench, she took flight. It was as though her subconscious clung to the hope that by removing herself physically from the area she could also expunge the words she'd heard and the violence she'd experienced.

She let out a sob of gratitude when she turned a corner between two tall hedgerows and discovered that it opened up onto the rolling green lawn beside the manor itself. As she reached the graveled pathway that led around the building, Megan clung to the security of being surrounded by other milling visitors. She forced herself to stop and turn back to survey the scene below her. It was the same beautiful, serene view that had enchanted her not more than a couple of hours before. The backdrop of mountains, the blue sea scintillating in the sunlight, the lush hedgerows and blankets of green grass that encircled flowerbeds of kaleidoscopic colors—these things were all the same, but somehow the place had lost its magical charm and Megan felt cheated that something so wholly out of her control had had the power to mar her experience at Plas Newydd so completely.

She turned and gazed up at the majestic building beside her one last time, then with fear still stalking her, she walked briskly back to the car. Instinctively, she locked the doors as soon as she was seated, and then in that comparable safety, she bowed her head and offered another prayer—this time one of gratitude for the protection she had received and a request for peace and wisdom as she dealt with the memories of her experience.

Ugly images tormented her as she returned to the hotel. Snippets of the men's conversation came back in disjointed fragments, but it was not the words per se that concerned Megan now; it was the ambiance of evil that permeated them that disturbed her most. She found that she could not separate the two, and so her frustration and distress mounted; as convinced as she was that the men and the "job" they described were at odds with the law, she had no tangible proof at all. If being in a foreign country and ignorant of the law enforcement system was not deterrent enough, Megan realized, with bitterness, that no Welsh police officer would ever take her seriously. She could supply no names, no faces, no places. She didn't even know what the "goods" were.

Megan slowed the car as she approached a roundabout. Mechanically, she worked the gears, following the stream of vehicles heading toward Menai Bridge, and as she did so, she tried to organize her thoughts. What did she really know? Well, some kind of "job" was about to take place that involved at least one American and three Irishmen. She could remember the names Seamus and O'Connor, but was also aware that handing those to authorities would be like handing the names John and Smith to the police back home—only one stage short of useless. The job had been held up by a problem with the rail service because "the goods" were to arrive by train, be picked up by the American at the station, and transferred by the unnamed Irishman and Seamus to a ship offshore—a vessel that stuck out as different among all the yachts in the Menai Strait.

And then it hit her. Megan's heart began to pound, and as the implications unfolded in her mind, she discovered that her hands on the steering wheel had begun to tremble again. Not only did she know of a fancy blue-and-white motor boat plying the coast of Anglesey, crewed by Irishmen, she also knew of an American obsessively interested in the movements of that boat.

It had to be. It just had to be. Too many pieces of the puzzle fell into place to reject the theory outright, and yet, without knowing why, the thought that Joe Marks could be involved in something so scheming made her want to cry. She acknowledged to herself that her first impression of him had not been positive. In fact, she knew that if she were to share the events of this morning with Fran, her friend would have Joe clapped in irons and thrown into prison without a qualm. At the very least she would march Megan down to the local police station to file a report.

But as Megan pulled the car into the small parking lot next to the hotel, stopped, and took the key out of the ignition, she knew that she couldn't do it. She couldn't tell Fran right now. She couldn't go to the police right now. She may feel guilty about it for the rest of her life, but she couldn't accuse Joe Marks of orchestrating something heinous—whatever it was—without more concrete evidence. She couldn't believe that an evil nature so potent as to frighten her as a mere observer, could not have been felt while communicating with him one on one, as she had in Beaumaris.

Megan left the car and walked slowly up the hill to the hotel entrance. She would have to be on her guard. If she noticed anything that shed light on these intrigues, she would have to act. But for now she would conceal her suspicions about Joe and the mysterious motor boat—even from Fran. Somehow she was going to have to go on with her life as though the nightmarish experience in the maze had never occurred. She shuddered. Maybe that was possible during daylight hours, but she prayed her nights would be spared the specter of suppressed memories.

***

There was no sign of Fran at the hotel, so after freshening up and grabbing a small bite to eat, Megan decided to go in search of her. She walked down the hill past the hotel and the parking area, and on toward the sea. The lane meandered down a fairly steep decline with tall, gray, stone houses standing sentinel along each side of the road. Their front doors opened right onto the road, as the lane was too narrow to create a sidewalk. She could hear the distant humming of cars, but didn't meet a single vehicle herself. Even so, she stuck close to the edge of the pavement, afraid that an oncoming car would have little forewarning of pedestrians around the bends.

The sun was hot. Its rays beat down on the asphalt where they were soaked up, then released to shimmer upward in undulating waves. Megan pulled the wide brim of her sun hat a little farther down to protect her face, then raised her head in pleasure as she turned the last bend in the lane and felt the sea breeze touch her skin and fan away the heat that had seemed so oppressive only seconds before.

She had reached the small road that followed the coastline. Houses lined it on one side, facing out to sea. An ancient low stone wall, so commonplace in Britain but still a delight to Megan, followed the other side of the road. She walked over to it, leaned her hands on its scabrous surface, and looked out over the water. Immediately below her was a drop of about five feet. There was a narrow strip of rocky beach strewn with black and dark green slimy seaweed, a variety of crustaceans clinging to rocks, some waterlogged driftwood, and an occasional piece of litter. Less than two yards from the wall the sea licked its way forward, filling rock pools with swirling foam before ebbing and flowing again. The tide was still high.

Megan moved on, choosing to turn right toward the Menai Suspension Bridge. She had not received clear directions from Fran, but she thought this would have been the route she would have taken when she stumbled upon Church Island. Before long the rumble of cars became more distinct, and looking uphill Megan could see the tops of vehicles entering the access road that led onto the bridge. Then suddenly she was beneath them. A huge granite pillar stood to one side of her, its base anchored on an immense slab of rock below the stone wall. Flawless arches thrust upwards over her head, bearing the load of the road above. Two other pillars stood solidly beside the first, each connected by archways and the ribbon of road. Water lapped at their bases, and the rectangular-cut rocks, like oversized monolithic bricks, were discolored by the briny liquid. However, this did little to lessen their magnificence.

Megan stood in silence, marveling at the craftsmen who had the talent and vision to create such an edifice. It was difficult not to feel very small and insignificant beside the strength of the towering pillars. She shook her head in wonder, then stepped out of the shade provided by the cold stone above and continued down the road. Only a few yards farther on, a series of short cement poles stood in a row across the roadway, preventing vehicles from going any farther. Megan slipped through a narrow gap between two of the poles and entered the Belgian Promenade.

She had read a little about the walkway. It had originally been built by Belgian prisoners of war during World War II, and remained a popular footpath, although it was used primarily by local residents as its existence was not widely advertised to the tourists. There were no houses along the cement promenade. A continuation of the earlier stone wall separated her from the ocean on one side, and on the other the fecund hillside displayed its verdant offspring: grass, bushes, wild-flowers, and small trees. Farther up Megan could see groves of more mature trees, many of them evergreens, but all now in full leaf, displaying various shades of green. And then finally, just ahead, Megan caught her first glimpse of Church Island.

It was a tiny island not very far from the main island of Anglesey—less than a quarter of a mile, Megan guessed. Its entrance was marked by a wrought-iron gate that leaned slightly to one side, opening onto a narrow graveled path that led from the gate, over a slight rise, and then out of sight. A solitary building stood solemnly on the rise. Simple in style, it was built of a light brown stone with a steeply pitched slate roof. The only clue that the building could be ecclesiastical in nature was a diminutive bell tower that doubled as a steeple on one end of the roof. The remainder of the island was covered in grass, small shrubs, and gravestones.

As Megan drew nearer, she saw a break in the stone wall to her left. It led onto the cement causeway that cut across the inlet at that point and joined Church Island immediately below the sagging iron gate. Megan paused and looked across. The tide was beginning to recede, and the causeway was exposed on the two ends, but the center was still completely submerged.

As she stood deliberating, trying to estimate how long it would take before the causeway was dry enough for her to venture across, she heard a faint voice. She looked up at the island again, and there, standing on the top of the rise not far from the church, was Fran. Dressed in her khaki shorts and green T-shirt, it would have been easy to miss her as she blended in with her surroundings, but at that moment Fran was waving furiously and shouting to attract Megan's attention. Once she realized that she had it, she pointed at the flooded causeway and shrugged dramatically. Megan waved back and laughed. She could guess what had happened. Fran had made it to the island during the early morning low tide, but hadn't kept track of the time once there. She was marooned until the causeway reappeared.

Fran raised her sketch pad high and pointed at it. Megan waved again. She knew Fran would make the most of her time on the island and would be excited to show her the fruits of her labor later that evening. She watched her friend disappear over the rise again, then turned around herself and decided to follow the road a little longer to see where it would lead.

Not many yards farther on, she noticed a signed footpath that took off at an angle, weaving up through the trees to her right. On impulse, Megan decided to follow it. The coolness of the shade was inviting after walking so long in the blistering sun, and the carpet of pine needles a welcome change from the baking asphalt and cement. Gnarled tree roots wove in and out of the footpath, sometimes acting as natural stairs on the steep slopes, other times as obstacles to trip the unsuspecting walker. Delicate harebells, sky blue in color, thrived under the great trees' protection. Birds sang and flew by, seemingly oblivious to Megan's approach, and although she followed a well-worn path, she saw no one else until at last she emerged at the top of the hill and found herself at a lay-by alongside the main road leading into the town of Menai Bridge. She had made a big loop by going downhill on one side of the suspension bridge and uphill on the other, and had returned not more than half a mile from her hotel. Pleased with her discovery, Megan walked back into town and spent a pleasant couple of hours browsing through the small shops as she waited for low tide.

CHAPTER 5

The evening sun was lowering as Megan made her way down the lane once more. The sea breeze was stronger than it had been earlier in the afternoon, and as she followed the seawall, it teased the wisps of hair beneath her sun hat and cooled her skin. The tide was well out and had left behind a dark, damp wasteland over which seagulls swirled and swooped with territorial greed. The air was filled with their shrill cries, and the smell of salt was so strong that Megan could taste it.

She had almost reached the causeway when she met Fran, loaded up with art supplies, and heading her way.

"Megan," she called, "I'd just about given up on you. Are you still planning to go onto the island?"

Megan stopped and waited for her friend to reach her. "Yes, I was hoping to meet you there. I guess I waited a bit too long."

"Well, since I've been there *all day,* I thought I'd spend the evening elsewhere," Fran responded. "And besides that, I'm absolutely starving!"

Megan laughed. "You didn't watch the tide, did you?"

Fran's expression was sheepish. "I know, I'm an idiot. My stomach's been growling at me, telling me just what it thinks for hours. But," her face lit up, "I've got some great work to show for it!"

"I knew you would," Megan smiled at her friend. "And I can't wait to see it. But since your priority right now is eating, how about if I go over to the island while you get some dinner, then I'll meet you back at the hotel in a little while?"

"Sounds like a plan," approved her friend as she reshouldered her oversized canvas bag, gave Megan a small wave, and started forward again. She hadn't gone more than a few steps, however, before she turned and called back, "Megan, be sure to get inside the church before the sun goes down. There's a simple stained-glass window that's really beautiful. You'll miss it if it's too dark."

"Okay, thanks!" Megan called back and waved once more.

She quickened her pace and was soon at the break in the stone wall where the causeway began. This time it was completely exposed, and the warmth of the day had dried off any remaining puddles of seawater on the cement. Its whiteness was a stark contrast to the black, muddy sand and shale below. Megan walked across and opened the black iron gate. It creaked in protest when she pushed against it, and clanged shut heavily behind her as she passed through.

She decided to take Fran's advice and go straight to the church, but she glanced around with interest as she walked. The small gravel path was well tended, but the grass on either side was long and shared its growing space with weeds and wildflowers. Headstones of all sizes and shapes dotted the island, making mowing an impossibility. Some markers appeared fairly new: the polished stones retained their luster and the inscribed text was easy to read. Others, obviously much older, were leaning badly, or had begun to crumble as time and the salty air took their toll. A handful of hardy trees battled for survival on the island, along with some untamed bushes—gorse, broom, and blackberry among them. Although gnarled with age, none of the trees were excessively tall or large in diameter, and Megan guessed that perhaps the soil wasn't particularly deep or fertile on this rocky parcel of land stolen from the sea.

The church itself sat in a shallow hollow just over the crest of the rise. Not more than eighteen square feet, the ancient stone walls had been worn smooth by centuries of battering elements. A slate plaque hanging above the door stated simply: A.D. 960. Megan stood, gazing at it in wonder. How many thousands of people had crossed this very threshold? Individuals from countless generations, all drawn by their need to commune with God.

She grasped the large iron ring in the door and turned it. The metal latch grated against its casing as it moved upward and was released. Then Megan gently pushed the solid wooden door and it swung open over a single stone step. The step, hollowed into a concave shape by the feet of numerous worshipers and mourners, led down into the chapel itself.

The walls were whitewashed, and the floor of paved flagstones was polished smooth. A single aisle led up to a simple wooden lectern. On either side of the aisle were four wooden benches, wide enough to seat three or four people. Brass candlesticks containing half-burned white candles were placed around the room so as to light up the shadowed corners and pulpit. Narrow arched windows on each side of the room admitted the warm glow of the evening sun, highlighting the amber luster of the polished wooden pews, and spotlighting dancing dust particles that spun through the air. Spots of evanescent color and miniature rainbows pirouetted across the walls and stone floor as the solitary stained-glass window behind the pulpit proclaimed a valiant and final adieu to the setting sun.

Compared to the grand and elaborate stained-glass windows Megan had admired in the many cathedrals she'd visited during the past week, the one before her was very humble. Set back in a deep arched recess, it was perhaps three feet high and two feet wide. A simple cross in gold tones was surrounded by glass pieces in a myriad of hues. The pieces, of varying sizes and shapes, had been soldered together by a rustic hand to create an unpretentious work of art. Vivid blue, red, and green blended with subdued rose, violet, and turquoise to sprinkle the white-washed walls with soft color.

Reverently, Megan took off her sun hat and walked over to the closest pew. She sat in quiet contemplation for some time, enjoying the peace that seemed to radiate from the tiny chapel. Then, as she noticed the deepening shadows and the gradual fading of the flickering beams of light, she rose and quietly approached the old wooden collection box standing beside the door. She dropped a few coins in and let herself out into the twilight.

She paused at the church door, unwilling to return immediately to the cacophony of ordinary life. A glance at the sea reassured her that she had a little more time before the causeway became impassable once again, so rather than retrace her steps to the gate, she turned and continued down the path that meandered through the gravestones. She paused every so often to read a name or date on a headstone—so many young children, and so long ago. She looked up

into the indigo sky, the fingers of darkness closing over the light blue
of day, and wondered about these people of bygone eras. Were they
looking down upon her now?

The path led her gradually around to the iron gate entrance.
Once there, Megan turned and looked back at the church and
surrounding gravestones, silhouetted against the dark sky. The spirit
of the place was almost palpable, and she was thankful to have experienced it firsthand. She opened the weary gate, closing it carefully
behind her, then walked across the causeway.

Dusk lingered during British summers, so although the road was not
lit, Megan was able to see her way quite well. The sensation of perpetual
motion, created by the ocean waves, was echoed on land by the flickering shadows of the tree branches twitching in the evening breeze.

It was a few minutes before Megan registered the sound of footsteps drawing nearer—firm footsteps, not those of someone out for a
casual saunter beneath the moon, she thought. When the person
emerged from the shadows, she stopped.

"Hello, Richard," she said with surprise.

"Megan? It is Megan, isn't it?" he responded, stepping closer.

"Yes, that's right, Megan Harmer."

Richard Garrett looked down at her curiously. His pale face and
eyes seemed even more wan in the moonlight. Megan inwardly
squirmed at his unblinking stare and took an instinctive step backward. He must have sensed her unease, for he smiled.

"Whatever are you doing out here at this time of night? Is Fran
with you too?"

Megan gave a small laugh and glanced at her wrist watch. "No,
but I'm afraid Fran's tendency to lose track of time is rubbing off on
me. I hadn't realized how late it was until I started back from Church
Island."

She saw a flicker of interest in the eyes that hadn't yet left her face.
"You've been over to the island?"

"Yes," she replied and, unable to contain her enthusiasm added,
"what a wonderful place! Is that where you're headed?"

Richard raised his eyes for the first time and looked across at the
island over Megan's shoulder. "Yes," he said slowly, "that was my
intention. Just to look it over."

Megan followed his gaze. "You may have to hurry. The causeway was passable when I crossed, but the tide has turned and will move in quickly now." She paused. "It's going to be quite dark over there too. I didn't see anyone else, and there's no light at the church—I'm not even sure that it has electricity."

Richard nodded. "You're right of course, but I did bring a flashlight with me, so I'll make it a brief visit and watch for the tide."

"Well I'd better not keep you any longer then," Megan said, and moved to one side. "I hope you enjoy it as much as I did."

"Yes," Richard said automatically, still focusing on the island. Then he seemed to recollect himself and turned to Megan once more. He smiled at her and gave her a small salute with the pencil-sized flashlight that he'd just drawn out of his pocket. "See you later then!"

Megan watched him go for a few seconds. How peculiar that he would chose to visit the island when it was almost too dark to see anything. And even more peculiar was the fact that he came equipped with a flashlight. It certainly wasn't an item that had appeared on any of the numerous packing lists she'd prepared before her trip. She shrugged her shoulders. Well, it was really none of her business. She just hoped he made it back across while he still could.

A few steps took her to the seawall. Looking down, she could see the reflection of the water lapping farther down the beach. There were still several yards of shale to cover before the water began licking at the wall itself. Satisfied that Richard Garrett would not be marooned, she was about to move on when she heard an unfamiliar noise. At least she thought she did. The sea and the wind carried sound and distorted it, and Megan wasn't quite sure at first. She cocked her head and listened intently. Then she heard it again—a crying or whimpering. Frantically, she scoured the beach below her, wishing that she too had a flashlight.

After a few futile minutes of straining her eyes through the deepening darkness, Megan finally saw what looked like a small black mound, moving not more than four or five yards from her on the beach below. She leaned over the wall, desperately trying to ascertain what it was that she could see. She couldn't tell. She only knew that whatever it was, it was alive and in distress. Her heartbeat quickened as she placed her nervous hands down on the wall. What should she do? Should she run after Richard Garrett and try to find him on the island in the darkness? Or would aid then be too late? She looked around helplessly. There was no sign of anyone else nearby, only the sporadic and faint cries from the indistinguishable object below.

Offering up yet another silent prayer, Megan scrambled onto the low wall then let herself drop. It was difficult to do in the darkness. She could only estimate the distance of her fall and kept her knees bent in anticipation of an unseen landing. She hit hard and suddenly. It had not been as far down as she had feared, and a few scrapes on her knees and hands were the worst of the damage done. She stood up and brushed the sand and shale off. Then cautiously she moved toward the black shape.

As Megan advanced, all movement and sound ceased for a moment, then suddenly redoubled and became more frantic. She crept forward until she was only a yard or so away. A pair of baleful eyes looked up at her and a weak, pleading yelp brought her to her knees.

"Oh you poor thing!" she cried. "Whatever have you done?"

Gingerly, Megan eased her hand over to touch the dog. He flinched, but allowed her to move her hand gently over his back and down one leg, and then another. Even in the darkness, it took only seconds for Megan to discover the problem. Fishing wire. The dog was completely tangled in fishing wire, and his efforts to extricate himself had only compounded the problem. Not only was the nylon thread preventing him from standing or walking, it was now cutting into the dog's skin, and as Megan ran her hands over the animal's quivering frame she could feel blood, sticky on her fingers.

The dog's eyes glistened in the weak light and watched Megan's every move. She spoke soothingly to the animal and fondled his ears with one hand while the other one ran across his body once more. He was just too big. She couldn't tell what kind of dog he was, but he was far too big and heavy for her to lift. Removing the fishing wire would require a knife. She sat back on her heels and looked over at the water, drawing ever nearer. The tide had risen in just the short time she had been on the beach. By her rough estimation, she had less than half an hour to move the dog before he would drown in the oncoming water. There was no way that she could make it to the hotel, back, and free the animal from the fishing wire in that amount of time. She looked over at the black silhouette of Church Island. Richard Garrett was her only hope. Perhaps a man who carried a flashlight in his pocket would also carry a pocketknife. And if not, maybe between the two of them they could lift the dog to safety.

Megan turned her attention to the dog once more.

"It's alright boy," she soothed. "I'm going for help. Try not to struggle anymore." She patted the dog's back as she spoke, then rose and ran for the wall. Her feet slipped several times on the shale and damp seaweed, but she tried not to let it slow her down too much. Once at the wall, however, she stopped. It was six or seven feet tall, which meant that Megan would have to climb up a couple of feet before she could clamber over the top. There were many crevices and crannies in between the rocks, and under normal circumstances Megan was sure that she could have scaled it without much difficulty. In the dark, however, it was a more difficult proposition. Nevertheless she hunted for a firm handhold, and slowly began the process of feeling for nicks in the wall that could anchor her as she inched her way upward.

It didn't take long before her right hand felt the top of the wall. She took one more step up before putting her weight on her arms and heaving her body up and over. The stones grazed her legs unmercifully as she slithered over the edge, and loose rocks showered down to join the shaley beach below. She struggled upright with a sigh of relief just before a figure moved out from the shadows and grabbed her from behind.

Instinctively, Megan went to scream, but just as instinctively, the person behind her clapped a hand over her mouth, muffling the sound before it had time to truly form, and leaving Megan an immobile, mute, and terrified captive.

"A girl!"

Megan heard the surprise in her captor's voice, and with it the American accent. Memories of the conversation overheard at Plas Newydd came flooding back, and without warning, she felt herself starting to tremble. The man behind her must have felt it too, because without removing his hand from her mouth, he swung her around slightly so that he could see her face.

"Megan!" The shock in Joe Marks's voice was unmistakable, and he immediately dropped the hand that had been covering her mouth, although he continued to keep his other hand on her—more to keep her upright than to restrain her, Megan thought. "What are you doing here?"

Megan tried to speak, but found the words didn't come easily. "T. . . t . . . trying to s . . . s . . . save a d . . . d . . . dog," she sputtered.

"What?"

"Trying to save a dog!" Megan repeated more firmly, her initial terror beginning to subside. "What are you doing here? Or do you usually spend the evening accosting people?"

She knew she was playing with fire, but she also knew that Joe Marks had no idea that she had overheard a clandestine conversation earlier in the day, or that she had any suspicions about him. Furthermore, Megan Harmer didn't have red hair for nothing—her indignation was on the rise.

"No, I . . . I . . . " Joe was still coming to terms with finding Megan in his arms. "What did you say you're doing?"

"Trying to save a dog!" Megan repeated one more time, with impatience. "And you've wasted so much of my time that I'm not going to make it," she added bitterly. Then, as the realization dawned that she may have actually found aid sooner than she could have hoped, she added quickly, "Joe, d'you have a knife?"

"A knife?" he asked warily.

"Yes," Megan said, her agitation mounting. "You know, a pocketknife, or something—anything that could cut through fishing line?"

Joe let go of Megan and put his hand into his pocket. He drew out a Swiss army knife—the kind that had every type of implement imaginable—and showed it to her.

"Oh, that's perfect!" she cried. "Will you come and help me?" This time Megan grabbed his arm and pulled him toward the retaining wall.

"Come with you where?" Joe asked.

"Onto the beach, of course," Megan replied as if it were the most obvious thing in the world. "To get the dog," she added as an afterthought before she scrambled onto the wall once more and jumped down to the other side.

She heard Joe land heavily near her, but didn't stop to talk to him again. She started running in the general direction of the stranded dog, listening for any sound and straining to see his form in the deepening darkness. As she did so, she realized that she had put fear for her own safety aside automatically. Perhaps she was just too innocent and gullible, but she couldn't think of Joe Marks in the same evil terms as she did those faceless men whom she'd overheard. She didn't understand it. She only knew that when she'd realized who was restraining her on the pathway, her initial terror subsided rather than intensified. It made no sense at all, but she didn't have time to analyze it.

The dog gave a yelp as Megan approached. She moved closer and patted his back again. "It's alright boy! I've brought help this time," she said.

Joe moved up beside her. "Would you mind taking a couple of minutes to explain this to me?" he asked, but Megan noticed that he was already running his hands across the dog's body, feeling the fishing line and sizing up the situation himself.

"I was walking along the promenade, on my way back from Church Island, when I heard a whimpering sound coming from the beach. I could tell someone or something was hurt, so I jumped down to check it out. I found the dog here and knew I couldn't untie him or move him alone, so I was on my way to get help when you . . . ," Megan hesitated fractionally, ". . . er, found me."

"Didn't it occur to you to get help before you checked it out?" Joe asked, and Megan noticed that he was searching his pockets as he spoke.

"Well, yes," she admitted, "but I could tell it was a cry of distress, and there was the tide coming in . . ." She paused and looked over at the sea with alarm. "Joe, the water's much closer now. We have to hurry!"

She saw him nod, then there was a pinprick of light—a flashlight. Joe cradled it in his hand so as to minimize the glow. He shone it over the dog's body in a quick sweeping stroke then turned off the bulb and handed the flashlight to Megan.

"I'm beginning to think I'm the only person around here who doesn't carry a flashlight in my pocket," she said with surprise.

Joe froze, the scissors on his Swiss army knife only half open, and swung around to face her. "Who else d'you know with a flashlight in a pocket?" he asked brusquely.

Megan bristled at his tone. "Only Richard Garrett," she responded.

"You've seen him out here?" There was an urgency in Joe's voice that prompted Megan to pause and search his face before replying. He sensed her hesitation and reached out to her. He grabbed her arm, "Megan, I can't explain right now, but this is really important. When did you see Richard Garrett?"

"Just a little while ago," Megan said. "I met him right before I heard the dog. In fact I probably wouldn't have heard anything if I hadn't stopped to talk to him."

"He saw you too?" Joe sounded alarmed, and Megan began to feel the prickles of fear again.

"Of course," she defended. "We stopped and talked for a minute. He was going to Church Island, and I'd just left it. I told him he'd need to hurry because the evening tide would soon cover the causeway, and because it was getting dark. He showed me his flashlight and said he'd be quick."

Joe looked over at the distant black shadow that was Church Island and swore under his breath. Then he turned back to Megan. "Shine the light on the dog and I'll try to cut him free," he admonished. "And Megan, can you cover the light with your hand so it's not too obvious?"

Obediently, Megan put her hand over the bulb. Then she clicked the switch and opened her fingers marginally so that a narrow beam of light filtered through—just enough to reflect off the green strands that bound the dog so securely. Joe got to work quickly, and within seconds one leg was free. The dog started to wriggle, sensing release and unwilling to calmly wait for complete freedom.

"Hold on boy!" Joe put a restraining hand on the dog's back. "Give me a few more minutes, then you can really move."

Megan inched closer, trying to help quiet the dog while still directing the tiny aperture of light. It became more and more difficult to control the excited canine as the bands holding him down were broken. Megan could see Joe struggling to cut through the line around the dog's neck without further injuring the animal.

"Joe, if I let go of the top of flashlight I can help you," she suggested.

"No!" Joe gasped as he straddled the dog, wrestling him into submission for a few precious seconds. "I've almost got it. Shine it right here by his left front paw."

Megan did so and watched anxiously as Joe cut the last piece of fishing line that bound the animal. He moved away quickly as the dog staggered to its feet with a jubilant bark.

"Quick Megan," Joe said, "turn off the light!"

The click brought complete blackness. Megan could see nothing for a few seconds as her eyes adjusted to the dark, but within seconds she began discerning shapes again—the tall form of Joe by her side, and the bounding figure of the dog, reveling in his freedom despite his weakened state.

"Why are you so concerned about the light?" Megan asked. The question had begged asking since Joe had handed her the flashlight with such strange instructions. She hadn't dared interrupt him while he was focused on freeing the dog.

Joe didn't answer immediately. His silhouette and the dog's merged as the animal barked and jumped up to thank his rescuer. Joe laughed softly and said, "Get down you slobbery beast." Megan waited as Joe tried to calm the excited dog. Eventually the dog's noises became more subdued and Joe's voice spoke out of the darkness.

"I know I have some serious explaining to do, Megan. I owe you that for manhandling you back there. But this isn't a good place to do it. Can it wait till we're somewhere else?"

"I guess so," Megan conceded, her confusion clearly evident in her voice.

Joe appeared beside her. "Come on, I'll give you a hike up the wall!"

Megan gave a small laugh. "Alright, but what about the dog?"

Joe groaned. "Can't he go back the way he came?"

"I doubt it," said Megan seriously. "I'll vouch for the fact that it's a whole lot easier to go down than up."

"Well, I'll give him a hike too, if I have to. Come on!"

He set off quickly toward the retaining wall, and it was a scramble for Megan to keep up with him. She was so intent on pursuit, that she didn't realize he'd stopped until she plowed right into him.

"Oh, sorr—" Her apology was muffled almost immediately by Joe's hand. He removed it almost as fast, but kept his index finger over her lips, signaling her to silence. She didn't move, and above the rush of the coastal waves she heard the unmistakable sound of footsteps along the promenade. They were drawing closer.

Joe swung around, placing his body between Megan and the wall. The dog continued to hover nearby, barking occasionally and weaving circles around their legs.

"Megan," he whispered, "I've no time to explain. If you could just trust me one more time, I promise I'll explain this to you. Play along with me okay?"

"What d'you mean 'play along with—' " her question was stifled in one swift movement as Joe put his arms around her, pulled her close and lowered his lips to hers. Megan pushed against his chest, desperately trying to free herself, but his arms only tightened around her, pinning her even closer. And then she felt the gun, hard and cold under his shirt. She knew what it was at once, and felt the fear she'd suppressed since he'd first grabbed her on the promenade well up again.

She must have trembled in his arms, because she sensed Joe's iron muscles ease their grip slightly, only to have them retighten as the rhythmic footsteps faltered and stopped immediately above them. The dog's giddy movement ceased and he faced the wall and barked a few times. Suddenly a bright light hit them—a small, narrow beam, but blinding in its intensity, coming as it did out of the darkness. She felt Joe flinch, but he kept his head bent over hers. The light flickered over them once more, the dog barked, and after what seemed like an interminable silence, the footsteps began again, walking on toward the bridge.

Only when the footsteps had faded into the night did Joe release her. Megan pushed away from him, stumbling backward. He put out a hand to steady her, but she brushed it aside.

"And what," she spat at him, "was all that in aid of?" Her fear level was rising at an alarming rate, but she refused to give in to it, and so she lashed out.

Joe didn't answer her. Instead he looked down the beach following the direction the footsteps had taken. "You're a Mormon, aren't you?"

Megan stared at him in disbelief, and then anger got the better of her. "What's that got to do with anything? Just because I didn't fall into your arms in a grateful swoon and let you take advantage of me? Does that automatically label me a Mormon? Well, good. I'm glad you know we've got high moral integrity."

She saw his teeth glint in the pale starlight and realized that he was grinning. "I knew it!" he chuckled. "That's exactly what Katy would say."

"Who's Katy?" Megan asked, taken off her guard.

"Katy, you redheaded spitfire, is the wife of my partner and best friend, Rob Jenkins. They're both Mormons, and I admire them for it. My guess that you are too was based on the fact that both you and your friend turned down the alcohol Richard Garrett offered you, and on nothing more than a feeling I've had each time I've been with you."

Megan stared at him in disbelief. But he hadn't finished.

"I asked if you were a Mormon purely out of self-preservation. My partner, Rob, has saved our skins a hundred times over by praying us out of situations that seemed impossible. He's not here and we need some pretty powerful prayers going up on our behalf right about now."

"I don't know what you're talking about." Megan found that in her confusion she was backing away from him.

Joe must have sensed it too, because he reached out for her. "Megan, come here! I'm not trying to make light of your religion. If anything, it's the opposite. I'm asking you to share your faith with me—the way Rob does."

"You expect me to believe that of you? You, who haven't said or done anything that's made sense all evening?" Megan was shaking again. She'd had enough of this nightmare and wanted to leave. "I'm going home!" Then as the significance and stupidity of what she'd said hit, she sobbed, "I mean, I'm going back to the hotel!"

She swung around and began running to the wall, but Joe reached it before her. He put out a hand and took her arm. "You're shaking," he said with concern. "Are you cold, or do I really frighten you that much?"

Megan was not willing to admit her ragged emotional state to him. "Cold," she said.

"Here, put this on!" Before Megan could counter with an objection, Joe had slipped off his lightweight jacket and threaded one of her arms through the arm hole. He wrapped it around her and she was stunned by the comfort it brought her. It was warm and smelled faintly of men's aftershave—mingled with wet dog.

"Okay," he said, "if I give you a hike up this wall, will you promise me that you won't run off before I get to the top and have a chance to explain all of this to you?"

The idea of escape while Joe climbed the wall had already occurred to Megan, but the thought of the gun strapped to his torso was enough to deter her from following through with the scheme against his wishes. "I'll wait for you," she agreed quietly, and moved forward to allow him to boost her a couple of feet closer to the top.

CHAPTER 6

It was much easier to scale the rough stones the second time. Joe's hike put Megan within arm's length of the top, and it required nothing more than a good heave and a little leverage to shinny over. Once on solid ground again, Megan leaned over the wall and extended her arms for the dog. Joe hoisted the animal up as far as he could reach. Megan grabbed the dog's collar and helped pull as the animal furiously scrambled for footholds. She found herself digging into the wall with both knees to prevent herself from toppling over on top of the dog, but after considerably more effort than it had taken to get herself up, she was finally able to yank him over the last stone.

She couldn't bear to think of how much pain the climb had inflicted upon the already-wounded dog, but the deed was done; he was truly free to go home now. The dog wandered around for a few minutes, sniffing the wall, Megan's legs, and invisible patches on the cement. He raised his head and barked once as Joe emerged over the rim of the wall.

After regaining his footing, Joe walked over to the animal and gave it a last pat. "Go on home now boy!" he said. "Home!"

The dog barked, wagged its tail, and with a last long look at both Joe and Megan, obediently trotted off down the promenade toward Menai Bridge. They watched him go without speaking, then Joe broke the silence.

"There's a bench a bit farther down. Could you handle stopping there to talk for a few minutes?"

Megan pulled his jacket more closely around her neck, and nodded her assent. More than anything now, she needed some answers. She needed to know why this enigmatic man had accosted her twice and yet continued to treat her with consideration; why he was so concerned that no one see them in the darkness; and, perhaps most importantly, why, in Britain where any kind of firearms were illegal, he carried a gun on a shoulder strap beneath his shirt.

It took only a few minutes to reach the bench. Megan sat down at once, but Joe continued on until the promenade made a bend, then he stopped and listened intently for a few minutes before returning and joining her at the seat. Their backs were to the woodland and they faced the strait. The water was nothing more than inky blackness, but pinpricks of light from the buildings and roads on the mainland dotted the horizon. The soothing rush of the waves moving to and fro was the only sound to disturb the slumbering silence of the night.

Megan waited. Joe was staring out at the water, but Megan had the feeling that he wasn't really seeing it. He stirred and turned to face her.

"You've put up with a lot this evening, Megan," he said, "and for that reason, if nothing more, I need to explain some things to you." He paused, then added, "I've not been given clearance to talk to you about any of this, but I'm following my gut feelings. First off, I think you've got the moral integrity to keep what I tell you in confidence. And second, I have a strong feeling that your safety's at stake here, and the only way you can be on your guard is if you have some idea of what you're up against."

Megan felt sick. How had she ever become mixed up in this mess? She wanted to run back to the hotel and stay in bed with her head under the pillow until all these men vanished from her life. She yearned for the carefree summer vacation she had begun. Looking down at her hands clasped tightly on her knee, Megan tried to dispel the foreboding that was threatening to engulf her, and gave herself a mental shake. She couldn't turn the clock back. Forward was the only way to go, and Joe was right, she had to know what was going on, even if it frightened her.

She wasn't sure what Joe was expecting her to say, so she just nodded, and in a voice that sounded far too calm to have originated with her, she said, "Alright, tell me about it."

Joe cleared his throat. "I'm not sure exactly where to start . . . but I probably should tell you what happened tonight, and especially what's going to happen tomorrow, because I have a feeling it's going to involve you again. But I don't think I can explain it very clearly without giving you some background information . . . . How well do you know your Irish history?"

Surprised by the question, Megan grimaced. "Marginally better than the average American perhaps, but not well enough."

Joe nodded. "It's pretty complicated at best. Are you up for a brief history lesson?"

Despite her tension, Megan couldn't help smile. "You're asking me?"

"Okay—stupid question!" he admitted with a returning smile, and it seemed to Megan that some of the strain between them eased.

Joe leaned back against the rear of the bench, stretched out his legs and crossed them at the ankles. "Well, as you know, Irish history goes back centuries," he began, "but I'll begin in 1920. That's when the island was partitioned by the British. The northeast corner was made into a new entity called Northern Ireland—still governed from England, while the rest of Ireland was given its own autonomy.

"You see, most of the Irish in the south were Catholic and wanted their independence, but the north part of Ireland had a Protestant majority who considered themselves to be British. This Protestant majority said they would fight to maintain the right to be British; and so, since the government in London felt that it owed allegiance to its people in the north, the partition solution was created.

"Britain withdrew from Ireland in the 1920s, just like the northern states withdrew from the southern states after the Civil War. But the problem in Ireland was that the partition settlement was very much a compromise and left no one happy. Both sides believed they were the victims. The Catholics in Northern Ireland believed that they were on the wrong side of the border and had been robbed of their political heritage. They were joined by the Catholic majority in the south who wanted a united Ireland. The Protestants have a history in Ireland that goes back at least to the seventeenth century, and they believed they were the victims because they'd lost control of the rest of Ireland.

"As long as each group had that selective sense of history, they could do anything in the present and use history to justify what they did. That's why history's been such a potent force in the Irish conflict."

"Isn't that one of the greatest ironies of history?" Megan interrupted. "We're supposed to remember the past so we can learn from it, but too often we carry it with us as a chip on our shoulder, and use it to justify even more suffering in the future."

"That's for sure," Joe agreed. "This type of conflict happens throughout the world. But for Ireland it seems like it's been going on forever.

"In 1968 civil rights marches began when the Catholic minority in Northern Ireland, who for years had been trying to get some sort of equality under the British law, tried to emulate the policy of Martin Luther King and the Civil Rights movement in the United States. Their demands were quite simple. They said that if they were to be British subjects, they deserved British rights—such as good housing for Catholics, employment for Catholics, and more voice in the electoral system."

"Well, were they really being discriminated against?" Megan asked.

"Depends on who you ask," Joe replied. "One of the biggest problems was that in order to vote you had to be a local taxpayer, and since the Catholics were usually the poorest people and therefore less likely to own their own home or have a secure job, many couldn't pay taxes. And so they found themselves with grievances, but no political representation to hear their complaints.

"Unfortunately, the Irish have a tradition of being hotheaded and also have a history of resistance against the state—violent resistance against the state. So, although people joined the civil rights movement with the best intentions in the world, they found it difficult to adopt a policy of pure nonviolence. Radical groups emerged that pushed the mainstream to take more extreme actions. And so, when time passed with very little to show for their civil rights campaign, the Catholics were prepared to turn toward much more militant means, just so their voice would be heard. Enter the Irish Republican Army—or IRA as they're better known."

"But didn't the Protestants do something about all this? Couldn't they tell it was getting serious?" Megan asked.

"Of course, but they were fractured too. Some felt that the Catholics were using their civil rights agenda to undermine the state and to further the cause of a united Ireland. Others believed that their demand of one man, one vote was a reasonable one and should be conceded. Their own political parties began to split over the issue, and in the confusion a strong conservative government in England stepped in, determined to crush any signs of rebellion.

"It wasn't long before the political process in Northern Ireland was virtually nonexistent. Instead, those with the most strident voices and who could command weaponry were the people setting the agenda. The British army moved in and started using tear gas to control riots. Catholic communities feared for their physical existence and so their young people joined the IRA in droves. They were operating under the basic defense that if they didn't take control they would be wiped out."

"So, the British government really became one of the IRA's best recruiting agents," Megan concluded. She was completely absorbed by Joe's account and fascinated by the new perspective it gave her.

"You got it!" Joe seemed pleased by her grasp of the conditions he described. "And the IRA suddenly found themselves able to take more daring action because they believed they had the support of the people. They were able to go to the Irish elsewhere and offer themselves as the defenders of the Catholic community in Northern Ireland. They could then say they believed that the only solution was Irish unity, and that all Irish must help them. They were after world opinion, and they knew that the more victimized they appeared on global television, the better it would serve their purpose. They used propaganda to paint themselves as the representatives of the downtrodden."

"But it didn't wash completely, did it? I mean most people, even those who don't know much about Ireland, equate the IRA with terrorists, don't they?" Megan asked.

Joe shook his head. "You'd be surprised," he said. "The IRA itself splintered, and other groups, the Provisional IRA and Provisional Sinn Fein, were born. Their leadership built into the groups a sense of martyrdom, and dying for a united Ireland was revered. Those who were incarcerated began hunger strikes. They refused to wear prison uniforms and wrapped themselves in blankets. They portrayed the image of sacrificial lambs dying for a righteous cause, and it was very powerful within the Catholic community."

"How could they get away with that after all the senseless violence they'd instigated?"

"Violence, yes! Senseless, no!" he countered. "Think about it Megan. Belfast has never become a Beirut. There was control to almost all their violence, and usually there would be a warning—not often giving much time, but a warning nevertheless. When the bombings started they were really sending a message. They were saying, 'We're here. You have to talk to us, even if we have to bomb our way to the negotiating table.'

"Car bombs or letter bombs were used to cause as much economic destruction and embarrassment as possible to the British government, and killing British soldiers was their way of defending their own community.

"What they didn't promote was the fact that they killed Catholics too. In fact they've killed more Catholics than their opponents have. And they just couldn't hide the fact that too many innocents were dying, particularly children. Despite the fact that they were often able to paint the British government in a bad light, they couldn't escape the reality that they were killing, maiming, and destroying. No reasonable person is going to condone that."

"But we're not talking about reasonable people here, are we?" Megan said bleakly.

Joe shook his head again. "No, I don't think so. There may still be some purists among them, fighting for a historic and religious mission, but many are nothing more than blood-thirsty thugs—only too happy for an excuse to create mayhem and enjoying the power rush that comes from getting away with it."

"What about the Sinn Fein group? Haven't they been more involved than the IRA when it comes to negotiations with the British?" Megan asked.

Joe shot her a look of keen appraisal. "Either you know a lot more about Ireland than you let on, or my lecturing skills have improved dramatically."

Megan shrugged. "I just watch the news," she admitted.

Joe gave a mock groan. "Just as I thought I'd done something right by her!"

"You've been doing a great job," Megan encouraged. "Please don't stop. Tell me what the relationship is between the IRA and Sinn Fein. I've never understood that."

"I sometimes wonder if the leadership of each group has the same difficulty," Joe said. "Current views are that there are two separate operations. There's the militant Irish Republican Army on the one hand, and the political and more discreet wing of the Republican movement, Sinn Fein, on the other. But it hasn't always been that way. There have been times when they've stood solidly together.

"What makes a difference now, is that the leaders of Sinn Fein are, for perhaps the first time, making serious inroads politically. But the IRA is Sinn Fein's only weapon, so although it's in their interest to appear separate from the IRA at negotiations, they're not quite prepared to disown them. Past experience of betrayal at the bargaining table has left them wary, and they feel the need to keep that link to the IRA strong. Besides which, the Republicans are their voting public. Lose them, and their political party means nothing."

"So despite the recent cease-fires that have been touted on the news, you don't think IRA bombings are a thing of the past," Megan concluded.

"I wish I could be that optimistic," Joe said. "But I know too much. No matter what concessions Sinn Fein leaders wheedle out of the British government, they'll find they have little control over the IRA crusaders who'll stop at nothing until a united Republican Ireland is created. The IRA may lie dormant for a short space of time, but it's not going to dissolve. In fact my fear is that they'll use this downtime to regroup, reassess, and perhaps most alarming, restock their supplies."

"Supplies?" Megan asked. "You mean weapons?"

Joe nodded. "Small firearms, rifles, machine guns, ammunition, grenades, rocket launchers, explosives, detonators, even surface-to-air-missiles. You name it, they've got it or want it. Intelligence sources believe that the IRA already has enough weapons to maintain their low-intensity war indefinitely, but they're continuing to smuggle arms into Ireland and train their members."

"But where do they get their weapons?" Megan asked.

"The two main sources are the U.S. and Libya," Joe replied.

"The U.S.!"

" 'Fraid so," Joe said. "We're doing our best to put a stop to it, but the IRA's well established. Its tentacles are far-reaching, and when we cut off one source, before long another appears in its place."

"'We'? Who's 'we'?" Megan asked, sensing that at last they had reached a point at which some of her questions could be answered.

Joe leaned over and pulled a wallet out of his back pocket, drew out a card, and handed it to Megan. She took it and tilted it sideways to make the most of the faint starlight. She read the identification as Joe spoke.

"FBI," he said succinctly, then waited for her response.

Slowly, Megan handed the card back to him. He took the card from her and replaced it in his wallet. "Antiterrorism," he said, by way of clarification.

"And you're over here because of some connection between the U.S. and the IRA?"

That Joe Marks could be FBI had never occurred to Megan, and she was still struggling to accept the idea.

"I'm here," Joe was sliding his wallet back into his pocket, "to cut off one of those tentacles we just talked about."

Megan felt a chill run down her spine, and she shivered. Flashbacks of the hideous conversation she'd overheard at Plas Newydd suddenly flooded her mind and senses. The American, the Irishman, the goods that were to be delivered, the pervasive secrecy and evil—suddenly pieces of the puzzle began to fall into place.

Joe must have sensed her withdrawal. "You okay?" he asked, and reached out to touch her, but Megan was not ready for that. The last thing she wanted right then was to be any nearer to the gun concealed so deftly beneath Joe's shirt.

She pulled back and shook her head. "I'm alright. Just give me a few minutes to assimilate all this." Wrapping her arms around herself in a futile attempt to contain her shivering form, Megan turned to face Joe. "So let me get this straight, you're here on Anglesey to prevent some sort of arms smuggling between someone in the U.S. and the IRA?"

"In a nutshell, yes," Joe replied.

"And are you doing this alone, or are the bushes behind us crawling with other FBI operatives?"

"Look Megan, I know it sounds like 'cloak-and-dagger' material out here in the dark, but I can't risk talking to you at the hotel, and a few minutes ago you were pretty anxious for an explanation of this evening's activities. If I've made an egregious error in judgement here, and blown my cover to some smart-aleck girl, I've put a lot of lives on the line. I've either got to see some proof that I can trust you, or you're on the first flight out of here."

It was useless for Megan to feel defensive. Besides, she had no desire to start a duel. She desperately tried to put aside her feelings of confusion and fear, and sought for more clarification.

"I'm sorry," she said. "I overreacted. It's been a rough day, and I'm feeling way out of my league. I'll keep your confidence if you can help me understand things a little better."

Joe gave her an appraising look, and what he saw must have satisfied him, because he gave a slow nod and continued his account.

"The IRA propaganda machine made an appeal to Irish Americans. Many in that community haven't educated themselves on the situation in Ireland and have a very simplistic view of the troubles. They heard words like 'liberty' and 'oppression' and were immediately hooked. A gunrunning network was set up in the U.S., controlled by a veteran Irish Republican called George Harrison. His organization was finally shut down by the FBI in the 1980s, but he'd funneled so many weapons through the system that they're still in use today."

"But that didn't satisfy them. They needed another supplier," Megan volunteered.

Again Joe nodded. "It didn't take long. We had a basic idea of what to look for—an Irish background, good connections, and money. Suspicions have floated through our office for a quite a while, teasing us because we couldn't ever lay our hands on enough evidence to convict—until now." Joe gave a tense sigh. "If we play our cards right, this time we've nailed him."

Megan sat motionless for a few seconds, then in a voice devoid of emotion asked, "So what's Richard Garrett's Irish connection?"

It was Joe's turn to remain silent, but Megan was grateful that at least he spared her the insult of disclaimer. Just about the time she thought she'd overstepped the bounds of her "need-to-know" information, Joe spoke.

"His wife was Irish." It was obvious that Joe heard Megan's soft exclamation, but he continued as though there had been no interruption. "They met at the University of Chicago. She was an exchange student from Belfast—one of the Catholic minority we've been talking about. They'd been married three years when she went home to visit her family.

"It was during one of the many riots that city's known for that she was killed. A stray bullet. Another innocent victim. Her family blamed the British troops—I'm sure it was inconceivable to them that it could just have easily been an IRA weapon that took her life.

"Garrett was in Detroit at the time, already starting his way up the Ford Company corporate ladder. He flew over for the funeral, and my guess is that even then, in his grief-stricken state, he caught the attention of the IRA. I don't know how long it took them to contact him. Just long enough for his grief to turn to hate I imagine."

Megan sat staring unseeingly at the black void that was the ocean. Things like this only happened in the news, far removed from her own sphere. This had to be some sort of nightmare. Terror was knocking, crying for admittance, but she would not give way. Surely she would awaken soon. She closed her eyes and clenched her fists, praying that when she reopened them, she would find herself safely tucked in bed. But it was Joe's touch that brought her back to the present, and when he placed his hand on her arm, it startled her to realize how badly she needed human contact as she fought through the distressful fog of denial.

"I'm sorry you got mixed up in all this, Megan," he said. "Would you consider changing your vacation plans and moving on tomorrow?"

"But Fran hasn't seen anything yet!" Megan replied stupidly. "I mean, she's been down here sketching and painting, and hasn't been to any of the other interesting places she wanted to visit." She thought over the schedule that she had so meticulously planned—driving times, distances, and stops all worked out. Every evening's hotel or bed and breakfast reservation was prebooked. "We're only going to be here another two days," she added.

"So will Richard Garrett," Joe muttered.

Again the conversation she'd overheard at Plas Newydd came flooding back—understanding dawned. "That's right!" she whispered. "The goods will be here tomorrow or the next day."

Joe's hand on her arm tightened. "What did you say?" he demanded harshly.

Megan looked over at his face, shadowed in the moonlight but still showing strain and weariness. She took a deep breath. "I think it's my turn to tell you something," she said. "I told you earlier that it's been a rough day. You need to know what happened to me this morning."

And so Megan recounted her experience at Plas Newydd. She glossed over her visit to the manor itself, and the beautiful grounds surrounding it, but focused instead on what she heard in the maze. To her dismay, as she described the setting and the violent exchange she'd overheard, her emotions got the better of her. By the time she'd finished her account, she was shaking and tears were flowing unabashedly down her cheeks.

At some point during the telling, Joe had moved closer to her and placed a comforting arm around her slender shoulders. Emotionally spent, Megan buried her face in Joe's shoulder and he brought his other arm around to draw her close.

"Megan, are you absolutely sure they didn't see you?"

"Yes," Megan raised her head and reached for a tissue in her pocket. "I didn't see Richard Garrett at all, and if he saw me he must have assumed I was doing the tourist thing there, just like everyone else. He wouldn't have any reason to think otherwise would he?"

"Not then perhaps," said Joe grimly, "but he may have his doubts now—and that's what worries me."

"But I still didn't know he was involved in anything when I saw him on the promenade," Megan contended. "It was easy to act innocent—because I was!"

"I know that. But you've been in the wrong place at the wrong time more than once today. Try looking at your actions through his eyes, Megan. First you appear at the one tourist spot that he chooses to visit. Coincidence? Well maybe, but he's going to be more on his guard after the run-in with his Irish cohort. Next he meets you leaving the very island that he seems to have a special interest in—not during normal tourist hours and on your own, I might add. And then we've got the beach scene!"

Megan bristled at the memory, moved out of his arms and faced him. "Oh yes," she said, "you've still got that to explain."

Joe got up abruptly and walked over to the low wall. He stood there for a few minutes. The tide had now reached the stone barricade and was sloshing noisily against the rocks. Megan rose and joined him.

"I don't know how much he was able to see," Joe said quietly. Then he turned and continued earnestly, "I'm sorry I kissed you against your wishes. It was the only way I could think of protecting you."

"Protecting me?"

He nodded. "I heard the footsteps as we approached the wall. The last thing I needed was to be caught following Richard Garrett by Richard Garrett himself. The last thing you needed was to be caught so close to Church Island in the dark with me—someone he already seems to distrust. There weren't too many hiding places on the beach, so I improvised. I kept my head low, my back to him and—I hope to goodness—I kept you completely out of sight." Megan watched a small smile cross his lips. "As much as I like your golden hair," he said, "it makes you a little hard to camouflage."

Before Megan could respond to this, Joe turned back to gaze out to sea again. She had to step closer to hear his last words, spoken so softly against the rush of the swirling water below. "And that's why I asked you to pray—pray for us both—that Richard Garrett didn't see anything more than a local couple kissing on the beach as they walked their dog."

"I will pray, Joe," Megan said. "But you pray too."

Joe gave a short mirthless laugh. "I'm not well practiced in that art I'm afraid. I usually leave it to Rob."

"Where's Rob now?" Megan asked.

This time Joe's laugh was spontaneous. "Somewhere between here and Dagenham, holed up in a freight train. The last time I spoke to him he let me know just how unfair he thought life was, that I'm sleeping in a comfortable hotel bed while he's squished in between crates in a drafty, diesel-smelling boxcar."

"Where's Dagenham?" Megan was still confused.

"Dagenham is just outside London," Joe clarified. "It's best known for its automobile assembly factories. Ford has a large plant there." He paused, then continued carefully. "We believe that Garrett has been smuggling arms out of the U.S. hidden among the car parts destined for the Ford plant in Dagenham. It would be easy enough to do with a few strategically placed insiders at both ends.

"Two weeks ago we got lucky. We found the cache before it left. Detonators mainly—something the IRA can use from their most sophisticated Semtex bombs to their homemade mortars. And this time, for the first time, Garrett decided to come along. We haven't figured that one out yet. What's he doing here? Either he's getting paranoid about the way things are being handled, and wants to oversee it himself, or he's getting more involved somehow.

"Neither one of those scenarios bodes well for us. Trailing a guy who's got the jitters is a pretty scary thing. They tend to shoot first and ask questions later. But if, on the other hand, he's getting more involved with the IRA's inner circle, we've got to get to him before he does too much damage."

"So, you're assigned to keep an eye on Richard Garrett, while your partner keeps his eye on the goods?" Megan was struggling to keep all the information straight.

"Right—and we can't risk losing either one. Rob's followed the crate from Detroit to the Ford plant in Dagenham, and now it's on the train heading up this way. The main ferry terminal linking the United Kingdom to Northern Ireland is at Holyhead, on the other side of Anglesey. But the coast guard up there's pretty vigilant. We're guessing that before the train reaches Holyhead, the goods will be unloaded. We don't know where yet, but seeing as Garrett's hanging around here, and he's now been joined by a couple of Irish thugs in a speedy cruiser just offshore, my hunch is that they're hoping to load up on this side of the island to avoid dealing with officials and their inspections at Holyhead."

"But you can't prevent them on your own!" Megan cried.

"Do I detect a modicum of concern for my safety, or are you merely suggesting that I'm incompetent?" Joe asked, and Megan could tell that he was smiling. She couldn't help but smile in return, but she was saved from answering when Joe continued.

"Scotland Yard is aware of this operation, and so's the coast guard. The local police have been great in helping to keep tabs on Garrett. It would look pretty obvious if I were visiting every tourist spot at the same time he did."

"So someone was there, at Plas Newydd this morning?" Megan asked.

"Yeah, one of the locals. But he hasn't reported anything unusual, so he mustn't have been close enough to share in our friends' rendezvous—might have to bring that up with his boss."

"Perhaps he'd stick closer to his man if he could carry a gun like you," Megan suggested. She was still very uncomfortable with the fact that Joe was toting a concealed weapon, but found that her comment, rather than clearing the air, caused the descension of a frigid silence upon her companion.

She spoke again in an effort to smooth things over. "You can't expect to draw a girl into a close embrace and not have her feel a gun lying against your chest."

"I'll remember that next time," Joe said coldly, "and I'll ask you not to mention your discovery to anyone else."

"Of course I won't!" Megan cried. "I've already told you that I'd keep your confidence."

Joe drew a ragged breath. "I know. I'm sorry. I shouldn't have snapped at you. As hard as it is for you to comprehend what we're dealing with here, you'll just have to take my word for it—I wouldn't be carrying a gun unless I felt like I really needed to. The kind of men we're up against will think nothing of blowing my head off, or anyone else's who happens to get in their way. As great as the local 'bobbies' have been, they're not trained for this type of work—and I don't have much more backup!" He paused, then continued, "And just for the record, those who need to know at Scotland Yard and customs are aware of the fact that I'm carrying a gun."

Megan felt like a three-year-old who'd just had the dangers of crossing the road without looking explained to her. Embarrassment at questioning his professionalism caused her to look down. Joe must have seen the movement because he moved closer and placed his finger on her chin, raising it so that she was looking directly into his eyes.

"And that brings us back to your protection," he said. "Can I say anything that will persuade you to leave?"

Megan gave him a weak smile. "You've got enough to think about without worrying about me. I'll be fine. It's really quite possible that Richard Garrett doesn't suspect me of anything at all. Fran and I will stick together tomorrow, and even if we run into him during the day, there'll be someone keeping an eye on things, won't there?"

"Yes," Joe assented reluctantly, "but it might not be me. I can't get too close to him unless there's an obvious reason for it—like eating a meal at the hotel." He reached into his back pocket, pulled out his wallet, and drew out a small piece of paper. This he tore in two, and with a pen that he produced from one of his other pockets, he scribbled something onto one of the pieces and handed it to Megan. "My cell phone number," he explained.

Megan took it, slid it into her pocket, and as she did so they simultaneously became aware of the sound of footsteps approaching. They were light steps and coming fast. Megan glanced at Joe. His face was tense again, and he was listening intently. He looked down the promenade toward Church Island. The walkway stretched out behind them with nowhere to hide—even the beach below the wall was lost to them now that the tide was in. And so they turned to face the oncoming figure together.

CHAPTER 7

The moving shadow drew closer. They could hear shallow breathing and realized that the person was running—well before the limited moonlight allowed their eyes to confirm the fact. Megan sensed Joe's tension mounting until the runner was close enough for recognition to dawn.

"Fran!" Megan called out in surprise, and the figure came to an abrupt halt before them.

"Megan!" she gasped, "Oh Megan, you're alright!" Fran moved forward and threw her arms around her friend's neck. Then she stepped back and said accusingly, "Do you have any idea what time it is?"

Megan grimaced. "No."

Fran rolled her eyes. "Well, neither do I," she admitted, "but I know it's really late. I've been waiting for you for absolutely ages, and when you didn't come, and you didn't come, I began imagining all sorts of awful things—broken legs, drownings, maroonings on Church Island in the dark. You name it, I imagined it! I came *this* close to calling the police." Fran held up her thumb and index finger with a centimeter of space between the two. "Then I realized I didn't know what the number for the police is here."

Joe moved closer to the girls and spoke for the first time, "999."

Fran looked over at him with astonishment. "Joseph Marks?" she asked, then swung back to Megan. "D'you mean to tell me that I risked my life, limb, and sanity to come down here in the dark to single-handedly rescue you, and you were just down here shooting the breeze with him?" Fran jerked her thumb back in Joe's general direction.

"I'm sorry, Fran," Megan said in her most placating tone. "You have no idea what it means to me that you did this." She turned to Joe. "Fran's fear of the dark is superceded only by my fear of heights. It took immense courage for her to come down here now."

"You better believe it," Fran cried. "I've been running ever since I left the last street light—which was miles ago!"

Megan hid a smile. They both knew that the hotel was less than one mile away, so the last street lamp was significantly closer than that, but she didn't press the point. She merely gave her friend another grateful hug, linked her arm within Fran's and said, "How about we walk back together now?"

"Yes, please," Fran agreed, "and then maybe I can get some sleep without nightmares about your safety encroaching."

Joe raised his eyebrow in Megan's direction. "Wish I could say the same thing," he muttered so quietly that Megan wasn't sure she'd heard him correctly.

"Are you coming back with us?" she asked Joe.

"I'll walk you to the first street light," he said, "but I may not go back to the hotel just yet."

Megan knew what he meant. He didn't want to arrive back at the lobby in their company, just in case Richard Garrett was unduly interested in Joe's or her return. She gave him an understanding smile.

"That would be great," she said, and with her arm still linked through Fran's they began walking back toward the suspension bridge.

They said very little as they walked. Joe and Fran had not yet surpassed stilted pleasantries with one another. But as soon as Joe left them at the appointed lamppost, Fran swung to face Megan.

"Okay Megan Harmer, a complete account of your recent activities right now if you please! You've got a lot of explaining to do!"

Fran's words were an echo of her own only an hour or two before as she had confronted Joe. It made Megan realize how amazingly frank he had been, how much he had trusted her and truly confided in her. And it served to emphasize the precarious position in which she had been placed. Somehow she had to walk the narrow line between telling Fran the complete truth and compromising the information Joe had shared with her. Every response would have to be measured against a distasteful "need-to-know" framework.

Megan had always avoided lies and was unaccustomed to circumventing the truth, and so feeling as though she were walking on egg shells, she carefully outlined her visit to Church Island, and took pains to describe her delight with the place. She was purposely vague about how long she spent wandering through the gravestones and meditating inside the church itself, and mentioned running into Richard Garrett as a passing incidental. She thought it important to mention seeing him, just in case he approached her again and brought up their meeting in Fran's presence.

Describing her time spent with Joe Marks was more tricky. She didn't really want to mention that they'd been on the beach, despite the fact that it was the incident with the dog that had actually brought them together. How many people would be on the beach at that time of night with a dog she wondered? It just wasn't worth the risk of it being repeated and arousing Richard Garrett's suspicions.

So she told of accidentally running into Joe on the promenade—which was quite true, and subsequently stopping to talk with him for a while. Things became even more difficult when Fran asked pointed questions about Joe Marks—Where was he from? What did he do for a living? Why was he in Wales? Megan found that she either couldn't answer the question for fear of disclosing something she shouldn't, or that she really didn't know the answers. For the first time she realized how little she really knew about the man, and with that in mind, it was sobering to reflect upon how completely she had believed him—despite the far-fetched premise he had presented her. But as niggling doubts began to worm their way into her thoughts, Megan tried to re-create the feelings she had experienced during the day. She could not deny the fear that she had felt when Joe held her against her will, but it paled in comparison to the overwhelming terror that had gripped her during the sordid exchange in the maze. The thought of Joe now gave her a feeling of well-being, and that was enough for Megan. Until she knew more, she would pray for guidance and trust in her feelings.

***

Megan was not aware of any unusual interest in their arrival back at the hotel. The young man sitting behind the lobby desk gave them

a courteous nod as they walked through, and there was a background
drone of voices, the thud of darts hitting a board, and the clink of
glasses originating from the bar on the other side of the glass-paned
doors to their right. By the time they'd climbed the stairs and moved
into the richly carpeted hallway, the sounds below were lost to them.
The doors they passed were all closed tight, and Megan wondered
fleetingly which one was Richard Garrett's, and which one was Joe
Marks's. She felt a wave of unease at the thought that Richard
Garrett's room could be close to hers, and held out a fervent hope
that if it were, that Joe's door was between them.

"How about visiting a castle tomorrow?" Fran asked as they
reached their neighboring bedroom doors.

"Sounds great," Megan said enthusiastically. "Which one did you
have in mind?"

"I don't know. You've already been to Beaumaris, so maybe
Conway or Caernarfon."

"Caernarfon is where Prince Charles's investiture took place, and I
think they have an open air market outside the castle in the town
square." Megan had done her homework well.

Fran laughed. "Okay, Caernarfon it is. But if we don't get to bed
now we won't make it out of here until the middle of the afternoon
tomorrow!"

"I'm going! I'm going!" Megan already had her key in the lock.

She was tucked in bed a scant twenty minutes later, but sleep would
not come. Megan knew that she was exhausted, physically and emotionally, but her mind would not slow down. Pictures and snatched phrases
from her day mixed and mingled in random patterns through her
memory, heightening her anxiety, and causing all semblance of drowsiness to flee. After watching the clock for an interminable forty-five
minutes, Megan got up. She stood at her bedroom window and surveyed
the scene outside. The velvet darkness was starting to lift as the filtered
light of dawn began to manifest itself along the craggy ridges of the
Snowdonia mountain range. Minute lights still pricked the gloaming,
and even the broad ribbon of blackness that was the Menai Strait had an
occasional bobbing flicker from an anchored boat out in the water.

Megan wondered what her family was doing, far away across the
world. It was hard to believe that their lives were following their

normal routines, while she was having so many new experiences. For the first time since she'd left the States, Megan felt a wave of homesickness wash over her. She craved the security and familiarity of home—a bear hug from her father, her mother's famous enchilada casserole, her brother's obnoxious teasing, and defending her wardrobe from the clutches of her two younger sisters. Even her unpretentious apartment in Jackson Hole, or the madding throng filling the high school hallways held appeal at this lonely hour of the night.

But Megan was not in the habit of wallowing in self-pity or sadness. She gave herself a mental shake and got down on her knees beside the bed for the second time that night. This time Megan focused on offering a prayer of thanksgiving, and as she began recounting her many blessings, including the opportunity of visiting the United Kingdom, she felt the shadows of melancholy flit away. She rose with a happier heart and turned on the bedside lamp, climbed back into bed again, and opened her Book of Mormon. She had not read long when sleep overtook her, and she knew nothing more until Fran's urgent knocks at her door woke her.

"You know," Fran said as Megan admitted her into the room, "if you've suddenly decided to put me in charge of being on time, we're in big trouble! I just tore downstairs, thinking that it was so late that you'd probably gone without me, only to find that you hadn't even emerged yet."

Megan laughed at her friend's good-natured reproof. "Give me fifteen minutes," she said, "and I'll join you for breakfast."

"Breakfast!" Fran replied in mock consternation. "Honey, breakfast's long gone—unless soup of the day sounds good to you!"

Megan pulled a face, looked over at the bedside clock, and gasped. 11:33 A.M.

"Fran, is it really that late?" she asked with horror.

"Yes, it is," she said matter-of-factly, and sat down on the edge of Megan's bed, "and you've got precisely twenty-seven minutes to be dressed, ready, and waiting at the hotel front doors."

"What . . ." Megan began, but Fran waved her into the bathroom impatiently.

"I had breakfast with Richard Garrett," she called through the bathroom door, and Megan froze with her hands on the taps of the shower. Her anxiety deepened as Fran continued. "He asked what our plans were today, and when I told him we were thinking of going to Caernarfon Castle, he said he'd had the same idea and suggested that we go together. He's picking us up outside the lobby at noon."

Megan could think of nothing she'd like less than to spend the day with Richard Garrett, but she had no idea how to get out of it. As she hurriedly showered, dressed, and applied the barest touch of makeup and a liberal amount of sunscreen, she furiously considered—then rejected—dozens of improbable solutions. She looked at her face in the mirror. The sun had given her a pink glow and scattered a few more tiny freckles across the bridge of her nose. Her damp golden-red waves bounced back as she ran a comb through them and teased them into place. There was no way that she could get away with feigning illness—she looked the picture of health.

She could argue against going to Caernarfon in lieu of Conway, but since she'd pushed for Caernarfon only the night before, Fran's suspicions would be aroused. And how could she explain not wanting to see Caernarfon Castle when she so desperately wanted to do so?

Saying that she didn't want to go with Richard Garrett would appear petty and selfish, unless she could furnish a logical reason for her aversion, and stalling in her preparations would only cause irritation. She knew Richard Garrett would wait however long it took to have her under his watchful eye, and purposely provoking him by dragging her feet wouldn't help.

So at five minutes before noon Megan found herself following Fran down the stairs, still frantically trying to contrive some excuse to be elsewhere. As they entered the lobby, the main doors swooshed open and Joe stepped into the entryway. Megan called his name, and for a split second she thought she saw relief flash across his face, but in a moment it was gone. She kept her eyes on him, willing him to see her distress.

"Hi," he said as he approached. "Are you just now setting off for the day?"

"Yes," Megan replied. "I'm afraid I slept in longer than I should have." She saw his lips quirk as he fought back a smile at her confession. All humor left his face, however, as Megan continued. "Richard Garrett has invited us to go to Caernarfon Castle with him this afternoon." She tried to keep her voice upbeat, but her eyes still pled with him for help, and she prayed he'd understand.

"Sounds like a great idea," he responded, matching her enthusiastic tone, "I've been wanting to go there myself."

Megan recognized the lifeline as soon as it was thrown. "Why don't you come with us too?" she suggested. Hope that had begun to blossom within her, however, was crushed almost immediately by a voice at the doorway.

"I wish I could echo that invitation," Richard Garrett said as he walked toward them, "but I'm afraid I only have room for two passengers in my car."

"No problem," Joe said, "I may have to leave for another commitment before you're ready to go anyway, so I'll just follow behind you in mine."

Richard's smile did not reach his colorless eyes. "If you can keep up!" The veiled challenge was obvious.

"I'll do my best," Joe replied, and all emotion in his face and voice was immediately shrouded. He gave a seemingly nonchalant shrug and added, "and if I lose you in the traffic or crowds, I'll meet up with you at the castle."

They made their way to the doors. Richard held it open for the two women, and when Megan exited she saw his car for the first time. It was a silver, two-door sports car that oozed opulence so completely that the presence of the metallic feline perched on the tip of the hood was quite superfluous. While Fran and Megan gazed at the car, trying not to appear overawed, Joe stepped quickly away to retrieve his own vehicle from the parking area below the hotel.

Megan heard him go and immediately moved forward to ask Richard about his car. She was banking on the fact that a few strategically placed questions about the make and model of the vehicle—that he was so obviously proud of—might buy Joe enough time to pull his car around behind them. She was right. She didn't understand half of what Richard told her about horsepower, engine size, or computer-aided controls, but she maintained polite if somewhat artificial interest until a modest navy blue Renault pulled up behind the Jaguar. Then she allowed Richard to help her into the backseat of the car.

At least Richard Garrett hadn't lied about space in his car, Megan thought, as she squeezed in behind the driver's seat, grateful that she wasn't wearing a long dress or high heels. Graceful entry or exit would be almost impossible. The car was truly intended to be a two-person vehicle, but if Megan sat sideways, there was just enough leg room for her to fit on the cramped but cushy leather backseat.

Once Fran was ensconced in the passenger seat beside Richard, he started the engine. The car leaped to life and Megan was reminded of the vehicle's mascot. The engine purred and even the passengers could sense the repressed power in the machine, like the tensed muscles of a living, breathing jaguar preparing to pounce on an unsuspecting victim. Richard put down his foot and the car sprang forward and into the traffic on the main road.

Megan surreptitiously tightened her seat belt and noticed Fran doing the same thing. Within minutes they were out of the town of Menai Bridge, cutting through the countryside and merging with the stream of cars entering the Britannia Bridge. From this bridge, Megan could look out across the water to the Menai Suspension Bridge farther down the strait. Even from this height the swirling water between the bridges, known as the "swellies" for the freak currents and whirlpools, was readily apparent. There was more cloud cover than there had been since their arrival on Anglesey, and without the reflected blue above, the sea looked gray and cold.

All too soon the bridge was behind them and they sped on through the green countryside. Fran and Richard were conversing amicably, and Megan found that she was only called upon to make a comment occasionally. This suited her well. She focused instead on checking for Joe's vehicle behind them, and deep breathing through Richard's obviously reckless speed. She did not want to give him the satisfaction of seeing her discomfort, but the entire journey was accomplished with a prayer for safety in her heart.

Apart from Megan's irritation over Richard's blatant disregard for the rules of the road, she was also chagrined that the one time she didn't have to concentrate on the driving, they were traveling too fast for her to enjoy the scenery. Small villages passed by in a blur of gray stone buildings, while meadows, groves of trees, and private land added streaks of green to the moving picture. They flew past other cars with the buzz of an angry hornet, but each time she hazarded a peep through the rear window, Megan caught a glimpse of blue—evidence that Joe was still behind them. He was not always right on their tail, but close enough to be reassuring.

Within fifteen minutes they passed the road signs welcoming them to Caernarfon, and thanks to the increase in traffic, Richard was forced to slow down. The road was well marked with signs for the castle, and they followed them until they reached the center of town. Immediately in front of them, and stretched out for yards on the cobbled square, were the colorful awnings of open-air stalls selling fruits, vegetables, clothing, household items, tourist paraphernalia, and sundry knickknacks. Local residents and tourists mingled amongst the booths, adding diversity to the picturesque scene.

Dominating the landscape, however, was the magnificent castle towering to one side of the marketplace. Richard followed signs that indicated a narrow road, sloping gently downward between the marketplace and the walls of the castle. He followed the road until it opened up into a large parking area at the base of the castle walls near the seashore. Multicolored yachts, rowboats, motor boats, and buoys bobbed merrily in the sheltered water, while seagulls wheeled above filling the air with their distinctive cries.

Although the parking area was crowded, Megan was relieved to see that there were several vacant stalls available. By the time they'd unloaded from Richard's car Joe had also parked, and within minutes had joined them.

"Glad to see you made it, Marks," Richard's words were civil enough, but the look he gave Joe belied the pleasant greeting.

Joe's only response was a curt nod.

Fran sidled up to Megan. "Whatever possessed you to invite him?" she whispered. "He's like a bucket of cold water."

"Which is a very good thing to have around when you're dealing with someone who could erupt at any moment," Megan whispered back.

Fran gave her a puzzled glance, but was prevented from any further conversation by Richard's hearty call, "Well, let's go into the mighty fortress, shall we?"

Richard's flippancy notwithstanding, Caernarfon Castle was a mighty fortress. Megan felt very small and insignificant as they made their way around the massive gray walls and up the slope that led to the main gateway and entrance. Although the overall color of the walls was chalky gray, stones of varying shades had been used during the castle's construction, creating bands of different colors that encircled the entire structure. Unlike Beaumaris Castle, which Megan had visited only two days before, the towers at Caernarfon were angular rather than round, and the serrated edge of the outer walls and towers was still in remarkably good repair.

The small group paid their admission fee and entered through the main gate. A wooden walkway met a gravel path that opened into a large grassy area within the castle walls. The lush, green grass was well manicured and a vivid contrast to the drab, cold stone that surrounded the area. Tourists milled along the narrow graveled paths that crisscrossed the open greenery. Markers were posted every so often drawing the attention of passersby to particularly well-preserved portions of the historic place, such as ancient halls, kitchens, gates, and private accommodations. There were also signs announcing a number of informative exhibits and displays housed in some of the towers, and after meandering through the inner courts for a little while, Richard suggested that they visit one of these displays in the Queen's Tower.

To her frustration, Megan found it unusually difficult to soak in the history of the castle. Instead she found herself focusing on the verbal exchanges going on around her. As they walked toward the Queen's Tower, Richard, Fran, and even Joe were pointing out unique features they noticed in the castle, commenting on areas of interest, and generally interacting in a congenial manner. It made Megan feel as though she were an interloper peeking in on a scene that was part of someone else's life. Surely if she pinched herself she would wake up, or at least learn that the information Joe had fed her the night before was a complete fabrication. It was so hard to believe, looking at Richard now as he stood indicating something on the ramparts to Fran, that he was really involved in illegal gunrunning, and that he could possibly be the vitriolic character she had overheard through the hedge.

Despite the increasingly overcast skies, it was a shock to the eyes and skin to enter the cool, dark tower, and it took a few minutes for

Megan's vision to adjust to the gloom. She rubbed the goose bumps off her arms and followed Richard's lead as they wound their way up the worn spiral staircase. The staircase opened up into a large chamber with a rustic wooden floor. Three large, glass-topped display cases stood in the center of the room, and around the walls were mannequins modeling suits of armor and military uniforms from bygone eras. Every piece of metal, from the armor to the brass buttons to the weapons, gleamed in the artificial light; scarlet overcoats, medal ribbons, and gold sashes brightly decorated the otherwise dun surroundings.

A brass plaque on the wall announced that they had entered the Regimental Museum of the Royal Welsh Fusiliers. Megan wandered past the row of life-size model soldiers, stopping every once in a while to examine the intricate chain mail and the hand-stitched jackets. As if in deference to those who had lived and died clothed in those uniforms, visitors communicated in hushed tones. It gave the room a mausoleum-like atmosphere.

She moved over to one of the glass cases. It was full of the relics of war. Bayonets, knives, pistols, and even a ball and chain attached to a rotted wooden handle were on display. Megan stood and stared at the glistening weapons, many with elaborately worked silver filigree handles and one with ivory overlay, and sighed.

Richard's voice startled her from behind. "Fantastic, aren't they?" he said.

Megan nodded. "I just can't believe how many people must have devoted their whole lives to make these things. Without all the machinery that we take for granted, it would've taken years to create chain mail for one soldier, or craft the handle of a single bayonet." She paused, then continued sadly, "And all that effort, just for battle—to kill and be killed."

"It was an honor to do it," Richard replied passionately. "Think of the adventure and glory. They were the best at what they did, and they dedicated their lives to the cause."

Something in his voice caused Megan to turn around and look at him. And that was when she knew. She saw it in his eyes—a wild gleam, a fiery brightness that smacked of insanity. He could barely suppress his excitement as he contemplated deadly battle. He may have deluded himself into believing that he was an avenging crusader, but Megan could not see it that way. She suddenly realized that his deep-seated, underlying motive for involvement in fatal conflict was far more base than she could have imagined—he found it a thrill.

A cruel smirk tugged at the corners of Richard's mouth, and it filled her with terror. All her daylight doubts about the validity of Joe's account fled, and Megan took an instinctive step backward. She had to get away before her revulsion showed. Mumbling something about needing to get some air, she moved quickly toward the closest exit, and without thought, groped for the thick hemp rope that acted as a makeshift banister rail for the stairs that wound upward toward the light above.

After following the narrow, spiraling triangular slices of stone stairs around and around until she was almost giddy, she suddenly came out into the open once more. She took a cautious step forward and looked around. She was at the top of the Queen's Tower, and from this vantage point the entire layout of the castle could be seen. The floor plan was unusual, shaped rather like an hourglass, with a crumbling wall separating the two parts at the narrowest point. A large disc of purple slate was positioned in the center of the upper enclosure, standing out against its green, grassy surroundings. Megan knew from her reading that the slate had been placed there as a podium for the investiture of Prince Charles, the current heir to the British throne. He had been crowned Prince of Wales on that very spot in 1969.

Tentatively, she moved closer to the wall for a better view. She tried to focus on the magnificent sight and block out what had compelled her to flee to the top of the tower, or for that matter, the fact that she *was* on the top of the tower. But it was no good. As she inched her way forward, she felt her stomach knotting up and her legs beginning to shake. It was so irrational it made her mad. She could argue herself blue in the face, but no mental cajolery would convince her body that, despite their crumbling appearance, there was nothing to fear atop these walls—they had stood the test of time for centuries.

Megan took a deep breath, then turned slowly toward the stairwell, but before she had taken another step, Richard appeared at the opening.

"Hi!" he said, but his smile didn't reach his eyes. "I thought I'd better check to see if you were okay. You left in such a hurry I wasn't sure."

"Sorry," Megan apologized, and as she couldn't think of any plausible excuse, she offered none. "I was just heading down again."

Richard ignored her and stood blocking the exit. He whistled through his teeth as he surveyed the scene below. "Wow, quite a view from up here!" he said.

"Yes," agreed Megan weakly, then added "Are the others coming up behind you?" There was only one thing she could think of that would be worse than staying up on the lofty tower, and that was being up there alone with Richard Garrett.

This time he shrugged. "Don't know. They were still looking over the uniforms when I left. They may not have seen us go." He smiled again, but there was cruelty in the way his lips bared across his flawless, white teeth, and this time Megan felt a chill run through her. He knew. She didn't know what he knew exactly—certainly not that she had overheard anything at Plas Newydd, or even that Joe had shared so much with her; but he knew that she didn't trust him, and somehow he'd sensed her fear. And it amused him. Much like a vicious dog, Richard looked at her now as though sizing up how far he could push, knowing he had the upper hand.

His eyes left hers for a minute, and he glanced down at the ground far below. "What's the round patch in the grass down there?" he asked.

Megan blinked. "It's . . . uh . . . it's the podium where they had the royal investiture in 1969," she answered automatically.

"Ah yes," Richard breathed, "the continuation of a line of puppet princes from England."

Megan stared at him. "Far better to have a ceremonial monarch than a tyrannical despot surely," she countered.

Richard glared at her. "Far better for the Welsh to be without either one. Look at this place!" he made a wide sweeping gesture. "D'you think Edward the First would have gone to the trouble and expense of building this, or the other half dozen just like it in North Wales, if the Welsh people eight hundred years ago had been as sappy as they are now? They were fighters. They knew what was rightfully theirs, and weren't going to sit by and let any pompous English king walk in and claim it. Edward the First had to build something this strong to protect himself from those valiant Welshmen."

Megan could only stare at him incredulously. She knew from her brief stay in the principality of Wales that the Welsh language and culture were alive and well. In fact, they were protected and revered. All public signs were posted in Welsh first with English translations beneath, and she'd heard the language spoken freely among old and young alike. The countryside was dotted with Welsh chapels, the towns still offered age-old folk festivals, and the shops were full of traditional Welsh items—from sheepskin rugs to slate, from wooden love spoons to pottery. Indeed, as far as she could tell, the Welsh people had lost very little since allying themselves with the English, except perhaps a continuation of bitter conflict and the human tragedy that accompanied such contention.

Richard was watching her face as these thoughts flashed through her mind, a cynical expression playing across his own. Megan knew she must tread carefully, as every word and every gesture would be weighed for or against her, and she rather suspected that Richard was looking for any excuse to confirm his suspicions about her feelings.

"Heavenly Father," she prayed silently, "please help me know what to say and do. Protect me from this man, and let me find a safe way down from this tower."

With her heart hammering so hard that Megan felt sure Richard would hear it, she tried playing for time. "I've never thought of it quite like that before," she began.

Richard snorted. "Oh come on, Megan! You can do better than that." His demeanor had transformed. He seemed almost maniacal in his intensity. "Fran told me you're a history teacher, so you're not ignorant of what's happened on this fair isle over the centuries. The English are obsessed with ruling other countries. How many countries were under their thumb at the height of the British Empire? Think of how much innocent blood sullies the hands of Britain's leaders, and how much they hate those who try to oppose them? Even now they just can't let go. Countries still not freed from their domineering grasp continue to suffer."

Megan would have loved to point out that many colonial countries fared far worse once the English withdrew, but thought it too impolitic given the circumstances. It was obvious that she was being given the condensed version of Richard Garrett's justification for supporting the IRA, without so much as one specific reference to Ireland being made. His blatant half-truths painted a frightening picture of self-delusion.

He took a step toward her, and instinctively she took one back, unwilling to allow the space between them to lessen. He saw the move, gave a sardonic smile, and Megan recognized with dismay that she had already given herself away. Richard moved toward her again, slowly and deliberately. Megan realized in panic that she had nowhere to go—in two short steps she had backed herself into the waist-high tower wall. Frantically, she forced her eyes to stay focused on Richard's face, trying to suppress all images of what lay below, but her whole body was quaking and she felt tiny beads of sweat breaking out along her hairline. She hated the expression of demonic delight in the eyes of the man before her, particularly as she knew that it stemmed from the misconception that he'd singlehandedly brought on her current state of panic. As vehemently as she wanted to deny that, she was reluctant to admit her weakness for vertigo—to give him any further ammunition for terrorizing her.

"Help me Heavenly Father, help me!" Megan begged inwardly as the first waves of dizziness began to wash over her. She reached a hand out behind her to grasp the cold stone. Centuries of weathering had worn it smooth, and as her fingernails dug deep, tiny particles of grit loosened beneath them. But it was solid enough. It was something secure to cling to as other objects began to sway.

"Do I frighten you, Megan?" He was close enough now that she could feel his breath, and Megan turned her head away.

Suddenly, he turned away too. The clatter of feet taking the stone steps at a tremendous rate reached them from the stairwell. Megan heard Richard curse as Joe Marks appeared at the entrance, and although he took an inconspicuous step away from her, he stood his ground as Joe approached.

"Hey, we wondered where you two'd gone," Joe greeted them both as though he were completely oblivious to the emotionally charged atmosphere crackling between the tower's occupants. Without waiting for a response, he stepped toward Megan, whose rubbery limbs refused to move away from the wall. She gave him a watery smile, but he must have seen the anguish in her eyes.

"What's the view like from up here?" he asked, and as he leaned over the parapet, he placed one hand directly over Megan's. She felt his strong fingers curve around hers, prying them off the wall, then he held on tight. "Wow, you can see all the way over to the coast of Anglesey," Joe exclaimed enthusiastically. "No wonder you guys have been up here so long."

"Well, I've seen enough," Richard was doing little to hide the contempt in his voice. "I'll see you at the bottom, Megan." Then blatantly ignoring Joe, he turned on his heel and disappeared down the stairs.

Megan and Joe watched him go. As soon as his footsteps faded, Joe turned back to Megan and pulled her gently toward him by the hand that he still held. She stumbled into his arms and clung to him until the trembling subsided.

"Thank you! Oh thank you!" she repeated the muffled words into his broad shoulder.

He said nothing, but held her tight with one arm while the other hand rhythmically stroked her glossy hair until, with a final shudder, Megan raised her head.

"You okay?" Joe asked.

Megan nodded. "I will be once I'm off this tower."

"Did he hurt you?" The question was almost brusque, but Megan sensed that his short manner masked strong feelings—held in check only by tremendous self-control.

"No," she said, and Megan felt some of the tension in the arm that held her subside. "But he was sure enjoying my discomfort up here," she added.

"Your terror, more like," Joe's self-control slipped for a second, and Megan glimpsed the fury foaming within. He looked down at her, his dark eyes meeting her green ones for a second, then he looked back at the stairwell. "In deference to you, I'll refrain from calling him the foul names he deserves, but we both know what he is!"

Megan shuddered again. "Let's go," she whispered. "Let's find Fran."

Joe took her hand once more and guided her downward. Megan's legs were still very wobbly, and courtesy demanded that descending visitors walked on the inner portion of the triangular stairs, while those on their way up kept to the wide end. This meant that there was no rope to cling to—just the smooth, stone spine of the staircase jutting through the center of the tower. Megan had to keep her eyes down, watching her footfalls to ensure she didn't slide off one of the narrow stone wedges.

The steps themselves were worn almost concave by the millions of feet that had climbed them, and in the gloomy light they appeared wet because they'd been smoothed to a glossy shine. Megan knew that even under the best of circumstances it would be easy to slip, and in her present condition it was likely. She was grateful for Joe's reassuring presence just ahead of her.

The thought made her wonder about his fortuitous arrival at the top of the tower. "Joe," she called out into the semidarkness. He stopped and turned to face her. "How did you know to come up the tower when you did?"

"It was Fran who saw you," he said. "We were down in the courtyard because we couldn't figure out where you'd gone, but we thought if we hung around in the open we'd meet up before too long." He paused. "Fran was snapping a million photos. I think she must have caught sight of you through her telephoto lens, because she suddenly gave out a gasp and said 'Megan!' in a way that you don't ignore. I saw you then, and took one look at the way Garrett was hovering over you and didn't need Fran's reminder about your fear of heights. I bolted up the tower, and I imagine Fran was close behind me, but she must have met 'Mr. Snake Oil' coming down and been reassured that we were still sightseeing."

He gave her hand a squeeze. "I lived through hell coming up these stairs—and when I got up there and saw the fear in your eyes, and your sunburned face bleached white, I wanted to kick his teeth down his throat!"

"Joe!" Megan remonstrated automatically, but found that on reflection she wasn't as concerned about Richard Garrett's dental work as perhaps she ought to have been.

"Well," Joe growled, "he's got it coming pretty darn soon—and it's going to be a whole lot worse than losing a few teeth!"

They were prevented from any further discussion by the sound of footsteps and voices echoing off the cylindrical stone walls. As the people drew nearer, Joe faced downward again, and anxious to prevent any congestion in the tower continued his descent with Megan closely in tow.

Megan wanted to weep for joy when she saw the first beams of light around the last bend. Within seconds they were outside on terra firma once more, and Joe released her hand. Fran was waiting for them. She'd been hovering near the entrance, unsure whether to try going up again and run the risk of being caught in a stream of people going the wrong way if she needed to turn around. As Megan and Joe exited, she gave a small cry and ran to embrace Megan.

"Are you alright?" she asked. Then, without waiting for a response she continued, "Whatever possessed you to go up there?"

Megan didn't want to go into details. Apart from the fact that she didn't know what to tell her friend, she also didn't want to relive the experience right then. So instead she just said, "I'm okay, but I'm sorry I scared you."

"Where's Garrett?" Joe's question brought the women back to the present.

Fran looked surprised. "He's gone. He told me he hadn't realized how late it was and he had to head back to meet someone. He said he'd mentioned that to you at the top of the tower, and that you'd offered to drive us back to the hotel."

Joe let slip a mild expletive, pulled a cell phone from his jacket pocket, and while dialing moved a few yards away.

"Would someone please explain what's going on here?" Fran said with frustration. "I feel like I did at my first Italian opera, where everyone seemed to follow the plot except me. And don't," she said looking pointedly at Megan, "tell me I'm imagining things!"

Joe returned in time to catch the last of Fran's remarks, and Megan looked at him beseechingly. "You can trust her, Joe. You've got to tell her."

"Yes, you've got to tell me!" Fran agreed, looking from one to the other in complete confusion.

Joe frowned, but must have realized that he had few alternatives, for he pointed to a bench positioned against a wall a few yards away. "Let's go over there and talk," he said.

Obediently, the two women followed as he led them to the seat. Megan noticed that it faced the courtyard and that there were no entryways or openings in the wall anywhere near enough for eavesdroppers. She sat down immediately, grateful to rest her still-shaky legs. Fran sat down beside her and looked up expectantly at Joe, who continued to stand above them.

Joe wasn't looking at them, however. He was leaning against the wall, casually enough for the occasional passerby to walk on without a second thought, but Megan could tell that he was far from relaxed. She watched as he scanned the castle up and down, then when he seemed satisfied, he inched closer and began to talk quietly but urgently, and in a manner that neither Megan nor Fran contemplated interrupting.

"I'll give you a concise outline, Fran, and Megan will have to fill in the details later—but only when you're absolutely positive you're alone," he warned. Then, after an infinitesimal pause, he cut right to the chase. "Richard Garrett is illegally smuggling weapons out of the U.S. and putting them into the hands of the IRA."

Fran gave an involuntary gasp, but her eyes never left Joe, and he continued as though he'd heard nothing. "He's waiting for a consignment to arrive by train anytime now. When he picks it up and transfers it to a boat that's lying off the coast of Anglesey, and manned by a couple of IRA thugs, my partner and I—aided by the local police force—are planning to put an end to his gunrunning activities."

"You're going to kill him?" Fran croaked in horror.

"No . . . " A small smile flitted across Joe's lips. "You've been watching too many movies. We're going to arrest him. And hopefully do it in such a way that the incriminating evidence will put him out of commission for quite some time. He's got enough money and connections to pull in the wiliest, big-name defense lawyers in the States, so we have to make sure we don't leave them a single loophole." He ran his fingers through his short dark hair, and Megan could see the tension in his face.

"When does Rob arrive?" she asked, knowing that Rob's presence would lighten Joe's anxiety.

"Rob?" Fran asked.

"My partner," Joe clarified. "This evening, I hope. He called to say that they should have the train on its way again this afternoon."

He glanced at his watch. "But Garrett's departure has me worried. I called the local sergeant who's been helping me out, and he's got one of his men tailing him right now—but something's not right. I can feel it."

"Well, you'd better not ignore feelings like that," Megan said with conviction. "Come on, let's go." She stood up and Joe gave her a grateful look.

"I'm sorry to make you leave before you've seen the whole castle," Joe said.

"I've taken plenty of photos," Fran assured him, following Megan's lead and arising quickly.

"And I don't want to go anywhere near another tower," Megan added emphatically.

CHAPTER 8

The skies were still overcast as they exited the castle grounds through the huge arched gateway. The colorful awnings of the market stalls across the town square were bright spots in an otherwise gray scene. Megan looked over at them curiously, and as she did so, she noticed a row of glass-canopied benches immediately across the road from where they were standing.

"Hang on just a minute," she called to her companions, then with a glance both ways she darted across the road and over to the first of the large transparent cubicles. An oblong plaque was attached to one side of the glass announcing a bus schedule. Megan scanned it, but seeing no destinations that looked familiar, she quickly moved on to the next one. By the third cubicle she was beginning to lose hope, but at last, near the bottom of the list, she found the name she'd been searching for: Menai Bridge.

"Joe! Fran!" she called, and within seconds they had joined her. "Look, there's a bus that leaves here . . . " she consulted her watch, ". . . in an hour that could drop us off in Menai Bridge." She looked up at Joe. "Why don't you leave Fran and me here and go do what you need to. We'll only slow you down. Fran and I can easily spend an hour wandering through the market, then we'll make our own way back to the hotel without you having to worry about it."

"Are you sure?" Joe asked, his relief at the suggestion marred only by his overriding concern for their safety.

"It's a great idea," Fran piped in enthusiastically. "I've already mastered the bus system in New York—this'll be a piece of cake in comparison."

Joe gave her a dubious smile. "Alright," he agreed. "Have you still got my cell phone number?" he asked turning to Megan. She nodded, but still he hesitated.

"Go Joe!" Megan urged. "Don't worry about us, we'll be fine. Besides," she added, "it was 'Mr. Snake Oil' who ditched us, remember? Not you!"

Joe grinned at her use of the epithet he'd created for Richard Garrett. "Be careful!" he admonished once more, then without another word and without turning back, he took off at a steady jog for the parking lot.

The two women watched him go for a few seconds, then Fran turned to Megan. "Okay, Megan Harmer, 'Woman of Mystery,' how about those details Joe promised you could provide?"

Megan gave a resigned sigh. "I know, you must be going crazy with unanswered questions, but I have one condition that must be agreed to before I'll tell you anything." Fran raised an eyebrow expectantly, and Megan continued, "I've got to get something to eat first!"

Fran looked at her in amazement. "How can you think of food at a time like this?"

"Hey, I didn't have any breakfast," Megan countered, "and I've decided that if I ever want to feel sturdy on my legs again, I've got to get some calories into this body!"

"Oh, alright," Fran groaned with impatience. "Come on, let's see if there's anything edible at the market—or will I need to carry you?"

***

Once Megan's hunger was appeased by a quarter of a freshly baked, oval loaf of bread, torn off in barbaric style, and a succulent peach that dripped all over her hands and chin, she proceeded to tell Fran about her previous activities and conversations with Joe Marks.

She began with their first meeting at Beaumaris and his interest in the motor cruiser in the bay, and finished with her encounter with Richard Garrett and Joe's subsequent arrival at the top of Queen's Tower.

Megan found grateful release in confiding this new and startling information to her friend. She trusted Fran implicitly, and had not liked withholding information from her. Nevertheless, she couldn't be completely open about the more intimate moments she and Joe had shared, since she wasn't sure how she felt about them yet. So she found herself glossing over the fact that he'd held her in his arms, had kissed her—albeit unwillingly on her part, and that once or twice she had wondered if he were truly coming to care for her. Neither would she allow herself to analyze whether or not she was beginning to reciprocate such emotions.

The marketplace proved to be a perfect foil for their serious discussion. Their conversation ebbed and flowed as they wove their way between the stalls, admiring handcrafted items of pottery, knitting, and woodwork. They passed Pakistani tradesmen, their raven-colored hair, dark eyes and skin seemingly at odds with their clipped English accents, each displaying tables laden with cotton shirts, shorts, and neckerchiefs of every hue imaginable. Local farmers' wives stood behind stalls, their countertops overflowing with fresh produce: potatoes, carrots, cauliflower, broccoli, peas, beans, and turnips. Other tables featured fruits, some locally grown such as the apples and strawberries, while others, like the apricots, cherries, and peaches, were brought in from the warmer growing areas in southern England.

Children loitered near stalls that sold cheap toys, souvenirs, and postcards, and a stray dog brushed by, nose to the ground exploring every crevice—despite an obvious sensory overload. The air was filled with the babble of voices, distant car engines and horns, the cry of the seagulls, and the rhythmic rushing of the sea.

"It's all so far-fetched," Fran mused aloud as they paused in front of a display of china pieces. There was no complete set, but Fran began sifting through a crate of mismatched egg cups, pulling out a few whose patterns intrigued her. "Are you really sure of all of this?" she asked Megan. "I mean, Joe's ID could be a forgery you know."

"I've already thought of that," Megan replied. "I even thought of it at the time—after all, I couldn't even see it that well in the dark."

Fran shuddered. "Don't remind me!"

Megan smiled at her. "Well, anyway, I've tried not to approach this like the naive country bumpkin that I am, but the bottom line is, I'm way out of my depth. So all I can go on is my feelings, and there's something about Richard Garrett that scares me—a deep-down inexpressible fear." She looked over at her friend. "Have you felt anything like that?"

Fran shrugged. "I guess I was too flattered by his attention to be very sensitive. After all, Richard's as smooth as . . . as . . . "

Fran was struggling to come up with a suitable word, so Megan helped her out. "Snake oil?" she supplied.

"That's not exactly what I had in mind," Fran responded wryly. "And what the heck is snake oil anyway?"

"I don't know," Megan replied, "but it fits Richard Garrett perfectly!"

Fran rolled her eyes. "Well, Joe wasn't overly impressive either I might remind you!"

"*'Wasn't!'* Hmm, do I detect a moderating opinion?" Megan asked, one eyebrow raised. "Is it possible that the failing pupil could yet redeem himself?"

"Let's say he's on probation," Fran conceded with a small grin. Then she stalled any further discussion of Richard Garrett or Joe Marks by handing the wizened old woman behind the table half a dozen assorted egg cups. As the gnarled hands carefully wrapped each piece of china in white paper and stowed them carefully in a paper bag, Fran reached for her purse.

"Thank you, dear," the elderly woman said in a lilting Welsh accent.

As the woman and Fran exchanged money for the bag full of egg cups, Megan had the wherewithal to glance at her watch. She gasped when she saw the time. "Hurry Fran, or we'll miss the bus, and then we'll have to put in a call for another rescue!"

Thankfully, Fran needed no second bidding. With a smile of gratitude to the bewildered saleslady, she chased after Megan, who was forging a narrow path through the crowds of shoppers, and arrived at the bus stop just as the bright green double-decker bus pulled up.

***

Their return journey from Caernarfon to Menai Bridge was the antithesis of their outgoing one. Megan was pretty sure that the lumbering bus never reached a speed above thirty-five miles an hour—and for that, both women were grateful. They had chosen to climb the stairs beside the door and sit on the upper deck of the bus. It was a novelty, and it also afforded them the best view of the countryside as they passed by. However, they soon learned that if the bus was traveling at even a moderate speed when approaching a curve, the top of the vehicle swayed alarmingly. When this occurred, they each clutched the handrail attached to the seat in front of them, and scanned the road ahead for any traffic or a bus stop that might slow the vehicle down once more.

Megan was immensely grateful that her seat on the upper deck did not induce vertigo, and the vehicle's decorous speed helped alleviate her anxiety. She soaked in the sights as they passed: the ancient stone walls, and the dark green hedges—some trimmed immaculately around equally immaculate gardens, and others taking the form of riotous wild bushes clipped only enough to contain cattle within their prescribed boundaries. But most of all she enjoyed watching people board and disembark the bus.

From her elevated vantage point, she observed tight knots of teenagers clustered around the bus stop signs. They broke apart only long enough to step into the bus before regrouping again within the moving vehicle. There were tired women carrying large shopping baskets from the market, some all the more harassed by the young children clinging to their skirts whining for tea or sweets. A few young men came and went. They sat on the back row and seemed to recognize each other. They smoked voraciously the entire time, filling the air with the rancid smell of cigarette smoke. Megan tried opening the sliding window beside her in an effort to circulate a little more fresh air, but to no avail. The window had obviously not been opened in some time, so she finally gave up, sighing inwardly with relief when the smokers moved down the stairs as another stop approached. One elderly man traveled on with them, but he sat several rows behind and was completely absorbed in his newspaper.

After passing through a handful of tiny villages and alongside acres of pasture land, the road opened onto a large roundabout and the bus moved forward, joining the traffic merging onto the Britannia Bridge. Megan gazed out at the Menai Strait far below them. Despite the overcast skies and the gray water, small yachts were relentlessly tacking back and forth against the prevailing wind, their navigators skillfully avoiding the eddies so obvious from the bus above and so treacherously hidden to the sailors below. She was so mesmerized by the sight that it took a poke in the ribs from Fran to bring her back to the reality of another phenomenon closer at hand.

"What's going on?" There was a hint of panic in Fran's voice. "Can you feel it? Can you hear it? Is it an earthquake?"

What had begun as a distant rumble was now stronger and louder. Megan felt the sides of the bus vibrate and turned quickly to scan the faces of the other passengers. Not one of them showed any indication of being even minutely perturbed by the low reverberating sound, but before she could say or do anything more, she heard it— the piercing sound of a whistle coming from far below.

"Fran, it's the train!" Megan almost choked on the words. "The rails runs over this same bridge, underneath the road we're on."

Fran's face began to regain its natural pallor. "That," she said with no preamble, "was a very scary train!"

Megan looked thoughtful. "I wonder if it's the train Richard and Joe have been waiting for?"

Fran gave her a piercing look. "Then it's a doubly scary train, and you and I are going to have nothing to do with it. Right?"

Megan wanted to respond with a resounding "Right," but it wouldn't come. Instead she gave a tentative nod of her head, looked out of the window for a few seconds, and then, when she realized that Fran was still watching her, said quietly, "I have a really bad feeling about this whole Richard-Joe-IRA thing, but the worst part is that I don't know why. I mean, we're not really involved, are we?"

She saw a look of concern flit across Fran's face before it was smothered by slightly forced, cheery confidence. "Of course not! And stop worrying. Joe said there's not going to be a big shoot-out. Richard will probably be arrested quietly, and the event won't even make it onto the front page of the local paper."

Megan nodded again, but this time she remained silent. She couldn't tell Fran that she was becoming more convinced that her feelings of unease sprang from concern for Joe's safety rather than Richard's. Megan pressed her cheek against the cool pane of glass as the first drops of rain began to fall, and she offered up a silent prayer that Joe would be protected and guided to do the right thing.

***

The rain was falling hard when the bus eventually pulled into the bus stop on the high street in the town of Menai Bridge. Megan and Fran worked their way back along the narrow aisle of the upper deck, making for the steep staircase, and clinging to the handrail as the bus lurched to a standstill. Three people were waiting for the arrival of the bus, and had been taking shelter under the green-and-white striped awning of the greengrocer shop adjacent to the bus stop. Wordlessly, Megan and Fran exchanged places with them, and huddled together out of the rain as the gears of the bus ground into place and the lumbering vehicle moved on again.

Coatless and hatless, the women were glad that they at least had sweatshirts to put on over their T-shirts. The temperature had dropped significantly since they had first left the hotel, and with the damp air produced by the now-significant rainfall, they were both feeling the chill. Megan's navy blue-and-white sweatshirt had *BYU* emblazoned across the chest. Fran's in contrast was forest green and decorated with a single large bird soaring over a mountain top embroidered in white. The words *Jackson Hole, Wyoming* were written below. The girls stood quietly and looked around. There were still a few hardy shoppers darting in and out of stores along the high street, and cars continued to zip by, but the meandering throngs were gone.

"The hotel's just over there, isn't it?" Fran asked, pointing down the street.

"Yeah, it shouldn't take us too long to get there," Megan responded.

Fran looked doubtful. "I don't think it's going to matter how long it takes us. We're going to be soaking wet by the time we get there!"

As if to underscore Fran's words, the wind picked up at that moment, buffeting the awning under which they stood, so that the water collecting within its folds sloshed out in an unexpected wave.

"Argh!" Megan cried as her left arm was doused with cold water. "That's it! Come on Fran, let's go!"

Heads down, the two women darted out from beneath their rudimentary shelter and began jogging down the street. They had a clear run, as almost everyone else had taken cover, and although Fran's stride was longer than Megan's, Megan was fit and well able to keep up with her companion. And so it was not long before, puffing and panting, they arrived at the front doors of the Anchor Hotel.

"Whew!" Fran wheezed, out of breath. "That's my exercise for the day!"

Megan opened the door and nodded. Once inside, they both paused and bent over with their hands on their knees, taking time to catch their breath. When she finally stood up, rivulets of water ran down Megan's face from her sopping hair and dripped onto the floor.

"We're making a very big puddle," she said, as she became aware of the glistening water on the tile beneath their feet.

Fran grimaced. "I think a hot bath's in order right about now!"

"Great idea," Megan concurred, and followed Fran as they squelched their way across the lobby and up the stairs, thankful that they were able to reach their respective rooms without encountering anyone en route.

A hot bath was total bliss. Megan lay back, closed her eyes, and felt much of her tension slip away in the bubbly, scented water. But she could not quite erase it all. Her logical, orderly mind kept trying to reassure her ragged emotions, but it was not accomplishing its purpose as effectively as it usually did.

Despite all her mental arguments to the contrary, Megan worried about Joe. It made no sense at all. Why was she—a completely inexperienced young woman—fretting over a man as obviously capable and well trained as Joe Marks. She could do nothing to help him, and he undoubtedly had everything completely under control, and yet she could not get him out of her mind. In fact, it was beginning to irritate her. She slapped the water with her hand in frustration and a large wave rolled to the end of the bath, rebounded, and sloshed bubbles back at her. Megan groaned. It was time to get out.

It took only a few minutes to change into a dry pair of jeans and a clean white T-shirt. Megan checked her appearance in the mirror as she brushed out her damp hair. The white T-shirt made her look positively tanned—well, pinkish-tan anyway! Perhaps, as her mother had admonished her so many times before, she would one day be grateful for her delicate, clear skin that would never appear leathery or weather-beaten. She tucked a stray strand of golden hair behind her ear just as a knock sounded at the door.

It was Fran. She too had bathed and changed into jeans and a T-shirt. Her dark hair hung loose, like a thick curtain behind her, and she carried her large portfolio.

"Are you ready for company?" she asked.

"Of course," Megan replied. "Hang on just a minute." She hurried into the bathroom and hung her wet clothing over the shower rail to dry. When she returned to the bedroom, Fran was in the process of unzipping her portfolio.

"I thought since we're hotel-bound for a little while, I'd show you some of the sketches I've been working on."

"Oh, I'd love to see them." Megan walked over to the bed eagerly.

Fran pulled out the carefully stacked pieces of paper and spread them out on top of the quilt. There were about a dozen different renditions. Three of them were rudimentary sketches of the suspension bridge, and Megan could tell, by the way the strokes flowed, that Fran had been trying to capture the magnificent lines of the structure that she had commented on at first. Three others were landscape scenes drawn from different perspectives, but each encompassing the view across the Menai Strait—from the Snowdonia mountains to the seashore. Then there was a collection of work done while on Church Island. Megan recognized the small church itself, and a couple of sketches spotlighting a few of the many gravestones amidst the wildflowers and native shrubbery. Lastly, there were two drawings of people. One showed a youngish man with straggly, shoulder-length hair standing in front of a small dinghy. There was an emptiness to his face, and Fran had captured the hardness of his eyes.

"Who's this?" Megan asked.

"I don't know," Fran replied. "I was sitting behind one of the bigger trees on the island, sketching some of the gravestones, when a dinghy arrived." She shuffled through the remaining papers and drew out another sketch. This time the man portrayed was older—perhaps early forties. His unkept hair and unshaven face did little to improve his appearance. He looked like a prize boxer—complete with a once-broken nose. "That guy and this one," she handed the paper to Megan, "were on board and came onto the island. They weren't there very long. Just long enough to have a couple of cigarettes and drop the butts on the ground," she added with disdain.

"Did they see you?" Megan asked.

"I don't think so. They walked up to the church, but didn't go inside. They just walked around it a couple of times. Weird really. They had interesting faces to sketch, but they didn't seem like the kind of people who enjoy making small talk with strangers. And besides, I was enjoying my solitude too much. They didn't stay long, and I wasn't about to call them back."

Megan nodded. She knew how preoccupied Fran could become when she was engrossed in her art. That she'd missed the tide turning that day on the island was testimony to the fact that she'd been completely absorbed in her work, and any sort of intrusion would have undoubtedly been unwelcome.

"What's your last sketch?" Megan asked with interest.

Fran handed her the final piece of paper. "It's a really fancy cruiser that was at anchor on the other side of Church Island. The sky was so clear that you could see its reflection in the rippling water beneath the hull. Pretty, isn't it?" she added as Megan continued to stare at the drawing.

Megan found that her hand was trembling. "Fran," she whispered hoarsely, "did those two men come from this cruiser?"

Fran looked surprised, both by Megan's response to her sketch and also by the question. "Well, I suppose they could've," she said slowly. "I don't really know. I wasn't aware of them at all until they pulled the dinghy up onto the shale and I heard their voices. And to be honest, I didn't pay much attention to them after they left either. I heard the outboard motor start up and breathed a sigh of relief that I had the island to myself again."

"How well could you hear their voices?" Megan persisted.

"Just snippets carried on the breeze I guess," Fran replied, looking even more perplexed. "What's that got to do with anything? And why all this sudden interest in those men? I only sketched them because their faces were so interesting."

Megan knew Fran well enough to understand her meaning. Her friend saw facial features, expressions, work-worn hands, stooped backs and the like as outward manifestations of character within. Her ability to capture these things on paper was part of what made her the phenomenal artist she had become.

"Think hard Fran!" Megan urged. "Does it seem like these men had any kind of accent?"

"You're asking me that here?" Fran said, completely bewildered. "Honey, everyone around us has an accent—with the possible exception of Joe Marks and Richard Garrett!"

Megan gave a shaky laugh. "Point taken! But is there any way that they could have been Irish?"

Fran stared at her for a second, and Megan saw her expression change as the ramifications of Megan's questions fell into place. Fran picked up the drawing of the cruiser again and asked, "Is this the same boat you saw at Penmon and Beaumaris?"

Megan nodded. "It looks just the same, and I can't believe there are very many of them. It certainly stuck out as different when it was anchored near the other boats there."

"And so you're wondering if those two men I saw are the crew?" Fran asked as she retrieved the other two sketches. She looked at them again, and Megan drew closer and studied them with her. Her eyes were drawn to the small dinghy. Fran had lightly penciled in a few letters along the hull.

"What's that?" she asked.

Fran studied her rendition. "There was a name on the boat," she said slowly, and squinted as she struggled to make out her own pencil marks. "Dom . . . no, Don . . . Donegal . . . that's it!" she cried. "It was *Donegal Lady*. I remember wondering about the name!"

"It's Irish," Megan said, marveling at how calm her voice sounded, despite her racing heart. "Donegal Bay is on the northwest coast of Ireland."

"So you think it's them—the Irishmen involved in this awful smuggling!" Fran stated matter-of-factly.

"I think," said Megan, "that it's a blessing you didn't make yourself known. I'll bet they're not too crazy about being watched—or sketched for that matter!" She saw the implications of her words hit, and Fran chewed her lower lip nervously. Megan continued, "What d'you think they were doing there, Fran?"

Fran shrugged. "Nothing, as far as I could tell. Maybe they just wanted the exercise. If I'd been stuck in a boat for days I'd probably want to do laps around the church too."

Megan was unconvinced. "They don't strike me as exercise types. You don't smoke like a chimney and live on beer if you care that much about your body."

Fran shook her head and shrugged again. She obviously couldn't come up with any other explanation, but before either of them could say another word there was a knock on the door.

Within a split second, Megan had gathered up Fran's artwork. Ignoring the panic in her friend's eyes, she thrust the innocent sketches of the suspension bridge at Fran, who slid them into her portfolio. The other papers Megan hastily shoved under the bed, and with a brief scan of the room, to be sure that no telltale sheet of paper remained to be seen, she walked over to the door.

She ran her sweaty hands down the sides of her jeans, turned to give Fran what was meant to be an encouraging smile—but in truth, fell sadly short—and then gingerly opened the door.

"Joe!" Megan wanted to weep with relief.

"Hi! I just wanted to check . . ." He stalled midsentence and studied her face. Then he took a step forward and reached out to touch her arm. "Hey, is something wrong?"

"Come in!" she said urgently.

Glancing up and down the hallway, satisfied that no one was observing him, he entered quickly. He must have sensed rather than seen Fran's slight movement as he entered, for he checked himself fractionally before recognizing her and proceeding into the room.

"Hi Fran," he greeted her. "Glad to see you both made it back." Then as Megan closed the door behind him, he added more quietly, "Did you have any problems?"

"No," Megan replied, and with a wry smile she added, "unless you count getting soaking wet!" Then she walked over to the bed, knelt down, and retrieved the papers she'd so recently stuffed beneath. "We've got something to show you."

The tension in her voice must have been evident. She saw a furrow of concern cross Joe's forehead as he stepped closer and took the papers from her.

"What're these?" he asked.

"Fran came in to show me the drawings she's been working on during the last couple of days," Megan explained.

Joe whistled through his teeth in approval as he sifted through the first couple of papers. "Fran, these are amazing!"

Fran gave him an appreciative smile. "You haven't reached the really good stuff yet!" she said, and as he continued to look through the pile in his hands, she began to tell her story. With a few inserted clarifications by Megan, Fran told Joe about her experience on the island—in particular, about the arrival and subsequent activity of the two men illustrated in her drawings.

Joe listened politely until he reached the picture of the cruiser, and then he froze. When he slowly raised his eyes, he looked directly into Megan's, and she knew he could see her fear reflected there. "It's them, isn't it?" she whispered.

He didn't answer immediately, but surveyed the room. The bed was strewn with Fran's artwork and large black portfolio. There were only two chairs in the room—one of which was piled high with maps, guidebooks, and brochures. The bedside table was too small to function as anything more than a surface for a watch or alarm clock, and so, with resignation, Joe sat down on the floor. He leaned back against the end of the bed and spread three drawings out in front of him: that of the cruiser, the older man, and the younger man beside the dinghy.

"Alright," he said in a businesslike tone, "let's sit down and go through this again." He waited while the two women joined him on the floor. Fran sat opposite him, familiar enough with her drawings to view them upside down. Megan, however, moved closer. As she sat down beside him, he smiled at her, and Megan felt her spirits lift a little. She was very glad he was there, and drew strength from his calm, pragmatic approach to the situation.

"From the top please, Fran," he requested. "I want to hear everything you can remember before, during, and after these two," he gestured to the faces looking back at him from the sketches, "arrived on Church Island."

And so Fran rehearsed it all over again, and Joe listened attentively, inserting a few questions every once in a while, but for the most part allowing her to tell the tale uninterrupted. Megan sat quietly at his side, tinglingly aware of his presence without the need to look at him. What was it about this man, she wondered, that attracted her so much? That he was extremely good-looking went without saying, but it wasn't just that. He had the ability to make her feel safe and protected—something that she often missed in her life as a single woman—without feeling as though she were being stifled. He was tender with her in a way that enhanced rather than detracted from his strength. Well . . . , all except the time when he'd kissed her against her will. That had been a display of brute strength. But as Megan reflected upon it, she wondered with a small pang if her response would be different now than it had been then; and she found herself wishing that he would take her in his arms again and kiss her because he wanted to, not because he had to. The intensity of this desire caught her by surprise and she took a sharp breath. Joe must have heard it, for he turned to look at her questioningly.

Megan felt color rush into her cheeks at his glance, and she fervently hoped that he had not added mind reading to his other investigative skills. His eyes held hers for a few seconds before he released her from his gaze and returned his attention to Fran and her drawings. A spark of hope flickered within Megan. Perhaps it was her wishful imagination, but it seemed to her that for a few short moments it hadn't been easy for Joe to resume the work at hand.

She watched as Joe took a small notepad and pen out of his pocket and began scribbling down notes. When he'd finished, he took another long, appraising look at the pictures on the floor.

"Can I keep these for twenty-four hours, Fran?" he asked.

"Yes," Fran answered without hesitation. "I'll probably never be able to look at them again without feeling uneasy," she added.

Joe gathered the papers together and stood up. He held out a hand to Megan, who grasped it with surprise and allowed him to pull her to her feet. She did not immediately withdraw her hand, and he curled his strong fingers around hers. It was immensely comforting, and instinctively she drew closer to him.

"You've given me more to go on in the last few minutes than I've dug up in the last few days," he said. Looking over at Fran, he smiled at her gratefully. "Thanks for these, Fran." He lifted the papers in his free hand, and she smiled at him in return.

"Hope they help," she said.

"I'm headed for a computer right now," he confessed. "If we can come up with a positive ID on these two, we'll really be making headway. At least we'll have a better idea of who we're up against." He paused, and changed the subject abruptly. "What are your plans tomorrow?"

The two women looked at each other. One day on vacation tended to blur into another, and it was often hard to keep track of the days of the week. It had come as a welcome surprise to Megan, when she'd realized a little earlier that day, that the next day would be Sunday.

"We were hoping to go to church in the morning," she said. "We looked up local LDS churches on the Internet before coming. The nearest one is in Gaerwen, about ten miles from here, and their meetings start at ten o'clock."

Joe nodded and seemed pleased. Megan wasn't sure if his pleasure sprang from their desire to remain faithful to their Sunday observances, even while on holiday, or from the obvious fact that they would be safe and out of the way for three hours or more.

"Is Rob here yet?" she asked, not knowing whether this was information he'd be willing to share or not.

Joe shook his head. "Nope, but I'm expecting him late tonight." He offered no further details, and Megan didn't push. "Hopefully, I'll have more information for him by the time he arrives," he added, bringing the conversation back to the pictures. He gave Megan's hand a gentle, affectionate squeeze before finally releasing it and walking toward the door.

"When do you move on?" he asked with his hand on the doorknob.

"First thing Monday morning," Fran replied. "We'll probably spend most of tomorrow afternoon packing up."

Megan stifled a smile. She could organize a suitcase in a matter of minutes. Fran took hours, and would probably need the better part of a day to pull things together, since she'd had three or four days to spread her belongings all over the hotel room.

"I'll get your drawings back to you before you go," Joe promised. "Stick together tomorrow, and stay as far from Richard Garrett as you can get!"

"Hmm, church is a good option then," Fran said tongue-in-cheek, and Joe gave her a grin.

"Perfect!" he agreed.

He opened the door quietly and checked the hallway for occupants. Apparently satisfied, he turned back to them again. "Be careful!" he admonished, looking right at Megan.

"*You* be careful!" she responded.

Then he smiled, and with a soft click of the door he was gone.

Fran and Megan stared at the closed door before Fran broke the silence. "Are you sure you know what you're doing, Megan?"

Confused, Megan turned to face her. Concern and compassion were the expressions that met her. "What d'you mean?" she asked.

Fran moved over to the bed, sat on it and looked up at her friend. "You're falling for him—falling hard!" she said.

Megan turned away. She wanted to deny it, but she knew deep down that she couldn't—especially to her best friend, who knew her almost as well as she knew herself.

"Megan!" Fran urged, "I know he's incredibly good-looking, and I'll even grant you that once you get to know him he's a very nice guy, but . . ."

Fran squirmed uncomfortably, and Megan sighed. "I know. He's not LDS!" she supplied.

Fran nodded unhappily. "And he lives on the other side of the American continent."

Megan picked up the lightweight jacket that lay across one of the two chairs in the room, tossed it to the ground, and plopped herself into the seat. "Well, maybe that's a good thing," she said with a reluctant smile. "It makes our chances of seeing each other again close to nil." Then she wondered how such a *good thing* could make her feel so miserable.

"But you're starting to really care for him, aren't you?" Fran pressed.

Megan looked down. "He's not like anyone else I've ever been out with," she admitted, mentally reviewing some of her previous dates. Many had been fine, honorable men, and handsome besides—but none elicited the intense and deep emotions she experienced when she was with Joe. She felt a closeness to him that transcended verbal communication. He was not LDS, she hardly knew him, and yet she felt more complete when they were together—more so than she had with any other man. Nevertheless, these feelings put in peril the single most important goal she'd held since childhood—a temple marriage. And that really frightened her.

When she looked up again, the compassion in Fran's expression threatened to shatter Megan's fragile composure. She swallowed hard and tried to think of something she could say that might lighten the mood. "Don't worry about me. Joe's here to do a job and doesn't have time to give me a second thought. Once we've left, I'll be nothing more than a minor notation on his report."

"Hmm!" Fran's face exuded disbelief. "The way he looks at you, you may be the *only* thing he remembers for his report."

Disconcerted, Megan wasn't sure whether to feel happy or sad—happy that Fran thought Joe might reciprocate her fledgling feelings or sad that if he did, far more soul-searching lay ahead for her.

CHAPTER 9

The morning brought pale blue skies and weak sunlight filtering in through rain-spattered panes of glass. Megan lay in bed listening to the song of birds in the tree beneath her window as they joyfully announced the coming of the new day. She padded softly to the window and opened it a crack. Moist, cool air assailed her and she breathed deeply, invigorated by its freshness and fully awakened by the tingling shiver that ran through her as the breeze teased her hair and caressed her skin. Her spirits lifted as she surveyed the sparkling clean world outside. Then she moved from the window and into the bathroom where, unbidden, she began to hum a familiar hymn: "Welcome, Welcome, Sabbath Morning." She smiled to herself. She was looking forward to attending church.

Fran was already up when Megan knocked at her door, so it wasn't long before they were seated at a table downstairs eating breakfast. The patio tables and chairs were still wet, so this time they ate indoors. None of the other early risers at the hotel were dressed for church, so the two women received several curious and admiring glances from their fellow diners.

Fran wore a simple knit cream dress with a narrow brown leather belt, and an intricately carved jade necklace that had been a gift from a friend in New Zealand. Her dark hair was pulled up into an oversized clip, the same color brown as her belt and shoes.

Megan's dress was teal green, and made of a light airy chiffon that complemented her slender figure while creating the illusion that she was floating when she walked. A narrow gold necklace was her only piece of jewelry, apart from her small wristwatch which she glanced at occasionally during their meal.

"We should probably head out soon," she said. "Since we don't know exactly how long it will take us, I'd rather be there early than arrive late."

"Why am I not surprised!" Fran responded with a smile, but after taking a last drink of juice, she announced that she was ready.

They saw no sign of Richard or Joe as they left the hotel, and Megan wondered if the men had already left. She didn't bring up their absence to Fran, and was grateful that her friend didn't mention anything either. She was determined not to dwell on what might be happening to both men that day—particularly since it likely involved events wholly out of her control. But it was hard, and she found herself humming another hymn just to keep her mind occupied.

The car was parked in a honeycomb of muddy puddles. After surveying the area for a few minutes, Megan suggested that she be the one to try and circumvent the water, enter the car, and drive it out onto the road to pick up Fran. Fran, looking at her impractical church shoes with something akin to loathing, agreed to the plan, and waited patiently for Megan to complete the maneuver. It didn't take long, and soon the women were headed out of Menai Bridge, following the road that took them toward the center of the island.

Within minutes they passed the Britannia Bridge, and soon afterward Megan pointed out the road that led to Plas Newydd. Then they were in new territory. Megan slowed the car as they approached the first village along the road.

"Look at that!" Fran's tone was incredulous as she pointed to the sign welcoming visitors to the village.

Megan glanced at the sign as they passed and started to laugh. "I read about this place," she said, "but I didn't realize we'd be passing through today."

"Well, there's no way that name's for real!" Fran exclaimed.

"It is!" Megan said. "It's supposed to be the second longest place-name in the world."

"Good grief!" Fran muttered. "I'd hate to see the longest one!"

"It's a Maori name," supplied Megan, taking one hand off the steering wheel long enough to grab her purse lying between the two front seats. "Here," she said, thrusting the purse at Fran, "see if you can find it in the guidebook."

Fran rolled her eyes. "You're taking your guidebook to church?"

"Yes," Megan replied without compunction, "and aren't you glad I brought it?"

Fran could only laugh, and soon had the guidebook open to the correct page. "Llanfairpwllgwyngyllgogerychwyrndrobwllllantysilio-gogogoch," she spelled out, then continued to read aloud, "One of the world's most prosaic place-names, it means 'Saint Mary's church in a hollow by the white hazel close to the rapid whirlpool by the red cave of Saint Tysilio.' Exhausted locals have long since shortened it to 'Llanfair P. G.' " Fran snorted. "Even that's a mouthful!"

"Well, maybe not if you're a fluent Welsh speaker," Megan suggested, but Fran appeared unconvinced.

"Look," she said, and pointed to a long sign on the other side of the road just ahead of them, "there's the name all written out again. D'you want to stop and take a photo of it? Your camera's in your purse too."

Megan slowed the car down to a crawl and scanned the vicinity for a parking spot. A large car park was located immediately beside the long sign, so she turned off the road to enter it. As she did so, however, she realized with misgiving the purpose of the sign. It stood with bold white letters on a polished red background, announcing the village to all passengers arriving at the railway station.

"Fran," Megan said, with Joe's warning still ringing in her ears, "it's the train station!"

Fran leaned forward and looked over at the cement platform immediately beyond the sign. A few people stood in clusters, but it was impossible to judge if they were tourists or passengers. "I vote we drive on to the church," she said with somewhat artificial enthusiasm.

Megan nodded gratefully, put the car into gear, and entered the traffic on the main road again without another word. It didn't seem to matter how many hymns she hummed after that, Megan's thoughts kept wandering back to the railway station, to Richard Garrett, the Irishmen on the boat, and to Joe—mostly Joe.

It only took another fifteen minutes or so to reach the village of Gaerwen. The village itself was straggled along the main road and didn't seem to have any specific center. The two women scanned the roadway anxiously for any sign of a church, and were about to turn back and ask for directions when Fran spotted the sign behind a stone wall. Megan pulled into the small car park, stopped the car, and looked over at the building with pleasure.

It was so familiar. The chapel itself was smaller than ones she was used to, and undoubtedly had a different floor plan, but there was something about all LDS chapels that gave her a sense of being home. She wasn't sure what that certain something was—"The Church of Jesus Christ of Latter-day Saints" logo, the simple, uncluttered building design itself, the care and cleanliness that went into its maintenance, or the knowledge that she shared a peculiar faith with the strangers entering at the chapel door.

She and Fran were welcomed warmly. They met the bishop briefly before the meetings started, and stopped to talk to the two dark-suited missionaries. Megan got the feeling that they were glad to have some contact, however tenuous, with the United States.

Once they were seated for sacrament meeting, Megan looked around her with interest. There were perhaps forty people in attendance, but many of them were young children. One young man and an older man sat at the sacrament table, and the sacrament was passed to the congregation by a single boy and one of the missionary elders. The bishop and his two counselors sat behind the podium, and their seats were the only ones that were permanent fixtures. The congregation sat on plastic chairs that had been placed in rows on the wooden floor. The chairs shifted often, particularly those bearing squirming youngsters, and so their shuddering movement added a new dimension to the whispering, crying, and rustling noises that Megan was already accustomed to. Despite the distractions, however, Megan felt the peaceful touch of the Spirit in the meeting and was glad.

Megan and Fran helped the ward members reorganize the seating immediately after sacrament meeting so that the large room could be partitioned into smaller classrooms. Megan watched the younger children disappear into another part of the building for their Primary classes, and joined one of the missionaries in helping a struggling mother to herd her offspring toward the door. When the task was complete, she voiced the question that had begged asking since she'd first entered the chapel.

"There seems to be a disproportionate number of women and children in this ward, Elder. Is that normal?"

The missionary shrugged. "Well, yeah, it's pretty typical. We're working hard, but it's a tough area. Everybody jokes that all the Welsh people ready and waiting for the gospel left with the early Saints! The people here are great, and I love 'em, but bringing a whole family into the Church doesn't happen very often. Most of the time it's the wife, and she brings her children to Church with her. The men are more stubborn I guess."

Megan gave him a sympathetic smile. "Well, you're doing a great job," she said, and cursed herself for not being able to come up with something less insipid, but the missionary's words had struck a chord, and as Megan sat down in Sunday School she found it very hard to concentrate on the lesson.

She glanced over at the few women sitting alone with their scriptures on their knees. They seemed happy, and most were participating in the lesson. But they were alone. For the first time in her life, Megan really pondered the consequences of marrying someone who was not of her faith. Did she really want to have to attend her church meetings without a companion? Did she want to have sole responsibility for raising her children in the gospel? What about family life without the support of a priesthood holder in her home? The thought left her melancholy, and she knew her life would not be complete without a temple marriage.

Fran, too, appeared to be in a reflective mood as they drove back to the hotel. Megan was grateful for their quiet and uneventful journey.

When they arrived, they decided to forgo eating a late lunch in the now crowded dining room. The hotel restaurant was busy with Sunday afternoon visitors, and neither Fran nor Megan had any desire to enter the fray. The cacophony of voices, dishes, silverware, and clinking glasses that burst forth with every swing of the dining room doors was enough to dispel any feeling of Sabbath Day observance. They opted instead to order sandwiches that could be delivered to their respective rooms.

"The packing!" moaned Fran as they reached their doors.

Megan gave her an encouraging pat. "You can do it! And if I finish first, I'll come in and give you a hand."

"'*If?*' What d'you mean, 'if?' *When* you finish first, I'll be grateful for any assistance you can offer!" Fran replied abjectly.

Megan was still smiling when she entered her room.

***

As expected, Megan's packing went quickly. Thanks primarily to the orderly unloading of her cases, little effort was needed to replace items. She changed out of her dress into jeans and a T-shirt, and packed all her shoes but her open-toed sandals. These she slipped onto her feet and did a last tour around the bedroom and bathroom, checking the corners and underneath furniture for mislaid items. Other than her pajamas and toiletries, everything seemed to be safely stowed away. Her lightweight jacket still lay across the arm of one of the chairs and her sun hat . . . Megan walked over to her jacket and gave it a shake. Her sun hat was missing.

Perplexed, she scoured the room once more, but there was no sign of her hat anywhere. Megan's heart sank. She loved that hat and had owned it for years. It probably wasn't the most flattering headwear in the world, but it had seen her through girls' camp, a hike down the Grand Canyon, several excursions into the Tetons, and at least half of her visit to Britain. She perched on the edge of her bed and tried to mentally turn back the clock, hour by hour, day by day, to the point at which she knew she had been wearing it.

She did not think that she had used it at all on Saturday. Even on their excursion to Caernarfon Castle she couldn't remember having it with her. Admittedly, she had left her room in haste that morning, but even before the rain began in earnest the skies had been overcast and she'd had no need for a hat. So she thought back to Friday.

Friday morning she'd spent at Plas Newydd, and she knew that she'd had her hat with her as she'd toured the gardens. Could she have left it in the car? Later that day she'd walked down to Church Island, and she remembered pulling down the brim of her hat as she faced the blinding rays of the setting sun. Then there'd been the dog rescue. She strained to remember. She pictured herself running her hands through her hair in frustration as she tried to free the dog alone—and there was no hat.

Suddenly, Megan knew what had happened. When she had entered the small chapel on Church Island, she had taken it off and placed it on the bench beside her. Twilight was upon her when she left the building, obviating the need for a hat. With its service no longer required, she had completely forgotten to pick it up.

Frustrated, Megan walked over to the window. The sun was beginning its final descent, showering the sea with coruscating beams of light. She stood mesmerized by the view, watching pink-tinged wisps of cloud wing by, adding glorious color to evening's fanfare. It was stunning in its intensity, and Megan was not content merely playing a spectator role; she wanted to be part of it.

Hurriedly, she left her room and knocked at Fran's door. Fran opened the door to reveal cosmic chaos.

"Fran!" Megan exclaimed in disbelief. "Was it a tornado, hurricane, or an atom bomb?"

Her friend surveyed the scene from the doorway with dejection. "It's not really as bad as it looks from here," she tried to persuade Megan. Then with hope in her voice, added, "Have you come to help?"

Megan laughed. "Not quite yet. I'll help you get things in the cases after you've located all your bits and pieces." Then she ruefully added, "I've just realized that I've done a stupid thing. I left my sun hat in the chapel on Church Island."

"Oh no! Not your 'I've-taken-this-everywhere' sun hat?" Fran was taking impish delight in the fact that Megan, for once, had done something absentminded.

"Yes, that one!" replied Megan defensively. "So, I'm going to run down to the chapel right now in the hope that it's still there." She paused and looked at her watch. "D'you think the causeway will be passable?"

"What time is it?" Fran asked.

"Almost seven o'clock," Megan replied.

"I think you'll be fine then," Fran said. "It was later than that the last time you went, wasn't it? And I don't imagine the tide has changed very much in two days."

"Okay, I'll give it a try. I won't be long, and when I get back I'll lend you a hand."

Fran looked back at the disaster zone and grimaced. "Oh, I daresay I'll still be at it," she said with chagrin.

Megan laughed, waved, and was quickly on her way.

***

The road that led down to the shore was quiet. Shadows were lengthening across the asphalt and an old tabby cat stretched out luxuriously on the hood of a parked car, soaking up the last rays of the summer sun. The lackadaisical feline epitomized the aura of peaceful slumber that pervaded. Even the soft click of Megan's sandals seemed unusually loud as she stepped lightly down the hill.

Megan soaked up all the sights, sounds, and smells. She knew that it was probably the last time she'd visit this beautiful place, and she wanted a clear mental imprint that would remain vivid and true for years to come. She smiled as the Menai Strait came into view. The air, so tangy that she could taste the salt, and the cry of restless seagulls over the rhythmic rush of waves would be her memory of this secluded spot.

Walking under the towering arches of the suspension bridge and onto the Belgian Promenade took very little time, and in minutes she was within sight of Church Island. Megan quickened her pace until she reached a point on the promenade where she could see the causeway. It was still clear of water. Happily, she crossed onto the island.

She followed the gravel path confidently, and as she approached the small chapel she noticed, for the first time, a small bulletin board hanging slightly askew next to the heavy wooden door. She paused to read it. A laminated paper was tacked to the board announcing a meeting schedule. To Megan's surprise, a worship service was still held in the lonely church twice each Sunday—from ten o'clock until eleven o'clock, and then again from five o'clock until six o'clock. Megan glanced at her watch; it was 7:10 P.M. She had obviously missed the worshipers, but what chance did she have of finding her hat if two meetings had been held since she was last here? Her heart sank.

Carefully, she raised the ancient latch and pushed the solid door inward. It opened easily, as if the hinges had been oiled. Megan stepped into the chapel and waited for her eyes to adjust to the gloom before moving forward, away from the door. A fresh spray of flowers had been arranged and left on the lectern at the front of the room, and their faint scent mingled with the musty odor intrinsic to the place. Slowly, Megan walked along the narrow aisle toward the front of the chapel. She peered down each pew, and even went down on her hands and knees to check beneath each wooden bench, but her hat was not there.

Disappointed, Megan turned back toward the door, but continued to scan the floor as she moved, particularly the dark corners, where very little light was able to penetrate. She had reached the wooden stand that held the collection box near the back of the room when she noticed another box, this one made of cardboard and brimming with an assortment of oddly shaped items. It was sitting on the floor beside the wooden stand, and as she drew nearer she recognized the object on the very top of the pile—her sun hat. She gave a small cry of pleasure and reached for it. As she did so, she glanced at the other paraphernalia in the box—cameras, odd shoes, sunglasses, a scarf, someone else's hat, and a purse. Suddenly, she didn't feel quite so foolish anymore. It appeared that she was in good company!

Clutching her hat in one hand, Megan walked over to the door, lifted the latch and began to open it. Then she froze. What made her stop at that point she never could explain, but she did, and by so doing she heard the men's voices well before they were aware of her presence in the chapel.

"Under the bush against the chapel wall! What kind of ruddy directions does he call that? Does he know how many bloomin' bushes there are around this chapel?" The voice was coarse and the accent strong.

Someone cleared his throat and spat, then a second person spoke. "Ah, shut up yer whinin' and start looking! We ain't got all day, and someone could come anytime now."

Megan recognized one of the voices, and immediately memories of the maze at Plas Newydd flooded her consciousness. She took a small step away from the door, but did not relatch it for fear of alerting the men with its click. Panic surged through her body, leaving her terrified and trembling.

Unseeing, she backed into a wooden bench and automatically sat down on the pew, where she stayed shaken, yet straining to hear the direction of the men's movement. Their voices still reached her through the crack in the slightly open door, but they were more muffled now, and Megan could not make out any words. She heard them tromping around the chapel, and before long a new scraping sound reached her, as though something heavy were being dragged across uncleared ground. Then it was gone.

Megan thought she heard faint voices a few minutes later, but they were distant and floated in on a gust of wind. Still she sat, motionless, afraid that even the slightest noise from within the chapel would bring them back. She watched the last rays of the setting sun shoot multicolored beams through the stained glass window, and as they danced lower and lower across the whitewashed walls, Megan realized that she did not have the luxury of waiting long. With every passing minute the tide would be lapping ever nearer the causeway, and she needed to leave before it was too late.

Gingerly, she rose and tiptoed to the door. She pulled it open slowly, an inch at a time, listening all the while for any unusual sound. Then she slid silently through the doorway and stood perfectly still on the doorstep, scanning the island as far as she could see for any kind of movement. Satisfied that the men had gone, she moved out of the shelter of the chapel, but instead of walking on the gravel path, she stepped onto the grass verge that followed it, avoiding the rattling stones.

She remembered Fran had said that the men she'd seen had beached their dinghy on the opposite side of the island, away from the causeway and Belgian Promenade. Megan hoped they had used the same beach again, for she purposely avoided even looking back in that direction, but focused instead on fleeing the island. She kept her head down low and moved quickly but quietly down the slope, toward the ornate gate and the beginning of the causeway.

Water was already beginning to make inroads onto the causeway. As the waves receded they left shallow puddles along the edge of the walkway, but the middle was still clear. Megan spared a moment to look over her shoulder just once when she reached the gate, but the only movement was a flock of blackbirds that took flight in unison from the largest tree on the slope. She watched them swoop low then swing around and flutter furiously for the mainland, and wondered, not without a twinge of misgiving, what had triggered their sudden departure. Then she turned and ran onto the causeway.

She was halfway across when she saw him. He had started toward her from the other end, and had obviously witnessed her hurried exit through the gate on Church Island. There was nowhere to go, and nowhere to hide, and so she slowed to a walk and then reluctantly stopped as he drew near.

"Megan! Where are you off to in such a hurry?"

Unbidden, the question, coupled with the sardonic leer on Richard's face, produced an image from Megan's childhood. For a second, she saw herself tucked in bed with her father sitting beside her reading the old fairy tale *Little Red Riding Hood*. But as the image vanished, she realized with a shudder that this was no bedtime story. She was facing her own wolf—just as conniving and just as deadly as the one in the storybook, but this time there was no guarantee of a happily-ever-after ending.

Tell the truth, she told herself. *Just act calm, innocent, and friendly.*

"I was racing the tide across the causeway," she said, forcing herself to smile at him. Then, in an effort to fend off further questions, she explained why she was on the island. "I left my sun hat in the chapel a couple of days ago." She lifted the hat in her hand, dismayed to see that in her agitation she had completely mangled it. She lowered it again quickly. "I ran back to see if it was still there—and it was!" This time it was easier to express genuine pleasure. "There's a whole box full of things that people have left behind in the chapel."

Megan saw Richard's eyes narrow. She swallowed hard and wished she could unspeak her last words about boxes and things left at the chapel. "What are you doing here so late?" she asked, hoping to divert his thoughts from her activities.

"As a matter of fact, I left something at the chapel too," he said with a saccharine smile. "Why don't you come and show me where you found the box?"

He placed his hand on her elbow and pivoted her around so that she was facing the island once more. Megan instinctively recoiled at his touch, and he must have felt it, for his grip tightened.

"Oh, you don't need me," Megan said, fighting a tidal wave of panic. "The box is on the floor right beside the small table inside the chapel door."

Richard ignored her and began walking toward the island, using his firm grip on Megan's arm to propel her the same way. *Stay calm! Stay calm!* The words echoed through Megan's mind as she fought to control the impulse to run. If Joe Marks toted a gun, the chances were high that Richard Garrett did too.

"It will be quite dark in the chapel by now," Richard said. "I may not find it without you."

"But we probably won't be able to get to the chapel and back before the causeway is covered in water," Megan pointed out desperately.

"Don't worry about that," Richard replied darkly, and Megan promptly hit a new level of worry. It bordered on terror.

Richard did not once relax his grip on Megan's arm as he led the way back to the island, through the wrought-iron gate, and up along the gravel path toward the chapel. Megan was careful not to look at him, but out of the corner of her eye she could see the tension in his face, and noticed that he turned often to check the path behind them. His obvious concern that someone might be tailing him was the only glimmer of hope Megan could find in her current situation. She knew that Joe, or someone working with him, could not be far away, and she prayed that he would reach her in time. Her fervent, silent prayers steadied her as she pled with her Heavenly Father for wisdom, courage, and aid.

Dusk had settled by the time they reached the chapel. Megan automatically stopped at the doorway, but Richard pulled her forward again and led her around to the back of the building.

"I thought you wanted me to show you where the box of lost items is kept," Megan began indignantly.

"I didn't go into the chapel," Richard replied tersely. "What I'm looking for was left outside." Then he looked directly into her face and hissed, "But I don't suppose I need to tell *you* that, do I Megan?"

Megan recoiled from the venom in his voice. "I don't know what you're talking about!" she denied vehemently.

It was as though he hadn't heard her. Megan clenched her lower lip between her teeth, preventing a cry as she looked into his maniacal eyes. He reached out and ran his fingers through her hair. The menace in his voice was abruptly replaced by unctuousness, which Megan found even more frightening. "Come now, Megan, where do your loyalties really lie? I'd have thought with your Gaelic name and coloring you'd come to the aid of your downtrodden kin without hesitation. What kind of hold does Marks have over you? Forget his poisonous words—"

"Take three long steps away from her, Garrett! And put your arms in the air!"

Richard Garrett's oath and Megan's sob found expression simultaneously as Joe Marks's words resounded between them. He was standing on a raised piece of ground no more than twenty yards away, with a gun leveled directly at Richard. In a split second, Richard swung Megan around by the elbow, so that she stood directly in the line of fire, and his free hand went into his pants pocket.

"Don't even think about it!" warned another American voice from behind. "We've got you covered Garrett, so just bring that gun out nice and slow, and toss it over into those bushes that interest you so much."

Richard froze at the sound of a second voice, and Megan watched as he slowly withdrew his hand from his pocket, bringing with it a small firearm. He raised the gun up over his head, then tossed it into the bushes that ran along the chapel wall. Joe began slowly moving toward them, his raised gun never faltering in its aim. Megan could hear footsteps from behind and, although she didn't dare move, she guessed that Joe's partner, Rob, was also drawing closer.

They were within four or five yards of her when yet another voice rang through the dusky air. "I'm thinkin' this would be a good time fer you boys to both drop yer weapons!"

It was Joe's turn to freeze. He looked up and must have caught his partner's eye—seen the inevitable reflected there, for within seconds both guns went clattering down, and two men materialized out of the darkness.

"On the ground!" The Irishman, whose voice was all too familiar to Megan, kicked Joe viciously in the shin, and Joe dropped to his knees. "All the way!" the Irishman growled again, and Joe lay down face first with his arms outstretched.

"Bring the other one over here Seamus!" he yelled at his comrade, and within seconds Joe's partner was similarly situated, prone on the ground.

With the two Americans out of commission, Richard galvanized into action. He dragged Megan with him to the bushes, where he'd thrown his own weapon, and quickly retrieved it.

"What took you so long?" he barked at the two Irishmen, and without waiting for an answer, he asked, "Is the boat loaded?"

"It's ready," the older Irishman's response was sullen. "We've bin waitin' fer you, we 'ave," he added defensively.

Richard glared at him, then turned to the other man called Seamus. "Take these idiot FBI agents into the chapel. None of these guns," he waved his own weapon disparagingly at the firearms on the ground and in the hands of the two Irishmen, "have silencers. Those old thick walls will be good for something. Take them in there," he repeated, "and kill them!"

"No!" screamed Megan, and she struggled to free herself from Richard's grip, heedless of the fact that he still held a gun. "You can't do that!" she sobbed. "You can't! You can't!" She beat her fists against her captor's chest, pushing with all her might to get away from him.

"Just watch me!" he said grimly through gritted teeth. "Move them Seamus!" he yelled over Megan's shoulder, then used both hands to cinch hers to her side. "Shut up, you little witch!" he hissed. "You're coming with me!"

"No!" sobbed Megan again, as she heard the chapel door slam closed and fought futilely against his grip.

"I said shut up!" Richard repeated, his eyes fiery as he moved her left arm across her body, clasping both arms in his left hand. Then he raised his right hand and hit her soundly across the face.

If she had not been held upright, Megan would have hit the ground. She swayed from the impact and the excruciating pain that filled her whole head. Sobbing incoherently, she stumbled after Richard as he dragged her toward the path that led away from the chapel, down the incline on the opposite side of the island from the causeway. She was vaguely aware of the older Irishman's presence ahead of them on the path, but no words were exchanged.

Within minutes the Irishman veered off the path and cut through some gorse bushes, and Richard, with Megan in tow, followed. The thorns on the gorse bushes caught on Megan's jeans and dragged her back as she passed, but it did little to impede Richard's speed. They slithered down a grassy embankment, and ended up on a small crescent-shaped beach. The tide, rising higher all the time, was within a couple of feet of the grass, and a small dinghy, drawn up high onto the shale, was securely tied to a nearby sapling.

"Get in!" Richard ordered, and shoved Megan toward the waiting boat.

Her face still throbbing, Megan staggered forward and clambered clumsily into the dinghy. She moved to the back of the boat, hoping to put as much distance as possible between herself and her kidnappers, but her way was barred by a large wooden crate.

"We've got enough weight back there." It was the Irishman who spoke this time. "Move up this way." He waved his gun at her and used it to indicate a seat closer to the front. Automatically, Megan obeyed.

The sound of sliding shale drew her attention to the embankment they'd just descended—it was Seamus, and he was alone. Numbly, Megan looked down, cradling her aching face in one hand, tears pouring unheeded down her cheeks and dripping onto her lap. *Joe!* her heart cried out in agony. She could not think about what had happened at the chapel—Rob, the partner she'd never met yet knew so much about, his wife, Katy, in the States and innocent of all that had transpired, and Joe. A lead weight settled where her heart used to be. She must not think about Joe—not yet, it hurt too much.

Seamus untied the dinghy and the men pushed the boat into the water. Richard climbed in and sat next to Megan with a hand securely around her arm. The two Irishmen continued to push the boat until it was truly afloat and clear of the beach, then with loud splashes they heaved themselves on board. The older Irishman pushed a button and a motor roared to life. Water surged behind them, and with the prow of the boat slightly elevated, he steered it in a wide arc and pointed it out into the Menai Strait. A quick adjustment to the throttle, and they were speeding through the water into the inky blackness beyond.

CHAPTER 10

A bulky shadow loomed out of the darkness. As the dinghy drew nearer, Megan could discern a single prick of light marking the vessel in the water. It was obvious that the men did not want to draw attention to the anchored cruiser, and yet were equally anxious that another vessel not run into it. The light was a token effort to ward off other traffic.

The older Irishman throttled down and the dinghy putt-putted closer to the cruiser until the sides of the boats grazed each other. Seamus put out a hand to touch the hull of the larger vessel and pushed off gently, guiding the dinghy along the length of the cruiser until they reached the metal-runged ladder attached to the hull. He grasped the painter and tied it securely to the lowest rung of the ladder, then called out to his companion, who immediately cut the engine.

Water sloshed around the dinghy as it bobbed drunkenly in the wake of the churning propellers, and the sides bumped alarmingly against the cruiser. Richard stood and braced himself with legs apart, then he pulled Megan to her feet, and without waiting for her to gain any sense of equilibrium, he dragged her over to Seamus.

"You go first, Seamus. She'll follow, with me close behind. Callum, you bring up the rear," Richard called over his shoulder.

Megan made a mental note of the other Irishman's name before Richard turned to her again. "Don't do anything stupid," he warned. "We've all got guns—and we're not afraid to use them!"

Without a word, Megan turned from him and moved toward Seamus. Her desire was to make a dignified exit, but another wave came in, causing the small boat to pitch violently. Megan stumbled and would have sprawled across the front seat had Seamus not caught her by one arm and pulled her upright once more. She staggered forward again, until Seamus released her and started up the ladder, pausing before climbing very far to ensure that she too had begun the steep climb.

It was the first time that Megan could ever remember climbing a ladder without vertigo paralyzing her midway. The only conclusion she could draw was that at that moment she was consumed by even greater fears. Within seconds she found herself being unceremoniously hauled on board the cruiser by Seamus, and barely made it upright before Richard was beside her, clasping her arm in his vicelike grip again.

Callum was close behind and didn't mince words once he got there. "Bringin' a girl along was not part o' the plan," he muttered belligerently.

"For once, I couldn't agree with you more," Richard replied. He looked out to sea, scanning the darkness for any unusual sight or sound, but he must not have detected anything that alarmed him, for he turned and gave Megan a forced smile. Then in a silky voice that made her skin crawl, he continued, "As soon as we're sure that we've no need of this little insurance policy, there'll no longer be a girl in our plan."

Callum grunted his approval and dug a battered packet of cigarettes out of his pocket. He lit one and passed it to Seamus, who grasped it eagerly and took a deep drag. Callum lit another one for himself, then offered the package to Richard, who shook his head disdainfully and brushed the offering aside.

"Where's the nearest room with a locked door?" Richard asked, his tone abrupt and businesslike once more.

Seamus walked across the wooden deck and opened the first door he came to. "The galley," he muttered, producing a key for the lock.

"That'll do," Richard said, and without another glance at Megan, or the room into which he thrust her with a malicious shove, he turned his back on her and left Seamus to close the door and turn the key.

Megan fell to her knees, and stayed there long after the men's footsteps and voices had faded into the night. When her uncontrollable shaking and tears finally subsided, she bowed her head and began to pray. At first her supplication was fragmented—pleas for Joe and Rob were mixed with pleas that her throbbing face would heal; pleas that she could think clearly with pleas for Fran—that she might be guided to find help, and throughout all of it were pleas for her own strength and guidance. Never before had Megan felt such an earnest need for divine assistance, and never before had she experienced so profoundly the power and comfort of the Holy Ghost. It was as if a blanket enveloped her, radiating warmth and calm throughout her being.

She rubbed her stinging eyes and took a deep, cleansing breath. The misery that had engulfed her was beginning to dissipate, and was being replaced by a burgeoning determination to escape. Groping her way through the darkness, Megan crawled over to the wall. She stood up and began running her hands over its surface, desperately trying to find a light switch. Eventually her patience was rewarded. Megan flipped the switch, then covered her eyes as the bright light momentarily blinded her. Seconds later, when her eyes had adjusted to the illumination, she surveyed her surroundings.

What appeared to have once been a beautifully appointed kitchen and dining area was now little more than a hovel. Megan had witnessed the clutter and grime of some men's apartments while a student at BYU, but none of them came close to the squalor of her current prison cell. Dirty dishes covered every surface and overflowed out of the small sink. The encrusted food was virtually fossilized. Discarded beer cans and cigarette butts covered the floor and accounted for a good percentage of the stains on the filthy linoleum. Megan wiped her hands down her jeans, aware that only minutes before she had crawled across that same floor.

Garbage that had long since filled the solitary can in the corner was mounded around the receptacle, and the stench from the corner was disguised only by the overpowering smell of stale cigarette smoke that had completely saturated the small room. The once-new fixtures each carried their own brand of abuse. The small gas stove was covered in scorch marks, the refrigerator door was nicked and scratched, and the microwave was covered in something brown and sticky.

The disgusting sight before her, coupled with her own experience with these men, convinced Megan that they cared nothing for anyone or anything but themselves. She quickly realized that her only hope for escape lay in exploiting their sole interest—that of self-preservation. But how to do this eluded her.

The only way off the cruiser, Megan reasoned, was by sea, and she had two strong motives for entering the water sooner, rather than later. The first was that her chances of ever making it to shore were far greater if she left the boat while it was within sight of Anglesey. Once they moved into the deeper water of the strait, they would be navigating the swellies, and while that was difficult in a boat, it would be suicide for an inexperienced swimmer. The second reason was that— little as she relished the thought of entering the frigid water—it was her one chance of survival. She had no way of knowing just when Richard would decide that he no longer needed "insurance."

Anxiously listening for the grinding of an anchor being raised, or the throbbing of the cruiser's engines, Megan paced the confined floor space of the galley, desperately scouring the foul debris that filled her jail, looking for something—anything that could provide a means of escape. Fighting discouragement, Megan stopped pacing, and as she did so, a solitary flash of light caught her eye. She turned, and for the first time noticed a set of metal brackets supporting a distress flare and a fire extinguisher. Moving forward to take a better look at the two objects, Megan examined the flare.

The aluminum launcher was shaped like a gun. Protruding from the inch-wide muzzle was a plastic cartridge with the words, *Red Parachute Aerial Flare* printed along its length. Carefully, Megan levered the launcher out of its mount. It was lighter than she'd imagined, and the directions, written in small print beneath the flare's caption, seemed fairly self-explanatory—engage the flare, hold the launcher at arm's length, and pull the trigger.

Megan placed her hand against the cartridge and pushed. It sank into the muzzle of the launcher with a solid click. The flare was engaged. Although she knew that she may not have an opportunity to use it, how wonderful it would be if she could . . . and someone saw it . . . and then responded to it. Mere thoughts of that possibility buoyed her spirits.

The fire extinguisher appeared to be a standard model with customary directions. Fervently she hoped she'd have no need of it, however, its presence was not only reassuring, but had actually planted the seeds of an idea—an idea that was rapidly germinating and developing into a plan. The more Megan thought about it, the faster her heart raced. It was daring—bordering on reckless—but it was probably the only chance she had, and she knew immediately that she was going to seize it.

Carefully, Megan placed the flare down beside the door before hurrying over to the kitchen cupboards. She tore them open, one by one, rifling through them, shoving the items within aside, and carelessly knocking things over in her haste. By the end of her foray, she had accumulated two pans, one a large, deep saucepan, the other a smaller frying pan; a lethal-looking serrated knife; a stained coffee mug; a box of matches; a half-full bottle of cooking oil; and a dishcloth—bone dry and stiff with encrusted food.

Megan stood with her hands on her hips taking inventory of the items on the floor before her. She sighed. It was a pitiful arsenal, but the best she could assemble under the circumstances. Yet she needed one more ingredient for her plan to work. Scanning the walls and ceiling, she was confident that an expensive cruiser would have it as standard equipment. Her hopes were realized when, at last, she spied a small round disc on the ceiling directly above the stove. Its minute glowing red light indicated that it was operational.

Letting out a deep breath, Megan moved over to the stove and cleared a space amidst the pots, pans, and plates amassed there. She set the dishcloth down next to the stove and placed the large saucepan on a burner directly beneath the smoke detector. After pouring the cooking oil into the pan, she turned the burner on high. Placing the box of matches beside the dishcloth, Megan picked up the knife.

She sat down on the floor, held out the bottom of her T-shirt, and punctured the fabric about six inches up. As fast as she could, without risking her fingers or torso, she began sawing through the material. By pulling and twisting, she worked her way around the shirt until she had cut away a six-inch loop. Again she applied the knife to the piece of fabric, this time cutting it across the width, so that she ended up with a long, rectangular strip of material. Quickly she picked it up and placed it across her face so that the ends wrapped around to tie behind her head. It was just long enough for a tight knot to hold it in place.

Satisfied, Megan took it off and carried it and the coffee cup over to the sink. First she filled the cup with water, then she held the fabric under the tap until it was completely saturated. Placing the cup near the stove and the sodden fabric on the floor next to the flare, she picked up the frying pan and placed it with the flare and wet fabric, then slid her sandals off her feet and tucked them under one of the chairs. Finally, she stood and gave her preparations one last mental check.

The possibility that she would asphyxiate before help arrived was very real, but Megan knew that unless she got off the cruiser, she would surely die. With trembling fingers she tied the soggy cloth around her face. It was cold and heavy, but she hoped that should the need arise, it would buy her a little time in a smoke-filled room. Once she had it tied tightly, she slid the front down below her chin so that it rested on her shoulders like a wet scarf. She was ready.

It was hard to light a match with shaking fingers. It took four times before the match stayed lit long enough for her to ignite a corner of the dry dishcloth she held in her other hand. Hungry flames spread rapidly, and when Megan threw the cloth into the waiting pan of boiling oil, she leaped back against the far wall, watching aghast as a huge yellow flame burst out of the pot. The fire roared as it ravenously consumed the oil, growing ever more ferocious, and for a few seconds Megan was convinced that she'd made an awful mistake.

Gingerly, she inched her way forward until she could reach the cup of water. She grabbed it by the handle, took another step backward then flung the contents of the mug at the fire. There was a deafening hiss as oil and water rejected one another and liquid spat out of the pot singeing all that it touched, but so too came steam and smoke—billowing up toward the smoke detector.

Megan ran to the door. She knelt beside it clutching the frying pan in both hands, and just as the smoke detector's first strident warnings rent the air, she began walloping the wooden door with the pan and yelling at the top of her lungs.

"Fire! Fire!" she screamed, banging and banging with all her might.

Perspiration was streaming down her forehead. The room was getting hotter and smokier by the second, and Megan wasn't sure how much more she could tolerate. Remembering all the "stop, drop, and roll" fire drills she had endured at school, she crouched down as low as she could, but kept her feet beneath her. She had to be ready as soon as she heard movement on the other side of the door. She prayed it wouldn't be long.

Reluctantly she pulled the wet cloth up off her neck, and covered her nose and mouth. With both hands free, she continued assaulting the door with the frying pan. Breathing was easier at first with the thick damp filter across her face, but it was not long before Megan started feeling light-headed. Debilitated she dropped the frying pan, and just as she wondered if all had been in vain, she heard the sound of a key in the lock.

Drawing on inner strength that surprised her, Megan grabbed the flare, slid out of reach of the moving door, and placed herself facing the crack in the doorway. She found herself leaning forward, preparing for a sprint just as she had when she'd run for her high school track team. It had been many years, but even without starting blocks the position came easily to her. Smoke swirled. Wheezing, she teetered in her place, straining to watch the door through stinging, watering eyes. As though in slow motion, she saw the crack of light widen as the door swung open.

It crashed into a wooden chair that had not been returned to its rightful place in the kitchen, and Megan saw Seamus stumble backward as the wall of heat and smoke hit him like an express train.

"What the . . . " he shouted.

But Megan didn't wait to hear the rest. As though a starting gun had just sounded on the most difficult race of her life, she leaped forward and shot out of the galley, running straight ahead for the cruiser's railings. She tore the cloth down off her face and gulped in deep cleansing breaths of fresh air as she ran barefoot across the deck. With lungs burning, she threw herself at the metal bars. She could hear thundering footsteps starting across the deck. Frantically, she climbed up and over the railing, her hands slipping as she attempted to keep a grip on the flare clenched in her left hand, and losing precious seconds in the process.

At last she stood perched on about nine inches of deck that stuck out beyond the railing. Seamus was almost upon her, and there was no escape but into the murky depths below. Desperate to slow his advance, Megan pointed the flare in his direction, pulled the trigger, and without allowing herself any time to contemplate what she was about to do, she leaped off the deck. She was vaguely aware of his screams as she hit the water, but then it was as though all the air had been sucked out of her lungs, and she found herself convulsing as the Irish Sea buried her beneath its frigid waves.

Raw instinct drove her upward. She could barely control her limbs as the shock of sudden immersion impacted her body, but finally her head burst forth into the night air. Megan took a rasping breath, swallowed water, choked, and went under again. This time, however, she remained near the surface and came up for air immediately after a wave rolled over her. Again she bobbed, and again she took a breath. Desperately, she tried to move with the rhythm of the water around her, allowing its motion to help rather than hinder her fight for survival.

Still shivering uncontrollably, but without the searing pain in her lungs, she shook the water from her eyes and looked up. To her amazement, the night sky still showed a few sparkling traces of the flare, spiraling slowly downward to the water below. Not knowing the exact path it had taken, Megan fervently hoped its illumination would bring a response.

Another wave washed over her, and as she surfaced once more a high-pitched buzz, like that of an angry bee, whizzed passed her head, entering the water beside her with a splat. Confused, she willed herself forward. Her body was becoming torpid, her arms and legs sluggish. Another bee sang past Megan's ear, but this time she saw it enter the water. Fear seized her as she realized they were no bees—they were bullets!

She flung herself away from the spot where the last bullet entered the sea. Her flailing arms and legs did little more than keep her afloat, and she relied on the waves to propel her toward the shore. A few more bullets zipped by, but Megan had neither the strength nor desire to look back. It was all she could do not to go under the water permanently.

When she reached the point of losing virtually all sensation, a searing pain tore through her right arm—a vicious confirmation that she was still alive. She cried out, instinctively pulling her arm close to her body, and immediately she floundered. As the water surged over her head, Megan foggily accepted her fate. She was completely spent—she had no more to give.

A huge surge of water lifted her up and spewed her to the surface. As Megan automatically took another breath, she was faintly aware of a rhythmic churning. In her stupor, it seemed that the night air was filled with the powerful throbbing of the cruiser's engines, and the vessel was moving away.

She knew that she should have felt relieved, but she felt nothing. She could not feel anymore; she could not think anymore; it was all too late. A bright light blinded her, and she wondered vaguely if she'd already died. Voices called out to her. Joe . . . one sounded like Joe . . . she must have died and Joe was there—that was a pleasant thought.

A large splash sounded beside her, then there were arms—pulling, dragging her. More voices. More people. Megan felt herself being lifted out of the water, and then she was lying on her back, shivering and shaking uncontrollably again. From a far distance she heard people shouting.

"Strip her, Fran! Quick! Get everything off except her underwear!" It was Joe's voice again. "Blankets! Where are the blankets?"

Hands pulled and tore at her clothing. Then there was Fran's voice, "Joe, she's bleeding! Look at her arm!" Megan wondered why her friend sounded so scared. She tried to reassure her—to tell her that her arm didn't hurt at all, but no words would come.

"Ian, we need your first-aid box, fast!" Joe was being bossy again, Megan's muddled thoughts churned. More hands and voices converged over her, followed by a shooting pain down one arm. Steady hands on her head, and a voice she recognized but could not place. Then nothing.

CHAPTER 11

The sensation of warmth and security was the first thing to filter through to Megan—and it felt wonderful. As she stirred slightly, strong arms tightened around her, and a soft voice called her name. She tried to open her eyes, but they were too heavy, so instead she snuggled down farther into the warmth and softness that surrounded her, and lost consciousness once more.

It was pain that aroused her the second time—a throbbing ache down one arm that was slowly spreading into her shoulder. Again she stirred, and again a soft voice called to her. Her eyelids fluttered open this time. At first she could see nothing but blackness, then gradually a face came into focus above her—a face gazing down at her so tenderly that Megan felt tears sting her eyes.

"Joe!" she croaked, her voice barely audible. "Are we dead?"

"No," he whispered back, his voice husky with emotion, "but you sure came close."

"Where are we then?" Megan was beginning to sense the presence of others moving and talking nearby, but apart from the dim lighting, her vision was also obscured by a thick woollen blanket wrapped around her from head to toe, mummylike.

"We're on the lifeboat, heading back to shore," Joe replied.

It was too much for Megan to comprehend. She felt her eyelids droop again, and moved her head slightly so that her cheek rested against Joe's strong chest.

"Stay with me, Joe," she whispered urgently. "Stay with me!"

"I'm not leaving until you're safely in a hospital," he reassured her, and ran a calloused finger over her cheek bone and down under her chin. "Hang in there Megan! Keep fighting, okay?"

Megan gave him a weak smile before she drifted out of consciousness again.

***

Someone was making too much noise and Megan couldn't sleep. She tossed her head to and fro. Her shoulder and arm moved up against something solid, and Megan cried out in pain. Joe cupped one large hand around the side of her face, soothing her with his touch and voice.

"It's alright, Megan. We're docking the boat, and the ambulance is waiting. Not long now and you'll have that arm looked at." He ran his fingers through her damp hair, rhythmically stroking her head.

A shout from the shore drew Joe's attention, followed by the sound of running footsteps.

"They're ready for her, Joe." It was Fran, a little out of breath. "I've given the ambulance crew an update on Megan's condition. They'll get her straight to the hospital." She moved closer and noticed, for the first time, that Megan's eyes were open. "Megan!" she cried, and reached out to touch her friend. Even in her muddled state, Megan could see that Fran's eyes were red and puffy.

"Hi, Fran," she croaked.

Fran leaned over and kissed her friend's forehead, fresh tears glistening in her eyes. Then she stepped back and with a slight break in her voice asked, "Can I do anything to help, Joe?"

"Nope, I've got her," was Joe's reply, then he turned to Megan. "I'll do my best not to hurt your arm," he said. "On the count of three we're getting up, okay?"

Megan gave a minute nod, and listened as Joe calmly counted, "One . . . two . . . three." With that he heaved himself to his feet, straining to prevent Megan from moving in his arms. Her arm throbbed with each of Joe's footsteps, but no racking pain ensued. She buried her face in his shoulder and allowed his even tread to lull her into a fitful doze.

"The gurney's ready for her, sir." Joe had come to a standstill, and an unfamiliar voice was speaking.

"Thanks," Joe replied, and Megan felt herself being lowered onto a narrow bed.

Wide straps were cinched around her body, then there was a slight jolt, and the gurney was moving. Joe stayed with her, holding her hand as she entered the ambulance, and he sat beside her once the gurney was anchored in place.

"Not long now, miss," the strange man in a white coat said, then he turned to Joe and asked, "Anyone else coming with us?"

"I am!" It was Fran.

"Alright, miss. Move away from the door now, and we'll be on our way."

Within seconds the vehicle was moving. Megan didn't have the strength to speak, and only flickered her eyes open for brief moments at a time, but Joe's tender solicitude and Fran's loyal presence brought her great comfort. Although she was virtually oblivious to her surroundings, she was aware of the loving care of those nearby. Even the strange siren wailing through the air, so different from the ones she heard at home, did not concern her—after all, it couldn't possibly have anything to do with her.

"If you could help me loosen the blanket just a little, sir, I'll check her vital signs." It was the strange man's voice again.

Megan was vaguely aware of hands and instruments touching her arms and chest, and the sound of voices talking quietly above her head. Then there were doors opening, bright lights, running feet, and more voices—and sometime during the ensuing confusion, Joe disappeared. She called his name in vain, trying to find him in the sea of unfamiliar faces—but he was gone. Just as panic welled up within her, Fran appeared beside her.

"Megan, I'm here!" Fran drew closer and grasped her friend's hand tightly. "Joe had to go. He's needed by the coast guard right now, but he'll come back, and I won't leave you!"

Gratefully, Megan squeezed her friend's hand and closed her eyes, but not before a tear escaped and rolled down her cheek. This surely had to be some sort of nightmare from which she would soon awake. She didn't even know where she was or why she was there. Desperately, she clung to Fran's hand and offered up a disjointed prayer.

It was as though she had entered some kind of vacuum, where time had no meaning. Megan lay on the hospital bed surrounded by monitors with illuminated displays and strident beeps. People came and went—drawing blood, taking her pulse, evaluating her blood pressure, and listening to her chest. IV bags were refilled, dressings placed on her arm, warm blankets wrapped around her, then exchanged for others; and all the while Fran stayed close by. There were times when Megan would open her eyes to see her friend asleep, slumped over in a nearby chair; and other times when Fran would be leaning over the bed anxious to converse for just a few minutes before Megan's strength failed her again.

Only when Megan opened her eyes to discover bright sunlight streaming through the window behind her bed, did she realize that she had survived the night and entered a new day. The warm summer sun did much to cheer her, and for the first time she felt that she could look around and observe her surroundings with a clear mind.

She was lying on a metal-framed bed between starched white sheets and woollen blankets. Her head was elevated on a firm fat pillow, and from this position she could see multiple wires running from various points on her body into a machine that sat beside her bed. A large screen on the machine displayed several flourescent green lines zigzagging up and down in a fairly even pattern, but she noticed that the lines immediately swerved from their regular course with the slightest movement of her body.

On the other side of the bed was a tall stainless-steel stand. This held a transparent bag of fluid that was hooked to its top and was connected by a long tube to an IV running into her right arm. Before entering her hand, the tube passed through a small box attached to the stand. Further scrutiny showed this to be some sort of timer that monitored the flow of liquid and warned when the supply was low. It appeared that there were twenty minutes left before some type of alarm would sound.

A dull throbbing in Megan's left arm drew her attention to the large dressing that wrapped its way from a few inches below her shoulder to just above her elbow. Gingerly, she flexed her fingers and then slowly bent her elbow. Although the pain intensified with the movement, Megan was reassured that she still had feeling and flexibility all the way down to her fingertips.

The only splash of color in the otherwise sterile environment in which Megan found herself, was Fran. Curled up in a sage green, vinyl-upholstered chair, her friend was fast asleep with her long dark hair falling in tangled waves across the arm of the chair. Her crimson T-shirt and khaki pants were looking considerably more wrinkled than they had when they were first donned. Fran's sandals had been discarded in a corner of the room, but Megan saw no sign of her friend's personal items—no purse, bag, or jacket.

This observation refocused Megan's attention on the absence of her own belongings. Looking down at the pale blue hospital gown she wore, she suddenly wondered where her own clothes were, and the questions that had echoed through her befuddled mind throughout the turmoil of the nighttime hours resurfaced. Where was she? What was she doing here? And what was going on around her?

A light tap on the door sounded, and Megan looked up anxiously, uncertain of what to expect. The woman who entered was short and slightly plump with tight gray curls covering her head. She was dressed in a white uniform with navy trim, and a gold pin on her left breast pocket announced that she was *Alice Jones, RN.* She observed Megan's alert expression and beamed, her small dark eyes almost disappearing as she smiled.

"Well now, you're looking much better." She glanced over at Fran's sleeping form on the chair and lowered her voice. "How're you feeling?" she added.

Megan gave her a weak smile. "Better, I think. I'm not sure." It felt like a very silly answer, but it was the truth. With no solid recollection of how she had been feeling hours before, it was hard to make any kind of comparison. However, she knew she didn't feel anything like she normally did.

"Well, let's have a quick check, shall we?" The nurse approached, still smiling, and unwrapped a stethoscope that was hanging around her neck.

Megan lay quietly as the nurse listened to her heart and lungs and measured her blood pressure, then she obediently raised her tongue for the proffered thermometer, and waited while the nurse jotted her findings onto a chart attached to the end of her bed. Once the thermometer was taken out of her mouth, however, Megan began asking questions.

"Could you . . . could you tell me where I am?"

The nurse looked up from the chart in surprise. "Why, at the hospital dear!"

"Uh, yes," Megan stifled her feelings of embarrassment at having to ask such seemingly juvenile questions and plowed on, "but which hospital?"

Putting the chart back onto the hook at the end of the bed, the nurse gave Megan a searching look, and must have seen the anxiety in her eyes because her own features softened.

"Bless my soul, you really don't remember anything that happened to you, do you?"

Megan shook her head woefully.

The nurse moved toward her and tucked the sheets back around Megan, and as she smoothed them down she said, "You're in the intensive care unit at St. David's Hospital in Bangor. An ambulance brought you in late last night, after the Beaumaris lifeboat crew pulled you out of the Menai Strait. You were suffering from severe hypothermia and a deep flesh wound down your left arm."

At the nurse's words, forgotten images flashed through Megan's mind—being in the ambulance with Joe and Fran, lying wrapped in a blanket in Joe's arms on a boat, the frigid cold water, sinking, the pain in her arm, escaping from the cruiser . . . It all came back so clearly and so fast that she gave an involuntary cry.

The nurse leaned over and patted her hand comfortingly. "It's all right, dear. You're going to be just fine." Then she stepped back and eyed the monitor readouts before adding, "I think once the doctor's seen you we'll be able to move you down to the regular ward." She smiled encouragingly at Megan. "Now, how about a nice cup of tea before he gets here?"

Taken off guard, Megan stuttered, "Oh . . . uh . . . no thanks!"

"Are you sure, dear? I'd have thought you'd have been dying for one by now! It's no trouble," she added.

"No, really," Megan assured the nurse, "not tea, but perhaps a small glass of juice?" She looked up hopefully, and it was Alice Jones's turn to look surprised.

"Juice? Well, I'm sure I can round some up. I'll go and see what I can find." She gave Megan a parting smile, then turned and slipped out of the room.

As soon as the door closed, Megan looked over at Fran. She was still asleep! It had been a long standing joke between them that Fran could sleep through anything, but up until now Megan had always assumed that Fran's heavy sleeping occurred only while she was horizontal in a bed. Her current cramped sleeping quarters took her to a new level in slumbering skills.

"Fran!" Megan called, frustrated that her voice was still so weak. "Fran!" she called again, and this time her friend stirred. Encouraged, Megan tried once more. "Fran!"

Fran raised a sleepy head and brushed her long dark locks out of her face. She blinked hard in the sunlight, and then as recollection of her environment came surging back, she sat up quickly and looked over at Megan.

"Megan!" she cried happily. "You're awake!" She got up stiffly and moved over to Megan's bed. She leaned over and reached out for her friend's hand. "How're you feeling?"

"Weak!" Megan replied with a grimace. "But at least I'm fully conscious and not fighting through the fog that surrounded me all night." She looked at her friend earnestly. "Fran, you've got to help me understand all this." With her free hand she gestured around the room, taking in the monitors, IV, and her own small form in the large hospital bed.

"I think there's going to be a lot of explaining done by several people today," Fran began grimly. She shook her head, groaned, and tightened her clasp on Megan's hand. "We came so close to losing you, Megan." Megan was moved to hear the break in Fran's voice. "If it hadn't been for Joe and Rob—"

"You've met Rob, Joe's partner?" Megan interrupted.

Fran nodded and continued. "Joe dived in for you and brought you up out of the water. Once he got you on board the lifeboat Rob gave you a priesthood blessing—right there on the deck." Fran stopped, and Megan could see the tears in her eyes.

"But Fran," Megan's emotions were close to the surface too, "I thought they were dead! I thought . . . I thought . . . Seamus had . . ." A lump the size of an orange had formed in Megan's throat, and she couldn't finish her sentence. Instead a sob burst forth, and Fran immediately rose and—regardless of all the tubes and wires—flung her arms around Megan's narrow shoulders. Fran held her close and cried with her as they released the pent-up emotions of the last twelve hours.

When their tears subsided, Fran pulled back and gazed at her friend from arm's length. "Well, I believe we both look absolutely stunning!"

Megan took in Fran's red, swollen eyes, her disheveled hair and wrinkled clothes, and had to smile. "At least you're fully dressed," she offered.

Fran pulled a face. "Which is more flattering, a shapeless light blue gown—clean and pressed, mind you!—or clothes that fit but are creased, dirty and smell . . ." she put her nose to her T-shirt and wrinkled up her nose, "like seawater?"

"My hair smells like seawater!" Megan said, and tried running her fingers through her short waves, only to have them become caught in the stiff tangles.

"Hmm." Fran surveyed her friend's matted hair, the usually glossy golden-red curls, dull and lifeless. "I bet you'd feel much better if we could get your hair washed. If I helped, d'you think you're strong enough to make it to the sink? Let's ask the nurse when she comes in."

As though she'd been waiting for just that cue, there was a light knock on the door and in walked Nurse Jones with a glass full of orange juice. She saw Fran at the bedside and smiled. "Oh good, your friend's awake." Then turning back to Megan, she said, "Sorry it took me so long, dear. I had to go down to the lower floor to get it. Is orange juice alright?" Without waiting for a reply, she pulled a small table on wheels away from the corner of the room, pushed it over to the bed, and after adjusting it to the right height for Megan, she placed the glass within her grasp.

"Thank you so much." Tentatively Megan reached for the glass. Her hand shook slightly as she lifted it to her lips, but the juice was pure ambrosia to the taste.

"There now!" said the nurse with a pleased expression. "The doctor's on his way, and all we need is a good report from him, and you'll be well on your way to feeling one hundred percent again." She turned to Fran. "I'm sorry I didn't bring up another glass. Would you like me to fetch you a cup of tea instead?"

"No, thanks," Fran smiled in return. "Is there a cafeteria or snack bar nearby? Maybe I could run and get something there while the doctor checks Megan?"

"That's a good idea," the nurse approved wholeheartedly. "The cafeteria is down the stairs and to your left."

"That okay with you?" Fran asked Megan. "At least I won't have to worry too much about running into anyone I know looking like this!" She glanced down at her crushed ensemble, rolled her eyes, and gave a small shake of her head. "Oh well . . . I'll see you in a few minutes," she said, obviously deciding that any further comment on her appearance would be superfluous, then she slipped out of the room just before the doctor entered.

Dr. Bill Hopkins, as he introduced himself, was a large burly man with a balding head and fine wispy white hair forming a halo effect around his crown. He wore a long white coat and half-moon spectacles that perched rather precariously at the end of his bulbous nose.

"Well now," he said as he reviewed Megan's chart, "looks like you've come a long way in just a few hours. Feeling better, are you?" He peered at her over the top of his spectacles.

"Yes, thank you," Megan replied, a little in awe of the large, blustering doctor.

"Splendid! Splendid! That's what we like to hear!" He put the chart down and proceeded to examine Megan and check all of her vital signs. He nodded to himself a few times, but said nothing more until he had completed all that he wanted to do. Then he looked up and gave her a smile.

"Well, young lady, I won't pretend that you didn't have a pretty close call last night, but I do believe we'll see you walking out of here very soon."

Megan felt her heart lighten at his news. "When can I leave?" she asked anxiously.

"Tsk, tsk, we're not treating you that badly are we?" the doctor asked with a twinkle in his eye.

"Oh no," Megan flushed. "I only meant . . ."

Dr. Hopkins waved off the remainder of Megan's explanation and laughed—a deep, infectious laugh, and Megan found her awkwardness evaporating and she smiled at the jolly man. He gave her a wink.

"It just wouldn't do for our colleagues in America to hear that we aren't operating up to snuff, see?" he confided, tongue-in-cheek.

"I'll tell them you were all wonderful!" Megan responded to his teasing.

"Ah, well," Dr. Hopkins turned to Nurse Jones who had been watching the exchange with a bemused air, "that seals it, Nurse Jones. I think Miss Harmer has just earned an early release from the ICU." Then his tone became more businesslike and he continued his instructions. "Let's unhook the monitors and IV and keep an eye on her for another hour or two. If she's holding stable on her own, move her down to the ward."

He turned to Megan. "I don't want you leaving until we're sure you're completely on the mend—especially as you can't be taken care of at home for a while. We'll keep an eye on you for twenty-four hours in one of our recovery wards downstairs, and all being well, you'll be able to check out tomorrow morning."

Megan couldn't prevent a stab of disappointment that she had to spend another day at the hospital, but had to concede that the doctor's advice was wise. "Alright," she said, "but d'you think I could wash my hair soon?"

Dr. Hopkins nodded. "As soon as you feel up to it, Nurse Jones here will help you," he offered, and the nurse was quick to agree. Megan smiled gratefully, and relaxed back on her pillow. A wave of tiredness hit her, and she closed her eyes. When she reopened them, the doctor was gone, and Nurse Jones was quietly disconnecting the many wires leading from the machine beside her to Megan's small body.

***

Three hours later Megan had showered, washed and dried her hair, and had been pronounced stable enough to transfer out of the ICU. She was stunned by how shaky she'd been on her feet when she took her first steps after the doctor had gone, and was grateful for the support of Nurse Jones on one side and Fran on the other as she'd slowly walked to the tiny bathroom and then relied on the solid railing to hold her up while showering. She couldn't deny that the excursion had exhausted her, but it also felt so much better to be clean and fresh smelling.

She had paused momentarily beside the mirror in the bathroom. Her reflection had appeared paler than usual, and she noticed a gray-blue bruise running across the length of one cheekbone. Touching it with tentative fingers, Megan thought back over her experiences the night before. She winced as she relived the vicious swipe Richard Garrett had made across her face, then quickly blocked the memory out, knowing that she was fortunate to have nothing more than a slight discoloration to show for it.

Mentioning nothing about it to Fran, she had allowed her friend to assist her back to bed, and as soon as she was there, Fran had announced that she couldn't stand her grubby attire any longer, called for a taxi, and promised to return to the hospital as soon as she'd showered and changed. She'd left for the hotel just before a friendly orderly arrived to wheel Megan out of her small room in the ICU.

He had been the first to inform her, while she was in transit, that she was receiving preferential treatment and being assigned to a private recovery room rather than to the larger ward she'd been expecting. As much as she enjoyed her privacy, Megan felt distinctly uncomfortable that a nameless, faceless someone had deemed it necessary to make these provisions for her, and she felt her unease rise as the orderly gave her a cheery farewell and left her all alone in the new room.

Except for fewer machines and a larger window, it was very similar to the room she had just vacated: the same stark white walls, scrubbed but worn linoleum flooring, and sparse furnishings. But this room, Megan noted, did boast two arm chairs, although neither of them looked especially comfortable.

Megan lay back in the bed with a sigh. She studied the ceiling above her and tried to sort through her tumultuous thoughts. There were so many questions and so few answers. She and Fran had had so little time alone since they'd awoken, that scarcely any information had been shared. The one thing though, the one truly wonderful thing she had learned, was that Joe's presence during the night had not been merely a hallucination. He and Rob were still alive. How?— she could not fathom, but she was overwhelmingly grateful. She closed her eyes and took advantage of the solitude to offer a simple prayer of thanks.

A sound at the door startled her, and she turned quickly. He was standing at the doorway, one hand still on the doorknob, another clutching a bouquet of fresh flowers.

"Hi! Am I disturbing you?" he asked hesitatingly.

"Joe!" Megan couldn't hide the joy in her voice, and instinctively raised her uninjured arm out to him. She saw the uncertainty leave his eyes as he crossed the room in three strides and took her in his arms. Megan buried her face in his shoulder, her senses reeling as the heady perfume of the flowers mingled with the leather of his jacket and the aftershave she'd come to recognize. She could feel his heart racing almost as fast as her own, and raised her head despite the fact that tears were running unabashedly down her cheeks.

"I thought . . . I thought he'd killed you!" her voice broke. "I tried to have faith . . . I tried to pray . . . but I . . . I couldn't see how . . ."

"Megan," Joe interrupted, his voice gentle yet insistent, "it *was* your prayers that saved us!" He cupped one hand around her face and tenderly wiped the tears away with the other. "Hasn't Fran told you anything?"

Megan shook her head. "We haven't had a chance." She sniffed and took a deep shuddering breath. "She's gone back to the hotel to change."

Joe grinned. "I know. I ran into her as I was leaving the lobby. She forbade me to look at her and then scurried off up the stairs faster than I've ever seen her move before!"

Megan's sniffs gave way to a giggle.

He gave her a tender smile. "That's better," he said.

She looked up into his eyes and saw emotion so deep that it caused her to tremble. He must have felt it, but he also must have seen something similar reflected in her own eyes, because he drew her close again, resting his cheek upon her head.

"Megan," he whispered into her hair, "Megan, I want you to know that last night—when I thought I'd lost you . . ." he paused and took a deep ragged breath. "It was the worst night of my life."

She said nothing, but knew that they were both recalling that grueling ordeal, and the many miracles that had brought her back into the security of his arms. It was several more minutes before Joe finally said with a bitter sigh, "It's no good. If we're going to exchange any meaningful information, I'm going to have to go and sit on the other side of the room!"

He released her, and Megan gave a small laugh as she realized that he was in earnest. He moved to sit on one of the two chairs, not quite across the room from her, gave her a crooked smile, and added, "Oh, and remind me to write to the National Health Department and compliment them on their attractive bed gowns!"

"Joe!" Megan cried, feeling color flood her face, and then it was Joe's turn to laugh.

To Megan's relief, the nurse chose that moment to knock and enter the room. It was not Nurse Jones this time, but a younger nurse with shoulder-length brown hair and a friendly smile. She wore the same uniform that the older nurse had worn, but her gold pin read *Yvonne Evans RN*. Joe stood up politely as she walked in.

"Can I interrupt for just a minute, to take your vital signs?" she asked, already unwinding the stethoscope from around her neck. Without waiting for a reply, she proceeded to take Megan's blood pressure, temperature, and listen to her heart. Joe and Megan remained silent, and although Megan purposely avoided looking at him, she could tell that he was watching the nurse's note-taking intently. Finally, the nurse loosened the bandage wrapped around Megan's arm, peeked at the wound beneath the dressing, gave a satisfied nod, and rewrapped it carefully but efficiently. When she had finished, Joe was the first to speak.

"How is she, Nurse?" Megan could hear the anxiety in his voice.

"Doing very well, indeed," responded Nurse Evans. "Is your arm giving you much pain?"

Megan shrugged. "It's sore, but not too bad."

The nurse looked pleased. "You must have a very healthy constitution, judging by how fast you've bounced back," she said to Megan. She then brought a smile to Megan's lips by following that remark with, "Now, can I get either one of you a cup of tea?"

"No thank you," Megan replied quickly, then turned to look at Joe questioningly.

"No, not for me either, thank you," he promptly added.

"Coffee then? I can get that just as easily."

"D'you have any juice?" Megan asked, hoping to redirect the conversation slightly.

"Yes, I think so," Nurse Evans replied in surprise, "apple or orange?"

"Apple juice would be lovely."

"Same for you, sir?" the nurse asked Joe.

"Sure, that would be great," he said.

She gave him a smile. "Would you like me to find a vase for those?" She pointed to the flowers now lying forlornly on the small table beside the bed.

"Oh yeah, that would be great!" Joe said, moving to pick them up again.

"I think I'll see if I can't rustle up a couple of sandwiches while I'm at it." She looked back at Megan. "You're probably ready to eat something by now, aren't you?"

"Maybe that will help cure my wobbly legs," Megan responded hopefully.

"Let's hope so," she said encouragingly, then let herself out of the room as quietly as she'd entered it.

Joe sat down again. "I never even asked you how you're doing," he said a little shamefacedly. "You just looked so wonderful when I walked in!"

Megan laughed. "I feel good—a bit unstable on my legs and aching in one arm, but otherwise I'm okay." She paused. "I forgot something too. I forgot to thank you for the beautiful flowers."

He handed them to her, and she held them close to her face, inhaling their fragrance—an assortment of multicolored fuchsia in pinks, purples, yellows, and white were intermixed with pink bachelor's buttons, yellow and white daisies, and other flowers that she failed to recognize. The whole effect was truly lovely.

"Thank you so much," she repeated quietly.

Joe bent over and brushed a soft kiss across her forehead. Then he turned abruptly, walked over to the chair, and purposely moved it another foot away from Megan's bed—sitting down on it heavily. He ran his fingers through his hair and groaned.

"I'm not getting anywhere. How do I explain to Rob, when he gets here, that all I've found out so far is that your legs are wobbly and your arm hurts?"

"Is Rob coming here?" Megan asked with surprise.

"Yes," Joe glanced at his watch. "Anytime now. He's been down at the police station. I escaped a little before he did. We were with the coast guard until this morning, trying to tie things up . . ." He ran his hand over his face, and Megan noticed for the first time the lines of fatigue and shadows beneath his eyes. He looked up at her again. "I'm afraid, if you're up to it, you'll have to answer a lot of questions today. Rob and I will have to fill out a report, as will the coast guard and the local police. We requested a private room for you so that, hopefully, you could do most of it from your bed."

"You're the reason for the room!" Megan exclaimed. "I wasn't told, and it worried me a bit."

"Sorry! I guess the staff knows not to advertise the fact when a request comes in from the police."

Megan bit her lip and nodded. "Joe," she said quietly, "before anyone else arrives, can you tell me . . ." She stopped, stunned by the shuddering reaction that the mere thought of Richard Garrett elicited. She wadded the edge of the bed sheet in one hand, and without realizing it, her other hand rose to touch her bruised cheek. "Did . . . did they catch him?"

"Yes," he said, and Megan saw his eyes rest on her bruised face. Self-control fought for dominance over his anger, and she heard the cold, hard steel in his tone, "Oh yes, they caught him!" One look at Joe's face told her that never again would she need to fear Richard Garrett.

CHAPTER 12

The nurse returned bearing a vase, two glasses of juice, and a plate of ham-and-cheese sandwiches, complete with two bags of chips (or *crisps* as they were labeled). After situating the juice and food within easy reach of Megan, she set about arranging the flowers in the vase, placed it on top of the solitary table, and whisked out again with an air of complete competence.

Megan watched Joe take a drink of juice, and he must have sensed her eyes on him, for he stopped and raised an eyebrow questioningly.

"You could've asked for tea or coffee if you wanted to, you know," Megan said, feeling awkward.

Joe smiled and bit into a sandwich. "Rob's been working on me for four years now. Drugs and cigarettes were never an issue—you don't have to be a Mormon to know that's dumb. Alcohol didn't take much persuading either; I've seen too many wrecked lives because alcohol took over. Tea and coffee . . ." he shrugged. "After a while it just got easier to share a hot chocolate with Rob. I haven't had tea or coffee for over two years."

Megan stared at him in amazement. This revelation was an uncomfortable reminder of just how little she really knew about the man before her—the man who (if she were completely honest with herself) she was in danger of falling head over heels in love with. There was something about him that drew her like iron filings to a magnet, and so far any new insights into his personality or past had only strengthened that pull. But it still terrified her that her heart was moving far faster than her common sense would normally permit. Nervously she cleared her throat.

"I guess I still have a lot to learn about you, don't I?" she said.

He met her eyes. "I hope, when this ugly business is behind us, we'll get a chance to really get to know each other," he replied.

"I'd like that," Megan said quietly, and she could tell by the softening of his expression that he was pleased.

A knock sounded on the door and Joe and Megan looked up to see Fran's face peek in. "Found you!" she exclaimed. "It's taken us ages to figure out where they spirited you away to!"

She opened the door wider and entered, closely followed by Rob. Megan recognized him at once, even though she had seen him only for a few minutes in the failing light on Church Island. Fran walked over to Megan and gave her a quick squeeze. "Doing okay?" she asked.

Megan smiled and nodded. Then Rob came forward. He extended his hand to Megan and she grasped it with pleasure. "Hi Megan! It's good to meet you—more formally—at last."

Megan studied the man in front of her. His sandy brown hair was cut short, his face was ordinary—in the nicest sense of the word, and in his blue eyes she saw intelligence and kindness. He was shorter than Joe, although still close to six feet tall, she guessed, and she could tell by his trim figure and firm grip that his physical strength probably rivaled his partner's.

She liked him immediately, and was chilled by the sudden thought that she could easily have never known him. With that in mind, she faced her guests and said, "Would you please tell me how you all ended up in the lifeboat? Even seeing you here in my room, it's hard to believe . . . " she paused to wipe a traitorous tear that had rolled down her cheek, and Fran immediately moved over to sit on the edge of the bed, a protective arm around her friend's small shoulders.

"Come on, guys," Fran said. "I know you came to pump her for information, but you owe her your story first. She barely knows how she got here."

Joe and Rob exchanged glances, and Rob gave a brief nod.

"Go for it," he said to Joe.

Joe took a deep breath and leaned back in his chair. Then, after exhaling slowly he began. "I guess I should go back to Saturday night. The train carrying Rob and the crate arrived in Llanfair P. G. at about eight o'clock, and soon after it pulled in, Garrett showed up to claim his goods. I was trailing him at the time, so Rob and I linked up and both got to see him load the crate into his fancy car.

"We followed him back to Menai Bridge, where he took a side road that brought him just about as close to the Belgian Promenade as you can get in a car. He hauled the crate down to Church Island by himself—which surprised me; I thought for sure he'd find some minion to do that for him! He did it under the cover of darkness, hiding the box in the bushes behind the chapel, and making it back over the causeway just before the tide came in.

"Then came twenty-four hours of nail biting as we waited for his next move. Rob and I traded off—one of us would watch the island while the other kept an eye on Garrett, then we'd switch. Garrett stayed well clear of the island all day. The only time he could cross the causeway was in the morning when church services were in session, so we figured all the extra people milling around the place was a big enough incentive to keep him away.

"About the time we were starting to think that he'd left it too late to catch the evening tide, things started happening all at once. Rob was stationed on Church Island, hidden in the bushes, and he saw a dinghy leave the cruiser—still anchored on the other side of the island—and head his way.

"He radioed through to warn me, but I was already heading down there because Garrett had suddenly decided to take his leave of the hotel. Only a minute or two later though, Rob sent a second call . . ." Joe paused and looked directly at Megan. "There was a girl approaching the chapel from the causeway . . ."

Rob glanced at his partner and took up the story. "I didn't know if you were friend, foe, or innocent bystander, so I started to describe you to Joe—I didn't have to go any farther than the color of your hair! Joe yelled, 'It's Megan! Get her off the island!'—but I knew I couldn't get to you in time. Seamus and Callum had pulled the dinghy up onto shore already, and the only chance we had against them was the element of surprise.

"Thanks to Fran's drawings, we already knew the identities of the two men on the cruiser," Rob threw Fran a look of appreciation, which she acknowledged with a humble smile. "But having Megan involved was an element we hadn't counted on. I knew Joe would get there as fast as he could, so I just sat tight and prayed for a miracle.

"I thought my prayers had been answered when you stayed in the chapel the whole time those men were rooting around the bushes, and didn't come out until they'd gone—but I was so focused on keeping you away from the Irish duo that I temporarily forgot about the possibility of you running into 'Mr. Snake Oil.' "

Megan shot a glance at Joe when Rob used the nickname she'd first heard Joe use. He returned her look, and his lips quirked as he controlled a grin at Rob's casual use of the name.

Rob didn't seem to notice the exchange and continued. "I watched Seamus and Callum load up the dinghy with the crate, and saw you slip away from the chapel and head back for the causeway. I couldn't follow your progress once you'd gone below the rise on the island, but thought you were in the clear, until I heard voices and saw you coming back with Garrett and heading for the chapel again. That's when I started to move.

"I thought I was in a pretty good position to back Joe up when he made Garrett aware of his presence, but I was an idiot not to double-check on Seamus and Callum first." Rob ran his fingers through his hair, and Megan recognized the same aura of exhaustion that she'd seen in Joe only a short while before. "I'm really sorry, Megan," he said. "I hate to think that if I'd done things differently, you wouldn't have had to go through all this."

Megan stared at him, sure that her stunned expression must be self-evident. "Rob, please," she begged. "I have nothing but gratitude for all you've done. It was no one's fault but my own that I was on Church Island in the first place. Joe even warned Fran and me not to go anywhere alone that day . . ."

"I did, didn't I?" Joe said, but Megan ignored him.

"The bottom line is that I endangered your lives and your case by being at the wrong place at the wrong time . . . I seem to have done that an awful lot recently!" Megan said unhappily, then added, "But, how did you escape? Once Seamus took you both away to the chapel . . . I couldn't . . . I mean . . . I . . ."

Joe saved Megan from further distress. "If Rob thinks he made a big mistake, then Garrett committed a colossal one!"

Megan must have looked as confused as she felt, because Rob picked up the story again. "Garrett had those two henchmen with him—Callum, who is older, more experienced, and as hard as nails, and Seamus, who's young, pretty malleable, and has a head full of crazy ideals. The error Garrett made was in choosing who should take us to the chapel.

"He knew neither one of them would hesitate to kill us—they've both got blood on their hands already, but where Callum's become completely calloused over time to any kind of divine mission, Seamus's belief in his people's religious destiny has kept some connection to his Catholic faith alive.

"Anyway, Seamus got us into the chapel with a few well-aimed shoves and kicks, but when he followed us down the step, he suddenly stopped. The light from the sunset was filtering in through the stained-glass window and hit the floor right at his feet. All at once he started crossing himself fervently—I think it was the first time he'd really thought about what Garrett had asked him to do: to murder within a holy house. It may not have been a Catholic cathedral, but it was apparently close enough for him. He kept us covered with the gun the whole time, but I watched his face . . . it was like something snapped.

"I could tell Joe'd sensed a change and was poised to launch himself at the man, but before either of us had a chance to act, Seamus was backing out of the chapel. He kept the gun trained on us, but it was more out of self-preservation than threat. He crossed himself one more time before heaving open the door and slamming it behind him. Joe and I reached the door just in time to hear the key turn. We were locked in."

Megan stared at him wide-eyed. "But when he joined us at the dinghy, he acted like he'd done it . . . like he'd sh . . . shot you both."

Rob nodded. "Seamus might not be the brightest crayon in the box, but he knew what his chances were if Garrett even suspected that he hadn't killed us. Men like Garrett can't conceive that anyone—especially a murdering thug like Seamus—could believe in any higher being. In the world Garrett's created for himself, he is God."

"But surely Seamus knew Garrett would find out eventually?" Megan asked incredulously.

Rob shrugged. "Who knows what he was thinking? Maybe he really thought we'd starve to death in there before someone found us—then Garrett would be none the wiser. Maybe he figured as long as he was gone before Garrett found out, he'd be fine. Then again, maybe he hadn't given it any thought at all. Like I said, not the smartest of young men!"

"Probably not," broke in Fran, "but let's be grateful he wasn't too calculating, or we wouldn't be here now."

"That's for sure," Rob agreed immediately.

"But how did you get out of the chapel?" Megan asked, returning the conversation to the events of the night before.

It was Joe who answered. "This is when your prayers come in, Megan," he said, and he gestured toward Rob with his head, "along with some pretty fervent ones that Rob was sending up."

"Fran, tell Megan your part in all of this." Rob suggested.

All eyes turned on Fran, and she squirmed a little uncomfortably.

"Remember how you'd left me in the debris of my room?" she asked Megan. "Well, I was plugging away, in my own disorganized way, trying to fit a quart into a pint pot, when I got a really strong feeling that I should go after you." She raised her hand, "Now before you go telling me how great it was that I was so in tune, let me say that I'm still not sure if I was following a prompting, or just using an excuse to get out of packing by myself.

"Either way, I ignored the feeling for a while—to start with I had no idea exactly how long you'd been gone because I hadn't watched the clock, and secondly, it was dark! But it didn't seem to matter how much I argued against it, the feeling persisted, and I wasn't accomplishing anything productive in the bedroom—I think I was undoing packing I'd already done by the end. So, vowing that I'd pack a flashlight next time I traveled, I set off after you.

"Once I left the outside lights of the hotel I ran. There was only that one lamppost between the hotel and Church Island, so actually I ran most of the way. I kept expecting to meet up with you, so when I reached the causeway and it was already about an inch covered in water, I really started to panic. I waded through the water, calling your name, hoping that if you were hurt or something that you'd hear me—because there was no way I was going to see you in the dark on that island."

"Fran!" Megan interrupted brokenly, "I'm probably the only one in this room who understands how much courage that took—for you to go into a strange graveyard alone and after dark!"

Fran waved her hand as though to brush Megan's remark aside, obviously not wanting to dwell on it, but Megan knew that their friendship had passed the highest test, and she gave Fran's hand a gentle squeeze.

"Well anyway," continued Fran, clearing her throat, "there I was on Church Island, screaming your name for all I was worth, with nothing but the sounds of the sea and the rustling of every living— and dead—creature in Wales in my ears, until I reached the chapel, and that's when I heard the thumping."

She looked accusingly at Joe and Rob. "If you think I was scared before, that noise pushed me to a new level of terror!"

The men responded with chagrined smiles, and Joe said, "Well, I'm sure glad you heard us, because the thick walls and door did a great job of soundproofing your calls. We had no idea you were out there, and I don't think that ancient door would've budged an inch, even if we'd pounded on it all night long."

"After I'd convinced myself that only a living person—and quite possibly Megan—trapped inside the chapel could make that much racket, I hurried over to the door and quite literally tripped over the key." Fran turned to Megan to explain. "It was one of those huge old-fashioned ones, made of heavy, dark metal with a big ring at the end. I'd noticed it hanging on a hook beside the door when I was sketching the chapel, but I really don't think I'd have been able to find it without a light, if it hadn't found me!"

"Seamus must have locked the door and tossed the key—he probably didn't even bother looking to see where it landed," Rob said.

"Well, the door opened up easily enough," Fran agreed, "and out burst these two on the run! They barely slowed down long enough to acknowledge who'd freed them, and certainly not long enough to explain what was going on. Joe just grabbed me by the wrist and dragged me behind him!"

Rob chuckled, but it was Joe who picked up the story. "Garrett had stripped us of our weapons, but he didn't take the time to get rid of our radios. We'd been able to call the coast guard and the

Beaumaris lifeboat crew from the church. They were both on alert, waiting for a call anyway, so the coast guard moved out to intercept the Irish cruiser, and the lifeboat took off to rescue us.

"We knew that by the time any help arrived it would have to come by sea, so we headed to the same small beach where the Irishmen landed their dinghy. Fran's arrival saved us a good thirty minutes, because by the time the lifeboat arrived at Church Island, we were already waiting at the beach. They got us aboard pretty fast, and then we headed out to find you."

He met Megan's eyes, and she knew without being told what agony that boat ride had been for him. Rob glanced at his partner too, and without comment, took up the story.

"I had a basic idea of where the cruiser had been anchored, because I'd seen it while I was waiting on the island. We didn't know at that point whether or not it had already moved on, but at least we were going in the right direction when the flare went up." Rob paused. "Was that you, Megan?"

"Yes," she said simply. "I was never sure if it really worked."

Rob smiled. "Well, it didn't go straight up, if that's what you mean, but it worked well enough to illuminate the cruiser, and to spotlight your jump into the sea."

"You saw me jump in?" Megan asked in amazement.

"Oh yeah," Rob said, "and that's what galvanized the lifeboat crew into action—the wet suits went on, and the searchlights flooded the water, converging on the area they'd seen you enter."

"But it was Joe who saw you first," Fran said. "He'd grabbed a wet suit too, and he dived right in and had you back at the boat before half the crew knew what was going on. A couple of the men helped haul you on board, and when they laid you down, we didn't know . . . we didn't know . . ."

Megan reached over and covered her friend's hand with her own. "It's okay," she said softly.

Fran sniffed. "No," she said, "it was not okay! It was awful!" Then brokenly she continued, "But we all did what we could—first aid, warm blankets, the crew turned that boat around on a dime and called the hospital to have the ambulance meet us, Rob gave you a blessing, and Joe held you until the paramedics took over."

Megan felt the tears well up in her eyes and tried futilely to prevent them from spilling over. "It's not very clear," she said, "but I can remember a few of those things."

Joe rose from his chair, walked over to the window, and rested his forehead against the glass, and Megan knew she should be grateful for her edited memories. She guessed that the rescue portion of last night's experience wouldn't haunt her as completely as it would Rob or Fran, or Joe. But she had her own vivid memories to deal with, and Rob, it seemed, was ready to hear them.

"D'you remember what happened before we reached you, Megan?" he asked, and although he was firm, Megan appreciated the kindness in his eyes.

"Yes," she answered.

"Fran told us you went to the island to find a lost hat," he prompted, and she nodded.

"It sounds terribly silly now, doesn't it?" Megan said. "But I'm afraid it's true."

She leaned back against her pillow and reflected on what had begun so innocently as a quiet Sunday walk to Church Island. Megan had been glad for an excuse to visit the picturesque spot one more time; and as she began her account for her listening guests, she confessed that when she made her way along the Belgian Promenade, she had worried about little more than beating the tide to the causeway.

She described arriving at and entering the chapel, and then hearing the men outside. When she told them of her anxiety about being discovered by the two Irishmen, Rob nodded his agreement.

"I just held my breath the whole time you were in there—praying that you wouldn't come out too soon. Judging by our experience, it was a good thing you didn't have the door all the way closed, or you'd have heard nothing, and had no warning that they were nearby."

"I did wait a while, even after their voices had disappeared, but I knew if I waited too long, I'd be cut off by the sea." Megan thought for a moment. "Maybe if I hadn't been in such a hurry, I would have seen Richard coming before he saw me—and been able to avoid him."

"He met you on the causeway then?" Rob asked.

"Yes," Megan said.

"I saw them," Joe spoke from beside the window. He had turned around and was leaning against the window frame. "I was close enough to see it happen, but too far away to prevent it." There was bitterness in his voice. "I tried to close the gap between us as soon as I got Rob's message, but there just wasn't enough time."

"You made good time, getting there when you did," Rob said, and Megan smiled at him gratefully. She knew that praise from his partner would do more to console Joe than anything she could offer.

"What did Richard say to you when you met on the causeway?" Fran asked.

"He wanted to know what I'd been doing on the island. I told him about my hat, but I don't know if he ever really believed me. He played along with it though, and asked me . . . well, no I guess it was more like he *told* me to go with him to help him look for something he'd left there too."

There was silence in the room for a few seconds, as the disingenuousness of Richard's words sank in. They each knew what had occurred once he and Megan had reached the chapel together, so Megan did not dwell on it. Instead, when she began speaking again, she described her departure from the island—being dragged down to the beach, waiting for Seamus's return in the dinghy, then casting off and motoring to the waiting cruiser.

At first, Megan wasn't sure if she could share all that she had gone through without some sort of physical or emotional reaction setting in. She knew that reliving the experiences in their entirety was beyond her stamina at that point, but she found that if she purposely distanced herself from the events and recounted everything factually, leaving out any feelings or emotions, she could do it. It was, she thought to herself, much like being a dispassionate television news anchor, reading a story of violence and terror that had occurred to faraway people in faraway lands.

Neither could she look at Joe. She sensed his tension and anger at the treatment she'd received at the hands of Richard, Seamus, and Callum, and wouldn't have held out any hope for the welfare of the three men had they been within Joe's striking distance as she spoke.

She held her audience captive as she described her plan for escape, but when she described the inferno she created, Fran instinctively cried out, "Megan, you could've been killed!"

To her surprise, she found that she could respond quite calmly, as though completely detached from the situation, "I think they intended to kill me sooner or later anyway."

Her statement was followed by complete silence. There was obviously nothing that either of the two men could say to refute her assessment—especially as they undoubtedly believed it to be true. Fran however, just stared at her friend until the impact of Megan's words truly registered, and then she abruptly got off the bed and began pacing between the vacant chair and the bed, distress clearly evident on her face.

Megan looked down at her hands on the bed covers and bit her lip. She hoped she hadn't been overly dramatic—although, truthfully it seemed to her, that in several instances she had underplayed the events, not willing to rekindle her own terror. But it was behind her now—apart from the nightmares that would surely come. Fran was dealing with the details for the first time.

Rob gave Fran a look of understanding, but decided against drawing her back into the discussion—wanting to give her time to adjust without the attention of everyone else in the room. Instead, he turned to Megan. "So by the time you jumped into the sea, you were probably already suffering from carbon monoxide poisoning and smoke inhalation?"

"I suppose so." It was the first time she had ever considered it. "I do know that I couldn't have lasted much longer in that room, if Seamus hadn't come."

When she had recounted the Irishman's arrival at the galley door and her subsequent escape, the shooting of the flare and leaping off the deck, Megan brought her narrative to a close, grateful to have completed it with her emotions largely intact. Little more needed to be said. After all, they had witnessed her desperate attempts to stay afloat; and the gunshot wound on her arm testified of the bullets that had sprayed the water beside her.

She tried to shut out the pain and terror these memories evoked, but found it was as futile as holding back a tidal wave. An audible gasp escaped her, and her body started to shake as images of her plunge and desperate fight for life in the frigid, briny deep were projected upon the canvas of her mind. The mental barrier she had erected could not halt the unrelenting assault of traumatic experiences upon her emotions.

Joe must have recognized the symptoms, because he was beside her in seconds. He took the place Fran had vacated on the bed, put a protective arm around her, and held her close as she cried uncontrollably into his shoulder. Nobody spoke nor tried to stem her flow of tears; they just waited patiently and compassionately. Joe laid his cheek on the top of her head and gently swayed, until at last—in complete exhaustion—Megan found her tears subsiding and the rhythmic movement calming her tumult and relaxing her trembling limbs.

When at last her ragged breaths evened out to something resembling normalcy, she raised her head and met Joe's eyes. The tenderness she saw there was almost her undoing, but he spoke softly to her. "You needed to get that out, Megan. As hard as it was, it will help the healing, and help you put those things behind you."

Fran approached and handed her a tissue without a word. Megan gave her a watery smile. She could only imagine how awful she looked—swollen red eyes and blotchy tearstained face, complete with runny nose. But she was too emotionally depleted to care. She leaned back against Joe's shoulder, drawing immense comfort from his steadying presence, and found Rob's gaze upon her. He gave a small shake of his head.

"Either you have a battalion of guardian angels, or you're one incredible woman, Megan Harmer," he said.

Megan had rarely felt less incredible than she did at that moment, but Fran spared her from responding by finally plopping down on the vacant chair and saying, "I think both of those apply," and then with a twinkle in her eye that suggested a return to her usual even-keeled disposition, she added, "but just remind me never to go on vacation with her again!"

***

The remainder of the day passed in a kaleidoscope of medical and legal protocol. Nurses came and went, checking her vital signs and her wound, and admonishing her to rest in the face of a room full of interrogators. There were times when Megan wanted to beg the nurse to be more forceful and evict the strangers so that she could sleep, but then she would glance at Rob, Joe, or Fran and see the weariness written in their faces, and know that she couldn't prolong this agony for any of them.

The local police came, accompanied by a very businesslike member of Scotland Yard, who'd driven up from London to represent the upper echelon in the British police force's antiterrorism branch. They asked for a full accounting of Megan's whereabouts since her arrival on Anglesey. Megan got the feeling that had the local "bobbies" been there alone, she would have seen a more relaxed, friendly group of men. As it was, they were thorough, to the point, and left with best wishes for a speedy recovery coupled with the warning that they would probably be in touch again.

The coast guard representatives arrived soon afterward, and were anxious for any and all details about the cruiser and her experience while on board. Under the direction of Rob, one of the coast guard officials informed Megan that they had apprehended all three men on board the *Donegal Lady*. Thanks to the radioed warning they had received from Rob, the coast guard on board its cutter in the Menai Strait was able to locate and move alongside the cruiser before it headed out into the Irish Sea. The cruiser by that time had sustained considerable fire damage, and although the flames had been doused, the vessel was not operating at full capacity. Officials had boarded the boat and seized the three men on board (along with their illegal cargo) with only moderate resistence. The men were being held in the local jail.

Rob and Joe came and went during the day. Sometimes they went outside to confer with the visiting officials, other times one or both of them would be gone for longer periods of time. Although they never gave detailed disclosures of their activities, Megan assumed that they were in close contact with the three apprehended men and were playing an integral part in their questioning and transportation from the local jail. Other issues far beyond Megan's scope were obviously at play, but she found that she didn't have the energy or desire to ask for details. Her role as injured victim and informer was more than sufficient for her to bear.

Fran stayed with her the whole day. She sat quietly through the interrogation sessions, and during the intervening times she encouraged Megan to walk around her small room to exercise her weakened muscles. Her enthusiasm for every little improvement in Megan's strength and stamina helped buoy Megan's spirits, and they even found occasion to laugh and tease, despite the difficult circumstances in which they found themselves.

It was only when early evening arrived, and Megan noticed Fran's head nodding as she valiantly fought overwhelming tiredness in the uncomfortable vinyl chair, that Megan began urging her friend to leave. The earlier frenzied activity that had surrounded them was waning, and it felt as if the hospital as a whole was preparing for a quiet night. Rob and Joe had been gone for some time, and Megan thought it likely that they wouldn't see them again until the next day.

"Fran, you need to go back to the hotel. You've had almost no sleep in thirty-six hours," she said.

Fran gave a reluctant nod. "I think I might have to, or I'll fall asleep while driving." She looked up with a grimace. "On second thought maybe not. I'd forgotten I have to negotiate three round-abouts, the bridge, and about six miles of twisty, winding roads. On the assumption the drive doesn't give me a nervous breakdown, it will at least keep me alert!"

Megan laughed. "Let's hope I'm up to driving tomorrow then."

"You'd better be!" Fran retorted with mock ferocity, then becoming more serious she added, "I looked up our itinerary when I went back to the hotel to change, and called the bed-and-breakfast in Hay-on-Wye to cancel our reservations for tonight. It means we'll probably have to bypass exploring the Brecon Beacons, but I think we can still make it down as far as the hotel we've reserved in Bath by tomorrow evening. Then we can just continue with our schedule from there.

"Oh, and I checked with the manager at the Anchor Hotel, and he felt so bad about you being hospitalized that he's letting us stay on tonight—and your room's free of charge!"

She looked so pleased with herself that Megan had to laugh. "Fran," she exclaimed, "you're showing signs of complete organization. I should be 'indisposed' more often!"

Fran rolled her eyes and stood up. "Don't even think about it!" she said. Then she walked over to the bed and dropped a kiss on her friend's forehead. Shouldering her purse, she walked over to the door, then just before she opened it she turned. "I'll see you in the morning, and I'll bring some of your clothes with me." Then with a mischievous look, she added, "And before you start thinking that I've turned over a new leaf, just remember, I'm still waiting for you to come back and help me pack my cases!"

Megan groaned and Fran grinned impishly, then waved and let herself out the door.

***

Soon after Fran left, Megan slipped out of bed and walked slowly to the window. Her legs felt stronger—there was none of the uncontrollable shaking that had accompanied her first venture out of bed earlier in the day. She rested her throbbing arm on the windowsill and gazed out at the scene below.

Dusk was settling in. Immediately below her was a large asphalt parking area, and cars were zipping in and out through a one-way entry/exit system that linked into the main road beyond. A red brick wall and dark green privet hedge formed a barricade between the hospital and the world outside. A few people were walking across the parking lot, coming and going through doors hidden from Megan's sight. One woman carried flowers, a few were in a hurry, while others took their time, perhaps loath to leave loved ones behind.

Megan watched for a few minutes. It was strange to think that for most of the people outside the hospital grounds, this had been just another normal Monday. For a few of the visitors their trip to the hospital may have broken with routine, but her own life, she knew, had been irrevocably changed during the last twenty-four hours.

Never again would she be able to listen to a news bulletin about the IRA with casual interest. Reports on her vacation to Wales may have to be edited to protect not only FBI operations, but also her own peace of mind. She wondered if the sea would ever hold any allure for her again—her respect for its power and ruthlessness had increased until it bordered on fear, but she hoped that emotion would fade with time. And her heart . . . Megan sighed and turned from the window.

She believed that Joe cared about her, but how much she wasn't sure. That she was falling more in love with him with every meeting, she reluctantly admitted. But where did one go with a relationship like this? She knew so little about him, and even when they were both in their respective homes, they lived almost an entire continent apart. Futhermore, he wasn't LDS—that in and of itself put them worlds apart. Leaving a portion of her heart behind when she and Fran left for Bath seemed cruel punishment on top of everything else she'd endured, but as Megan crawled back into bed, she tried to brace herself for what appeared inevitable.

A nurse came in minutes later. After checking that Megan's physical recovery was continuing to progress well, and that her patient did not require anything else before settling in for the night, she busied herself drawing the blinds over the window and straightening the bedding. When everything was to her liking, she dimmed the lights, wished Megan a good night, and slipped out of the room.

Megan lay in the semidarkness staring at the ceiling above her. She was physically and emotionally exhausted, but sleep remained elusive. Pictures and phrases from the last forty-eight hours flitted through her mind, and despite her total fatigue, Megan was afraid to let sleep come—afraid to allow in the nightmares she sensed were already knocking for admittance. She felt her apprehension building as time ticked by, one slow minute after another, so that when the phone on the small table beside the bed rang, she leaped like a scared rabbit.

At first, she could only stare at it, wondering why it would be ringing and whether or not she should pick up the receiver. She took a couple of deep breaths to calm her racing heart, then as it seemed that no one else was going to answer it for her, she leaned over and lifted the hand piece to her ear.

"Hello?" she said hesitatingly.

"Did I wake you up?" Megan could hear the concern in Joe's voice.

"No," she said, and lay back on her pillow, still holding the phone close, and smiling up at the ceiling that had been so oppressive only seconds before.

"I was hoping to come by and see you again this evening, but trying to get into that hospital after nine o'clock is like trying to enter Fort Knox, so I stooped to pulling rank on the hospital operator and demanded your room's phone number."

Megan laughed softly. "Who did you tell her you were, the president of the United States?"

"Oh, nothing that far-fetched. I went for passing as Tom Cruise!" he teased in return.

"Hmm! Close, but you're taller than he is."

There was a pause on the line, then Joe's voice came back, an echo of a question she had posed only a few days before, "Compliment?"

Megan smiled up at the ceiling again. "Compliment!" she concurred.

There was another pause, then Joe cleared his throat and asked, "How are you doing?"

"Better," Megan replied. "I'm a lot stronger on my legs, and even though my arm still hurts, the nurses seem pleased with how it's healing. I think they're planning to release me tomorrow morning."

"That's great. Is Fran picking you up?"

"Yes, with the understanding that as soon as we get back to the hotel, I have to help her pack!"

"How slowly can you get it done?" Joe asked.

"Slowly . . . ?" Megan asked, perplexed.

"I have to go back down to the jail first thing tomorrow," Megan could hear his hesitation, "but I was hoping to see you again before you head out."

"My bad arm and Fran's unique packing system should slow us down quite a bit," Megan said thoughtfully, then almost as an after-thought she added, "I'll make sure it does!"

She heard Joe chuckle. "Alright, I'll see you tomorrow then. Sleep well."

"You too!"

"I will now," Joe said, "but I still wish I was there."

"Me too." The words tumbled out before Megan could check them, and despite the fact that she was in a darkened room all alone, she felt her color rise. "Good night Joe," she said hurriedly. "Thanks for calling."

"Good night, Megan," he said softly, then the phone went dead.

She replaced the receiver and snuggled down under the bedcovers, closing her eyes and finally allowing herself to relax. Then at last, sleep came quickly and quietly.

CHAPTER 13

Fran arrived the next morning, just after the doctor had checked on Megan and pronounced her fit enough for release from the hospital. She had brought Megan's favorite light blue, short-sleeved shirt, and her khaki pants, along with a pair of canvas tennis shoes—which was the best she could do since Megan's sandals were irretrievably lost in the charred remains of the cruiser's galley. She had also thoughtfully included a hairbrush and Megan's makeup bag, so that by the time Megan emerged from the small bathroom, fully clothed with hair shining and a bare touch of mascara and lipstick to complete her grooming, she felt ready to face the world again.

Her arm remained bandaged, and the nurses gave Megan a small bag containing a clean dressing and a few pain pills should the discomfort become too unbearable. Then after signing a few papers, and thanking the staff, Megan followed Fran out into the sunshine and toward the parked car.

It was a beautiful day. Birds were singing cheerily from the shrubs and trees surrounding the hospital grounds. The air still sparkled with the dewy moisture of early morning, and a low droning that amplified as the two women passed by the bright yellow blossoms of a broom bush suggested that bees were already busy with their morning's work.

Megan recognized the parking lot as the one she had viewed from her hospital room window the evening before. There were fewer cars parked at this early hour, and it was not long before they were in their vehicle, following the exit signs out onto the main road.

Fran drove back to the hotel to spare Megan's arm a little longer. She muttered about having the route down, but Megan could tell she wasn't eager to drive on unknown highways in the days ahead. They arrived in Menai Bridge within twenty minutes, and Megan was glad to enter the hotel and reach her room without encountering anyone, particularly hotel staff who might have shown solicitous interest in her return. She was reluctant to answer a lot of questions about her experiences—she had reached her fill yesterday, and she was anxious for some sort of directive from Joe or Rob regarding just how much should be said outside the confines of an official investigative questioning.

It was almost a surprise to enter her room and find it just as she had left it. The only difference was that the jeans she had worn during her kidnapping had been laundered and lay clean and pressed in a thin plastic bag, hung over the back of the arm chair. How they had reached the hotel staff, she had no idea, but she was grateful for their thoughtfulness on her behalf.

Her torn T-shirt had obviously been unredeemable, and she noticed, somewhat ruefully, that the spot in her bag that she'd saved for her sun hat remained empty. Somewhere between the chapel and the dinghy beached on Church Island, she had once again lost track of her hat—but this time she had no wish to retrieve it. She covered the empty space with the laundered jeans, added her makeup bag and brush, then closed the bags and dragged them one-handedly to sit beside the door.

When she entered Fran's room, she found that the state of chaos had magnified rather than diminished during her absence, and Fran's despair was mounting. With a laugh at her friend's distraught expression, Megan fell to her knees and began sorting through piles of clothes, shoes, and various other bits and pieces, until in less than no time some semblance of order was achieved. Fran's mood lightened with every pile of clothing that disappeared into a case, and before long, Megan realized that they were close to completing the task, and that Joe had still not made an appearance.

She slowly rose to her feet and glanced around the room. "Fran, d'you think you can finish up these last few things?"

Fran looked up, concern on her face. "Sure. Do you need to rest?"

Megan smiled and shook her head. "No, I'm fine. I was just thinking that I'd like to walk down to the Belgian Promenade one last time—to see the sea and Church Island in the light of day. I'd like to remember it that way, rather than the way it was on Sunday night."

"D'you want company?" The concern had not left Fran's face.

"No, you stay and put away the last things. I'll take it slowly—and I promise I'll not go farther than the promenade."

"Alright, but you be careful," Fran warned, "and if you're not back in thirty minutes, I'm calling the police!"

Megan laughed. "My mother couldn't have said it better."

Fran pulled a face. "Well, someone's got to look after you!"

***

The narrow lane was becoming very familiar. Megan noticed that more dandelions had opened along the verge of the road, the owners of the narrow gray house with the navy blue door hadn't picked up their newspaper since she'd last passed by, the tabby cat she'd passed sunning itself before had been joined by a Siamese, and someone had dropped an ice-cream bar wrapper beneath the lamppost. Automatically she picked up the paper, wadded it into a small ball, and held onto it until she reached the litter bin she knew was just a little farther down the road.

Her footsteps slowed as she reached the suspension bridge, and she came to a halt beneath the huge arched pillars. She gazed upward one last time, trying to imprint their magnificence onto her mind, then as the chill of the large stones' shadow registered on her bare arms, she moved out again into the sunlight, and onto the Belgian Promenade.

She walked slowly alongside the retaining wall. It was almost high tide, and the water was lapping hungrily against the stones. The scene was much as she remembered it from her first visit to the spot—distant sails fluttering in the breeze, the smell of salt in the air, the perpetual motion of the rhythmic waves, and the raucous cries of the seagulls wheeling high overhead, completely obliterating the distant hum of cars crossing the suspension bridge.

Megan reached the wooden bench where she and Joe had sat and talked into the night, and she sat down. From her seat she could admire the view across the Menai Strait to the Snowdonia mountains beyond, and to her right she could see Church Island. The gray stone spire of the diminutive chapel was just visible behind the slope of the small graveyard. Ancient headstones, the black wrought-iron gate, and scrubby bushes broke up the smooth emerald-colored grass that appeared to rise magically out of the water. It was historically and picturesquely breathtaking, and somehow as she gazed upon it, Megan knew that despite all that had happened to her there, she would remember it that way—and she was glad.

Footsteps sounded, coming from the direction of the suspension bridge, and Megan turned to see Joe appear around the bend.

She smiled as he approached. "Uh oh! Are you the police?"

"Nope! But they'll be hot on my trail if Fran doesn't see the whites of your eyes pretty soon."

Megan laughed and rose from the bench. "She must have told you I was down here."

He nodded. "You okay?" He searched her face anxiously.

"Yes," she reassured him. "I just wanted to leave with happy memories of this place." She looked back at Church Island one more time, then turned to him. "We can go now."

"Sure?"

"Sure," she said.

Joe smiled and held out a hand to her. Megan took it. He curled his fingers around hers and they began walking back toward the hotel.

They walked in silence for a little while, but much as Megan delighted in simply being with Joe without the clutter of unnecessary conversation, she knew that their time alone would be limited. There were things that needed to be said—she just wasn't quite sure how to go about starting it.

"When do you leave Anglesey?" she tried—it wasn't brilliant, but it was a start.

"Probably tomorrow," he answered. "We've got a few more things to wrap up here, then we're heading down to Dagenham. There're a few loose ends down there we have to tie up before word leaks that Garrett, Seamus, and Callum are under lock and key."

"So there's been no publicity yet then?"

"Not yet, but we can't hold it off much longer. We've got people in the U.S. trying to follow Garrett's trail to the source of his weapons, and it'll be a whole lot easier to do while no one involved knows what's happened here. There'll be heads rolling in at least one of the military installations over this one."

Megan was silent. The magnitude of this operation was overwhelming, and she felt completely out of her depth. "What will happen to the three men here?" she finally asked.

"Scotland Yard will deal with Seamus and Callum, but an extradition order is going through for Garrett. He'll be tried in the States, and the list of felonies is growing by the hour. He hasn't said a word since we took him in, except to ask for his attorney—some hotshot lawyer from Chicago who's flying in today. Callum's been mute too. But young Seamus . . ." Joe gave a grim smile of satisfaction, "Seamus is singing like a bird. I think he took one look at Rob and me and figured he was more likely to see his next birthday helping us out, than if he went back to Garrett and Callum now that they know he didn't pull the trigger at the church.

"Oh, and you may be interested to know that he also seems to think we're going to go easy on him because he was the one who let you out of the burning galley!"

Megan stared at him incredulously, momentarily speechless, and Joe, noting her expression, gave her hand a squeeze. "Don't worry, it's not going to fly—but we may let him keep thinking it for a while. Who knows what else he'll share with us!"

"Yes, but who knows how much of what he says you can believe?"

Joe shrugged. "You're right, but sometimes these kind of leads are the best ones we have. The IRA is a tight organization, and not many leaks reach us in time to prevent tragedies. We'll take what we can get."

They arrived at the lamppost and turned to make their way up the lane toward the hotel. An elderly gentleman wished them a good morning as he strolled by with a terrier desperately straining to explore the tantalizing smells just beyond the reach of his leash.

"Have you been able to figure out why Richard Garrett was so personally involved this time?" Megan asked once the man was out of earshot.

"Like I said before, Garrett hasn't said a word, but if we give Seamus the benefit of the doubt, it appears that the IRA was recruiting him for his computer expertise." At Megan's puzzled expression Joe continued. "Remember that I told you the crate Garrett was transporting was full of detonators?"

Megan nodded.

"And I told you that the IRA's stash of weapons, explosives, bombs, and the like is pretty impressive?"

Megan nodded again.

"Well, in the late 1990s the IRA staged a bombing campaign in London—just to prove the vulnerability of England's capital. They even set one off in Downing Street. But despite their impressive show of military power, their campaign was not without problems. One bomb exploded prematurely, killing the IRA man who was about to plant the device. Another operation failed when a thirty-pound Semtex bomb planted under Hammersmith Bridge failed to explode.

"The people who study the IRA's activities are starting to suggest that the IRA's lost a lot of its more experienced bombers, and that even those they have left aren't educated enough to construct sophisticated timing and remote-control systems. The IRA needs a university-educated computer expert—especially one who can provide his own crate full of detonators—to set them up for another bombing campaign."

Megan felt a knot tighten in her stomach as she realized where this conversation was leading. "And Richard Garrett is a computer expert?" she guessed.

"He went into the Ford Motor Company with an MBA, but his undergraduate degree was in computer science, and he's been operating as CEO of Computer Client Services for the last two years."

Megan was starting to feel sick. She stopped walking and turned to face Joe.

"Joe, I had no idea just how important this operation was, and I don't know what's expected of me now. Do I just walk away as though I was never involved in any of it, or will my name forever be linked with these men?"

"I'd be lying if I told you that you'll never hear the name Richard Garrett again. There'll be publicity of course, but I'll do everything in my power to keep your name out of it. We know how to get hold of you if we need to, so you go ahead with the rest of your vacation, and we'll hope for the best."

"And pray," Megan added.

"And pray," he echoed.

***

Rob and Joe helped the two women load up their rented vehicle with their cases and bags. When everything was securely stowed they stood awkwardly outside the car. Rob was the first to move. He stepped toward Fran and gave her a hug, then embraced Megan.

"Hope that arm's completely healed soon, Megan. Keep in touch okay?"

Megan nodded, tears close to falling. Rob had given them the phone number of the office that he and Joe shared in Boston, and admonished them to call if they encountered any difficulties arising from the case they'd become so embroiled in.

Joe hugged Fran before moving over to Megan. He paused for a moment, then wrapped his arms around her and held her tight. Resting her cheek upon his chest, Megan closed her eyes, not wanting the moment to pass.

"Can I call you when you get home?" he whispered.

She nodded, unwilling to trust her voice as the tears started to flow.

With seeming reluctance, Joe released her. He took a step back and cupped her face in his hands. "Hey," he said, gently wiping the tears off her cheek with his fingers, "none of that! At least you've got Fran with you. I'm stuck with him." He gestured over to Rob with his head. "So I'm going to miss you a whole lot more than you'll miss me."

Megan glanced over at Rob who was manfully fighting a grin, and couldn't help giving a watery smile. "Look after each other," she admonished brokenly. Then, because she didn't want them to see her crying any more, she stepped into the car, sat down, and closed the door. Fran followed her lead, and within minutes they had started up the lane leading to the main street, and given a final wave to the men still standing sentinel in the hotel parking lot.

Megan drove through a mist of tears until she'd crossed the Britannia Bridge and entered the A55 heading east out of North

Wales. She was grateful for Fran's compassionate silence, and when at last she spoke, it was to comment on the scenery through which they traveled. And Megan had to admit, the gently undulating green hills and restful pastoral views were soothing even to her sore and tear-filled eyes.

CHAPTER 14

Less than a week later Megan and Fran boarded a Boeing 767 at London's Heathrow Airport, bound for JFK International Airport, New York. Once they had found their assigned seats and stowed their carry-on luggage, they sat down with their tiny white pillows and thin navy blue airline-issue blankets at their sides. The steady trickle of passengers continued to filter down the narrow aisles, opening and closing the overhead bins and bumping into each other as they maneuvered their bodies and bags around the confined spaces they had each been allotted.

Megan watched the seeming chaos slowly dissipate as seats were taken and the aisle emptied, then she turned her attention to the small oval window to her left. Half a dozen other airplanes were parked in single file beside the one she occupied. She recognized most of the flags and symbols on the aircrafts' bodies. They were from all around the world, and she couldn't help but marvel at the miracle of modern travel.

The ground crew were working feverishly, pulling up with wagons loaded with luggage, catering trucks, and service vehicles. Others stood with earmuffs on, orange batons in hand, waiting for the pilot's signal that would galvanize them into action and herald the airplane's departure. Beyond the vast cement ground-covering sat the terminal, its tinted windows mirroring the activity outside. And beyond the terminal, Megan could just make out the rich green English country-side.

She tried to swallow the lump in her throat. She had missed her family and loved her home, but she was loath to leave the British

Isles. The quaint villages, venerable historical sights, bustling cities where modern and ancient met, and idyllic landscapes had found a special niche in her heart. Perhaps it wouldn't have been so poignant if she'd known when she would next return, but since that day was likely far off, her heart was heavy as the stewardesses went through their routine check and orientation before takeoff.

Megan closed her eyes as the plane began taxiing toward the runway, and reviewed the last three weeks in her mind. At first there had been the excitement of London—the art galleries, theaters, and royal historical sights. Then there had been the drive up north, through Cambridge and Oxford with their elegant colleges, Stratford-upon-Avon and the Royal Shakespeare Theater, then through the Lake District and into Scotland. Exploring Edinburgh Castle had just whetted her appetite for the castles of North Wales, but nothing could have prepared her for the experiences she encountered on Anglesey.

Her thoughts flew to Joe—for about the millionth time since she'd left him. She wondered if he and Rob were still in the country. For the first two or three days after leaving Anglesey, she and Fran had anxiously scoured the newspapers each morning for any news of the arrest of Richard Garrett and the two IRA members, but they had found none. Their vigilance waned with the passing days, and they gratefully continued their tour through the historical city of Bath and the quaint small towns of southern England, then to Stonehenge and back to London.

Megan had been almost alarmed by how much she missed Joe. He was never far from her thoughts, and she caught herself more than once looking for his deep brown eyes, or his tall handsome form amongst the crowds they met on their journey. One evening she found the small slip of paper on which he'd written his cell phone number. Hesitatingly, she had dialed it, only to experience disappointment when a mechanical voice told her that the person she was calling was out of range and to try calling later. She never did.

The sound of the airplane's engines became more high-pitched and the lumbering aircraft suddenly surged forward, gathering speed and momentum with every passing second. Megan opened her eyes and watched through the small window as they left the ground, soared upward, then banked steeply and circled around until the position of the morning sun indicated they were headed west. The moving vehicles below soon took the form of ants crawling across a patchwork quilt of browns, blues, and greens.

"Good-bye," Megan whispered sadly to her last glimpse of English countryside, and then the plane pierced through a billowing cloud and all around was fluffy whiteness.

Lights flickered, beeps sounded, and the stewardesses went into action. Beverage carts were followed by lunch carts that were followed by dinner carts. A movie that Megan had never wanted to see flashed before her for over two hours; it was distracting despite the fact that she had her eyes closed at least half of the time, and could hear none of the dialogue. She and Fran chatted, read, and dozed until they were within one hour of their destination, then they decided to beat the last minute rush for the rest rooms and took it in turns to go and freshen up.

One of the many miracles of transatlantic travel, Megan mused as she gazed back at her bleary-eyed reflection in the tiny mirror of the claustrophobic rest room, was how someone could feel so utterly exhausted and horribly grimy after having done nothing but sit for eight hours. Her left arm, which had been healing well, was aching with every movement, and her eyes felt as though they had been dusted with grit. She sighed and, sparing her left arm as much as possible, filled the minute sink with water, washed her face and reapplied a little makeup. When she'd finished she had to admit that even though the weariness wasn't gone, she looked considerably better.

Cheered by this thought, and pleased that at least the first leg of their trip would soon be behind them, Megan walked back to her seat, passing the passengers who were now lining up to use the rest rooms. Fran was studying her ticket and looked up as Megan approached.

"We're not going to have much time to make the transfer," Fran said, and Megan scrambled over her friend's legs to her own seat.

She looked at her watch and then over at Fran's ticket. "Looks like we'll be getting in a few minutes late, and that gives us just under an hour to pick up the luggage, go through immigration, customs, and find the next terminal."

Fran grimaced. "JFK's a big place. D'you think we can make it?"

"If our luggage isn't held up, and we don't have to stop for long at the immigration or customs check points, we'll be okay. Let's get everything ready before we land, then we can be first off the plane."

Fran nodded her agreement, and stood up to open the bin above her head. She handed Megan her lightweight jacket, and pulled out her own. Then both women picked up the few items they had used during the flight, stuffed them into the bags at their feet, and were prepared for the final descent into New York, long before the announcement was made over the loudspeaker.

The stewardesses had just completed their last check of the cabin and were preparing to buckle themselves into their own seats when the head steward appeared at Fran's elbow.

"Miss Harmer? Miss Brown?" he asked.

"Yes?" the two women answered in unison.

"A special message just came through for you from the control tower." He handed a bewildered Fran a small yellow piece of paper. She thanked him automatically, and as he walked away, she turned to Megan and opened it so that they could both read the scribbled message inside.

Please do not disembark airplane until advised to do so.

They stared at it in stunned silence.

"What on earth does that mean?" Fran said. "D'you think it's some kind of joke?"

"I don't know," Megan replied hoarsely, her anxiety level rising with every foot of the airplane's descent.

"Well, one thing's for sure," Fran said bleakly, "if we stay on this airplane until everyone else has gone, there's no way we'll make that connecting flight."

Megan continued to stare at the note. She had never heard of passengers receiving messages via the cockpit before. Who could be behind it? And why were she and Fran being singled out? She straightened her shoulders and took a deep breath. They would wait. They had to. But if it turned out to be some sort of prank, someone, somewhere, was going to hear about it.

"We'll just have to hope that whoever has enough clout to send a message from the control tower can also cut through the red tape necessary to get us onto another flight," she said, trying to infuse some confidence into her words.

Fran gave her a miserable glance, then sat back to brace herself for the landing. A light thud was followed by the roaring of the engines and the airplane coasted down the runway toward the waiting terminal. The passengers all waited with eyes fixed on the illuminated *fasten seat belts* sign, and at the very moment that the light went out, the cabin resounded with clicks and people scrambled to gather their belongings and be on their way.

Megan and Fran sat silently and watched the frenzied activity all around them. Young children were squashed between strangers' legs; bags were slung over shoulders, narrowly missing other passengers still unloading overhead bins; jackets were donned or thrown over arms; and friends and family members called out to keep track of each other's whereabouts and belongings.

Eventually, however, the madding throng dispersed and the airplane's cabin sat empty of passengers, except for Megan and Fran. A puzzled stewardess moved toward them from the main exit, but before she could reach them, someone else boarded the plane. The woman had her back to them, but Megan could see her consulting with the head steward who had delivered the note. He nodded, then called back the stewardess who was heading their way, pointed out Megan and Fran to the stranger, and moved aside to let her pass.

Megan studied the woman as she drew nearer, and then rose with Fran to meet her. She was only a little taller than Megan herself. Her light brown, shoulder-length hair was pulled back into a ponytail and tied with a navy blue kerchief. Navy dress pants and low-heeled shoes were contrasted with a crisp, white cotton shirt, and her only jewelry appeared to be a wide gold wedding band and a thin, golden rope necklace. With her trim figure and conservative dress, she could easily have passed as an airline stewardess, but there were no identifying airline pins to be seen.

Her face lit up when she reached Megan and Fran, and she extended her hand to them in greeting. "Megan? Fran?" she asked.

"Yes," they both answered, wariness obvious in their voices.

"I'm so glad you got my message in time. I'm Katy Jenkins."

Megan took her hand and shook it automatically, racking her brains for some connection with this woman. Her confusion must have shown in her face, because Katy Jenkins smiled and said, "I'm Rob's wife."

"Rob, as in Rob and Joe?" Fran asked, as she too shook Katy's hand.

"That's the one!" Her blue eyes twinkled. "I'm just Joe's understudy when Rob's favorite partner's not around."

"It's nice to meet you," Megan said, and really meant it. She found herself immediately drawn to Katy Jenkins, just as she had been to her husband. "But what are you doing here? And why the mysterious message?"

Katy's face grew serious. "I received a call from Rob a few hours ago. He and Joe were at Heathrow—they must have only just missed you because they're on their way home right now. Somehow Richard Garrett's arrest was leaked to the press, and they had a big write-up on it in this morning's *London Times*. Your name was mentioned Megan, and Rob's worried about the response of the U.S. press. He asked me to get hold of you before the journalistic bloodhounds move in."

"But why go through the trouble of meeting us on the plane?" Fran asked, giving Megan time to adjust to this new information.

"Because when I arrived at JFK about an hour ago, and walked to the gate where your flight was scheduled to arrive, I found that I couldn't get near it. The place is swarming with photographers, news cameras, journalists, and the tabloid writers."

"They're waiting for us?" Megan could barely contain her horror at the thought.

"Yes, but they're going to be disappointed this time," Katy replied with satisfaction. "You're coming with me!"

With that, she helped Megan and Fran pick up their belongings, and led them to the exit. They followed her out of the airplane, but rather than continuing down the concourse into the terminal, Katy walked over to a small door almost hidden in the corner of the walkway, opened it, and ushered the women outside and down a narrow metal staircase that led directly onto the cement ground below.

Humid heat hit them like a wall as they left the air-conditioned airport facility. The roar of jet engines that filled the air precluded any verbal communication, so Megan and Fran just followed Katy as she led them across the cement and in through another door on the ground-floor level. When she pulled it closed behind them, it was like entering another world—quiet and cool.

"This leads down to international baggage claim," Katy explained, "and only passengers are allowed in there. We'll pick up your cases, get you through immigration and customs, then whisk you off again before any member of the press sets eyes on you."

They passed a large red-and-white sign that read: *Restricted Security Area, Violators Will Be Prosecuted,* and Megan looked at it nervously.

"Katy," she said, "how're you doing this?"

Katy smiled. "I wondered how long it would take you to ask," she said. Then she pulled her wallet out of her purse, opened it, and showed Megan and Fran a card inside.

"You're with the FBI too?" Fran said with astonishment.

"Yes, that's how I met Rob," Katy answered. "But we work in different branches of the Bureau. I work with security—airport security," she clarified. "And as luck would have it, I just finished a three week stint at JFK, which gave me a few inside connections for this little job."

"Like getting a message to the control tower?" Megan suggested.

Katy smiled, but she admitted nothing more. Instead she opened a door at the end of the corridor, and they found themselves transported, as if by magic, to the baggage claim area.

Their bags were the only ones still circling around baggage claim carousel five. Fran hoisted both cases off the moving conveyor belt—aware that Megan's arm was not up to that level of strain. They loaded them onto a cart and wheeled them through immigration, where a bored-looking official asked a few perfunctory questions, stamped their passports, and waved them on. Customs was even faster. They walked right through the *Nothing to Declare* gate unhindered, but stopped almost immediately afterward because they had reached the last barricade before entry into the main airport lobby.

Megan and Fran gave Katy a questioning look, and she promptly took charge again. They unloaded the cart, and carrying the cases between them, they left through a side door that read: *Airport Employees Only.* The door opened into a long corridor with other doors leading off from it. Small plaques nailed to the wall beside each door suggested that they led to individual offices.

Katy slowed as she approached the third door on the right, and turned to face the other women. "This is where you have to make a few decisions," she said. "I can find you another flight into Salt Lake City, if you want to keep to your original schedule. But I should warn you that the chances that the media are camped out there are pretty high, especially since they were thwarted here.

"If you have a good friend or relative that you could stay with at short notice, living in some other part of the country, I can try putting you through to another city. Or . . ." her eyes sparkled, "we can do what Rob suggested, and you could fly home with me!"

"To Boston?" Fran said, looking as stunned as Megan felt.

Megan's mouth was suddenly so dry that she didn't think she'd be able to say anything, but she swallowed hard a few times, then asked, "How long is this . . . this hounding going to go on?"

Katy shrugged. "I wish I could tell you. Rob seemed to think it would be a five-day wonder—the type of thing that will lose its dramatic appeal when it's old news, or when something bigger comes along to take its place." She gave Megan a sympathetic look. "I'm really sorry. From the little Rob's told me, I know this whole thing's been quite an ordeal for you both."

Megan ran a hand across her face. If only she wasn't so tired and jet-lagged, maybe she could think more clearly. Fran was looking at her, and she realized that her friend was expecting her to make the decision. With that realization came another one—in her present state, she was not physically or emotionally able to cope with an onslaught from the media. Merely contemplating falling back on Rob and Joe's physical protection and professional savvy, filled her with overwhelming relief.

"If it's really okay with you, I think we should go to Boston," Megan said.

Fran nodded her agreement and Katy beamed. "Let's go get some tickets!"

She knocked on the door behind her, and without waiting for a reply, entered and indicated that Megan and Fran should do the same.

"Hi Leon," Katy called, and a burly black man raised his head from behind a large computer screen.

"Hey, Katy, what are you doin' here? Are we in trouble again?" his deep jovial voice registered absolutely no fear of the FBI agent's presence.

"No, I'm just making a social call."

Leon snorted. "Yeah right! So what d'ya need this time?"

"Ah, Leon," Katy said, "You know me so well."

She leaned on his desk with both elbows. "How about three tickets to Boston leaving ASAP?"

Leon rolled his eyes, but his fingers went to work immediately, clicking through one computer screen after another, until with a grunt of satisfaction, he said, "Delta flight 1125. Leaves in twenty minutes."

He looked up expectantly, and at Katy's pleased nod he said, "Alright. What are the names?"

"Mrs. Jenkins, Miss Brown, and Miss Harmer—spelled H-A-R-M-E-R," Katy said.

A few more seconds of keyboard clicking ensued, then Leon looked up with a sigh. "Your boarding passes are waiting at Gate 26, Mrs. Jenkins."

"Leon, you're the greatest!" Katy said. "I owe you an ice-cream cone."

"An ice-cream cone!" Leon exploded, then shook his head in self-depreciation. "Oh man, the price you pay for dealing with a Mormon."

Katy burst into laughter, and the look of chagrin on Leon's face had Megan and Fran smiling too. Katy opened the door and gave Leon a cheerful farewell salute before the three women entered the corridor again.

"Okay, ladies," Katy said once the door was closed, "we're going to have to move fast to reach that gate in time." She paused and looked at Megan anxiously. "How's your arm holding up Megan?"

"It's throbbing," Megan admitted.

"Well, I don't have any luggage, so if you can manage your carry-on bag, I'll take your case. Are you alright with your stuff, Fran?"

"Yes," Fran said, already lifting her case off the floor.

"Okay, let's go."

***

Megan never was quite sure how they reached Gate 26 in less than fifteen minutes—but they did. Katy led them through a labyrinth of corridors, up an elevator, and even managed to hail a ride on one of the porters' carts for the last dash down the terminal. Megan kept her head low whenever they entered public areas, but Katy and Fran reported no sign of the media anywhere nearby.

They boarded the flight to Boston without difficulty, managing to hand over their cases as gate check-ins. After takeoff, the stewardesses barely had time to hand out bottled water and pretzels before they were gathering up wrappers, napkins, and cups, and preparing for landing again.

Despite all the sitting Megan had done during the past twelve hours, exhaustion was really beginning to affect her. The ache in her arm was starting to spread up into her shoulder and neck, but she lifted her carry-on bag onto her good shoulder and followed Katy and Fran off the airplane and into Logan International Airport's terminal, where thankfully, no one awaited them.

Having eliminated the need to wait at the baggage terminal, the three women were soon out of the airport and loading the bags into Katy's white VW Passat in the parking lot. Megan took the back seat, and knew that she had reached a new low in enervation, when even her innate sense of curiosity and delight in discovering new places could not rise above her need for sleep. She dozed fitfully and did not really show interest in her new surroundings until Katy drew the car up to the curb outside a row of tall, narrow town houses on an avenue lined with green, leafy maple trees.

CHAPTER 15

They gathered up the luggage, and Katy led the way through a small gate, up a short path to the front door. She dug a key out of her purse, put it in the keyhole, opened the door, and stood aside to let Megan and Fran in before her. The front door opened into a narrow hallway. A polished wooden floor led straight back to the far end of the house on the right side, and on the left, a staircase rose steeply, its banister railing the same polished wood as the flooring. The walls were painted off-white, and a few small paintings hung along the length of the hall. Fran moved forward to study them with interest.

Katy closed the door behind her. "Welcome to our home!" she said cheerfully. She gestured down the hallway. "First door on the right is the sitting room, second door is the dining room, and the one at the end of the hall is the kitchen. There's a small rest room back there too." She picked up Megan's case again. "Let's go upstairs and I'll show you the guest room, then if you want to sleep you can. You'll have plenty of time to look around later."

Obediently, Megan and Fran followed Katy up the stairs. "This first room," Katy said, as they reached the landing, "is the one Rob and I use as a study. Then there's our room . . ." she continued to walk down the hallway back toward the front of the house. "The bathroom's right here, with the guest bedroom next door." She pushed the door open and they walked in.

Megan loved it immediately. It was not a large room—big enough for two twin beds, a small dresser, and a wooden rocking chair. The walls were a pale sea-foam green, lace curtains were at the window, which looked out over the tree-lined avenue below. The two beds had hand-tied quilts, not matching exactly, but sharing many of the same scraps of fabric. The polished wooden floor that obviously ran throughout the house was covered in the center of the room with a pale-colored rug that was similar in hue to the walls. An antique wash basin and pitcher sat on top of the wooden dresser that separated the two beds.

"It's lovely, Katy," Megan said, and Katy looked pleased.

"Well, I'll leave you both to get some rest, but I'll be in the kitchen if you need me—right at the end of the hall downstairs," she reminded them.

***

Forty-five minutes later, Megan was lying on one of the beds watching the lace curtains billow gently back and forth in the breeze from the slightly open window. Fran was fast asleep on the other bed, and although Megan's whole body ached with fatigue, the time change and her nap in the car had completely muddled her system. As hard as she tried, sleep would not come.

She and Fran had used her calling card to place phone calls to their respective parents. Megan had asked that both her parents get on the line and had given them a sketchy outline of her experience in Anglesey, followed by the reason for their delay in arriving in Salt Lake City. She was anxious that they know about the incident from her before they heard her name on the news or discovered her photo staring back at them from the newspaper on the kitchen table.

Their responses had been predictable. Her mother was close to tears. Her father told her he'd be on the next plane out of Salt Lake City. Megan reassured them both that she and Fran were in very good hands, and explained to her parents that they might have to devote some time to contingency plans themselves. There was a fairly good chance that members of the media would approach them about their daughter's whereabouts. Her parents had ended the conversation by promising to cope with things on their end on the condition that Megan keep in close contact with them.

Fran's phone call home had been considerably shorter. Neither of her parents had been there, so she had called a neighbor, who told her that Fran's father was on a two-week river run and that her mother was attending an art show in San Antonio. Fran left a message for her parents simply saying that if she was not home when her parents returned, they were not to worry about her.

With that done, Fran promptly went to sleep, and Megan was left lying on her bed staring at the window with stinging eyes and a fuzzy head, but finding sleep completely elusive. After her sixth glance at her watch in as many minutes, Megan decided it was futile to keep trying. She changed her shirt, brushed her hair, and spent a few minutes washing her face and cleaning her teeth. Then feeling a little fresher, she went downstairs in search of Katy.

Megan found her in the kitchen. Katy had changed and was wearing a pair of faded jeans, a white T-shirt with a sunflower embroidered on the front, and her navy kerchief had been exchanged for a white ribbon. She was standing barefoot in front of the kitchen sink, humming softly to herself as she cut up vegetables for a huge tossed salad that was materializing in a bowl at her elbow.

"D'you mind if I join you?" Megan asked as she entered the sun-filled kitchen.

Katy jumped. "Hi, Megan! I thought you were asleep."

Megan grimaced. "My body wishes I were, but my mind won't switch off."

"Been there—done that!" Katy said with a laugh.

"Can I help you?" Megan asked hopefully.

"Sure." Katy opened a drawer and pulled out another paring knife. "How about cutting up the cucumbers?"

Megan moved forward, grateful for Katy's easy acceptance of her, and it wasn't long before they were conversing like old friends. Their shared membership in the LDS Church broke many barriers, and they found that they were able to connect via Church members they'd both known. Megan learned about Katy's graduation from BYU and subsequent employment by the FBI, about her meeting Rob, and their courtship and marriage a year before. She even learned a little about Joe.

His parents divorced when he was only six years old, and he was raised by his mother in the Boston area. He graduated from Harvard, majoring in history and European studies, and had been used as a resource specialist by the FBI for some time because of his graduate research into terrorist groups in Europe. When the Bureau finally persuaded him to work for them full-time, he was partnered with Rob, and they'd been best friends ever since.

Megan in turn told Katy about her home in Utah, her own education, and her work in Jackson Hole. She gave her a little background on Fran, and enthusiastically told her about their recent trip to Britain. Katy proved to be the most understanding audience she had yet encountered when Megan began describing the events that occurred on Anglesey. She had the advantage of being familiar with FBI past operations, and was therefore not stunned by the violence or terror that Megan encountered. But she was also a woman of similar age and background, and therefore Megan guessed, similar perspectives. Her empathy filled the space between them, and Megan received the distinct impression that no matter what happened in the future, Katy Jenkins would be a friend forever.

They had finished the green salad and moved on to emptying potato chips into a bowl and frosting brownies, when they heard a noise coming from the front door, and Katy stopped speaking mid-sentence. Her face broke into a beaming smile.

"I think we've got company," she said, and turned to face the kitchen door just as it burst open to reveal Rob, looking a little travel weary, but bearing the same expression of delight as his wife. He was closely followed by Joe.

The men took in the presence of the two women in one quick glance, then Rob crossed the room and took his wife in his arms.

"Katy, you wonder woman, I knew you could do it!" Then before she could utter a word, he kissed her long and hard.

Megan and Joe stood and gazed at each other for a few seconds, then he too closed the space between them. "You okay?" he asked quietly.

Megan smiled and nodded. "I am now," she said, and she saw the smile reach his eyes before he bent and kissed her. Instinctively her arms moved up around his neck, as she reciprocated his tender yearning completely.

When they moved apart, Megan realized they had an audience. Rob was looking their way, grinning broadly, and Katy's expression of stunned surprise and raised eyebrows expressed her feelings completely.

"Megan's been telling me about her adventure on Anglesey," Katy finally said, "but she obviously missed some key parts in the story!"

Megan felt her cheeks flush, but Joe slipped his arm around her small waist. "I'm sure she told you exactly what she told the police and the coast guard," he countered. "What else could you possibly want to know?"

"Joseph Marks, I've lined you up with every eligible maiden I know. If you've gone and beaten me again, and found a better woman without my help—one who'll even stoop to give you the time of day, I'll . . . I'll be most miffed!" She waved her frosting-covered knife at him.

Joe reached out, grabbed Katy's wrist, and took the knife. "Can I lick it?" he asked, just to torture her even more.

Rob roared with laughter, and Katy, valiantly trying to keep a straight face, snatched the knife back and said, "No, and if you don't start behaving better, you're not having any brownies either!"

***

Megan woke Fran up before they all ate. She was groggy, but coherent enough to know that if she didn't get up, she wouldn't be able to sleep later that night. She joined the others in the Jenkinses' small backyard, where Katy had put Rob to work barbecuing steaks, while she, Megan and Joe loaded up a small table with salad, baked potatoes, chips, watermelon, and corn on the cob.

Having filled her plate, Megan sat down on one of the chairs under the shade of a large cherry tree, and looked around with pleasure. The backyard was small and simple. A set of French doors led out from the kitchen onto a paved stone patio, where Rob stood monitoring the propane-fueled barbecue grill. From there, the rectangular lawn was bordered by terra-cotta-colored brick walls upon which a carpet of deep green ivy crept. The large cherry tree was the only tree in the yard, but its ancient branches shaded much of the area from the direct sun, while still allowing the filtered light to make the lawn beside its trunk a welcoming spot.

Katy had placed a rug and chairs at the base of the tree, and she and Fran joined Megan with their own plates of food. They chatted easily with each other, and Megan was struck again by how close a bond she already felt with people whom she'd known for such a short time. Constantly aware of his presence, she surreptitiously watched Joe as he helped Rob at the grill. They bantered back and forth, laughing and teasing over something; and Megan warmed to see Joe's expression, which had been so tense during most of his time with her in Wales, relax now that the stress he'd been under was beginning to lift.

She saw Rob turn off a couple of switches on the gas grill, then he and Joe made their way over to the women. They both chose spots on the rug—Rob near the center, and Joe right beside Megan's chair. Joe leaned back, resting against one side of her chair, and Megan was overwhelmingly conscious of his nearness. He was wearing jeans and a forest green polo shirt. His dark wavy hair shone in the sunlight, and his swarthy good looks were not lessened by the evening shadow that covered the lower portion of his face. In this confusing day of long-distance flights and time changes, he had not shaven, but it did nothing to diminish his extraordinarily handsome features.

Megan tried to focus on eating the delicious meal that Katy had provided, but it was almost impossible. Aware of every movement and comment Joe made, she had to keep reminding herself that he was not LDS. He participated fully in the conversation flowing around him—even when it turned to Katy's struggle over a Primary lesson and an elders quorum request for Rob to help a family move within the ward boundaries. Megan had seen him bow his head reverently when Rob offered a blessing on their food, and found herself wondering exactly where he stood when it came to religion.

But this was not the place for bringing up personal issues like that. Instead, after the general conversation died down, Fran brought up the problem of their unexpected presence in Boston, and the media coverage that had caused it.

"D'you have any idea how long this could go on, Rob?" Fran asked.

Rob gave a slow shake of his head. "It's pretty much anyone's guess," he said. "Garrett's in a prominent position at Ford, but he's no household name. My gut feeling is that it's not going to last too long.

Within a couple of days it will be old news, and if the media haven't had their exclusive photo or interview by then, they'll move on to something else. It's the drama around celebrities that tends to sit on the front pages at the checkout stands for months." He paused and looked up at her, wincing against the sun in his eyes. "If we're lucky another story will come up—with more public interest—and you'll be able to get back to your own lives very soon."

"So, are we under 'house arrest' until then?" Fran asked.

Rob smiled. "I think it would be a shame to spend your short time in Boston cooped up in the house, but having said that I wouldn't go standing on the steps of the state capitol with a name tag on either."

Fran sighed. "Okay. How about the Museum of Fine Arts without a name tag?"

Rob laughed. "That I think we can manage."

***

Megan snuggled down under the smooth cotton sheets of her bed about two hours later, replaying the events of the evening in her mind as the first hint of drowsiness began to descend. It had been a good— an amazingly wonderful—end to a completely shattering day. She did not want to think about the stressful journey that had brought her to this point; instead she dwelt on the friendships that had developed over the last few hours, and on the fact that she'd been granted a little more time with Joe.

By the time they'd all helped clear up the dinner dishes, jet lag was hitting everyone (with the exception of Katy) pretty hard. Joe had wished them all good night, but when he reached the front door, Megan was the only one still there to see him off. The others had quietly vanished.

The emotion burning in his eyes as he drew her close before leaving led Megan to believe that he would have done the same thing with or without an audience. She could sense his deepening affection in his kiss, and knew that she was responding in kind. Her head was screaming, "Megan, be careful!" while her heart pulsed, "This feels so right."

She had drawn away, and perhaps her confusion showed on her face, because Joe whispered, "We've got to talk." Then he paused in thought for a minute before continuing. "I have to fill out reports at the office tomorrow morning. Could we meet in the afternoon and go somewhere?"

"I'd like that," Megan said.

"I'll see you tomorrow then," he said with a smile, and pulled open the door. When he walked down the path toward his waiting car, Megan reentered the house feeling like a giddy teenager who'd just been asked out on her first date by the most popular boy in school.

And so now she lay in bed, desperately wanting to nurture her fledgling feelings for Joe, while realizing that one of the most important attributes she'd always wanted in a future husband—the sharing of her faith—was absent. It was an emotional battle of monumental proportions, yet it too eventually succumbed to her body's overwhelming need for sleep. She slept long and deeply through the night, and awoke only when the first light and sound of morning filtered in through the window.

CHAPTER 16

Megan tried rolling over and ignoring the beckoning day, but it was no use. Sleep had well and truly fled, so she slipped out of bed, and made her way downstairs. Rob was already in the kitchen, and greeted her cheerfully.

"Hi, Megan. Did you sleep okay?"

"Yes, thanks," she replied with a smile, and walked over to join him at the kitchen table. She sat down opposite him. The morning newspaper lay at his elbow, and he'd obviously been reading it while finishing his orange juice and piece of toast.

"Rob," she began somewhat hesitantly, "I haven't had the chance to really thank you for all you've done—arranging for Katy to meet us at JFK, letting us use your home, not to mention everything you did at the hospital." Megan paused, but before Rob could respond she continued, "I didn't want to say too much before, because I wasn't sure how much Joe would understand, but the blessing you gave me . . . I know that it helped. Thanks."

He gave a small shake of his head.

"You don't need to thank me. I'm just glad I could help. Joe's seen me give blessings before, and in his own way I think he even has a testimony of their effectiveness. Once, on a raid that we did together at an apartment here in Boston, I was the one who was shot. Joe rushed me to the hospital, but insisted that they find an LDS medic to administer to me before anything else took place."

Rob looked at Megan with serious eyes.

"Four years of working together have drawn us as close as any brothers could be. He's not LDS, but he lives like a Mormon. All he needs is a final commitment and a good dunking." He offered a small smile. "He cares a lot about you, Megan. Katy and I have watched him float in and out of a few relationships, but I've never seen him this way before."

Megan nodded, an uncomfortable lump forming in her throat. "I care about him too—so much that it scares me!"

"Because he's not LDS?" Rob asked.

She nodded again. "All my life I've dreamed of a temple wedding, and a gospel-centered family. I just don't know if I can let go of that dream."

To her surprise, Rob seemed pleased at her words.

"Good for you!" he said with an encouraging smile. "You hold on to your dreams, and we'll all start praying that Joe gets very wet, very soon."

Megan tried to emulate his hopeful attitude and quell her own misgivings by smiling in return.

Just then the kitchen door swung open and Katy entered.

"Oh Megan, I'm so glad you're up—now I won't have to leave a note," Katy said when she saw her at the table. "How did you sleep?"

"Great, thank you," Megan replied. "And my arm feels much better."

Katy looked pleased. "Well, have a relaxing day today, and just make yourselves at home here. Rob and I have to head to work in a few minutes." Using a piece of paper and pencil that Megan assumed had been intended for the now-unnecessary note, she wrote down a couple of phone numbers. "Here are Rob's and my phone numbers at work. I'll be there till five. Rob'll probably be done before then, but may have to go help with the elders quorum move afterward. I'm sure you'll see one or the other of us by five-thirty tonight."

She gave Megan a key. "Here's the front door key in case you decide to go out anywhere in the meantime."

Rob handed Megan the morning paper that had been lying on the table. It was most disconcerting to see her own face looking back at her from the front page. "You're still front page news," he said, "but at least you're not the main headlines today."

Megan took a better look. The article was only one column on the lower portion of the page, but she presumed it continued on one of the inner pages. A photograph of Richard Garrett was placed beside one of her.

"That's my faculty photo!" Megan cried. "How did they ever get hold of that?"

Rob shrugged. "I sometimes think the media's investigative network is better than ours. And having said that, just be careful if you do decide to go out. I don't think anyone's on the lookout for you in Boston, but it would probably be best not to draw attention to yourselves."

Megan glanced down at the paper again and nodded, chewing her lip miserably. "I keep thinking this whole thing can't be real, that any minute now I'll wake up."

Rob patted her arm. "I really don't think it will last long. You've done nothing wrong—quite the opposite, actually, so you have no reason to feel like a wanted fugitive. We just have to wait until the initial curiosity about you dies down, and it's amazing how fast the public forgets."

Megan gave a deep sigh, and impulsively Katy gave her a hug. "It'll all be okay very soon," she promised. "But until then, help yourself to anything. There's bread, fruit, cold cereal, yogurt, eggs . . ." Katy waved her hand expansively, "whatever you like."

"Thank you so much," Megan said, though the words seemed grossly inadequate.

"I'm just glad I got a chance to get to know you and be a small part of this adventure," Katy said, her eyes twinkling in a way that Megan was coming to recognize.

Katy picked up a set of car keys that were sitting on the counter, shouldered her purse, and walked out into the hall through the door that her husband was holding open.

"See you later!" she called over her shoulder, and Rob gave Megan a smile and wave before the door closed behind them both.

***

Megan read the entire newspaper article over a bowl of corn flakes. It was surprisingly accurate, but rather sketchy and lacking in details. Megan briefly wondered who'd been the reporter's source of information, but assumed she would never know. She just hoped that whoever it was had been adequately compensated, and wouldn't continue talking.

She was taking her empty cereal bowl over to the sink when Fran arrived.

"Have Rob and Katy left?" Fran asked, running her fingers through her tangled hair.

"Yes, they've gone to work," Megan said.

"I thought I heard car doors and engines starting up," Fran said, sitting down heavily on one of the kitchen chairs. "When will they be back?"

"About dinnertime, I think," Megan said. "We're to help ourselves to breakfast—and anything else we might need."

She slid the newspaper across the table so that it lay in front of Fran. "Read that and tell me what you think."

Fran looked down and raised her eyebrows as she immediately recognized the two photos in the lower corner of the front page, but she didn't say anything until she'd read the accompanying article.

"Well, at least they didn't claim that you were abducted by aliens, lived in Egypt three hundred years ago, or were born with a tail," she said, when she finally looked up again.

Megan stared at her for a few seconds, then started to chuckle, and before long they were both laughing so hard that Megan's side began to hurt. "Oh Fran," she finally gasped, "you are so good for me!"

***

It took Megan an unusually long time to shower and dress. She couldn't decide what to wear, and was further limited by the fact that every article of clothing that she had with her was smashed and wrinkled in her cases. She didn't feel comfortable rooting through Katy's cupboards in search of an iron, so she eventually decided on a pair of jeans and a white ribbed T-shirt—quite simply because they appeared to be the least creased. She brushed her hair until it shone, and the humid Boston air caused the natural wave to add a soft bounce as she moved. After adding a hint of makeup and perfume, she felt that she was as ready to greet Joe again as she could be, but she found the wait—watching the clock go around for well over an hour—agonizingly slow.

It was about twelve forty-five in the afternoon when he rang the doorbell. Megan answered the door—but not without checking through the tiny peephole first. He was standing on the doorstep wearing a light gray polo shirt, his hands in the pockets of his blue jeans. Self-consciously she welcomed him and led him into the living room.

Fran was sitting cross-legged on the floor sifting through some of the sketches she had made on their trip. She looked up as they entered.

"Hi Joe," she said.

"Hi," Joe replied, and when he saw what she was doing, moved closer with interest. He stood looking over her shoulder for a few minutes. "They're good, Fran. Really good!" he said. "Maybe you should take your portfolio with you when you go to the Museum of Fine Arts."

"Can we go?" Fran's enthusiasm lit up her face.

"Sure. I can take you there, if that's where you want to go." He turned to Megan. "How about you, Megan? Would you like to go to the museum?"

Megan hesitated. "I'd love to," she said, "but my face was on the front page of the paper today, and I guess I feel a bit wary of going anywhere quite that public."

Joe nodded with understanding. "Well, how about we drop Fran off at the museum first, then I take you somewhere less crowded, and we meet Fran back at the museum an hour or two later?"

Megan couldn't repress a smile. "You're taking a big risk, you know. If you let Fran loose in that place without an escort, we may never see her again—and certainly not at the appointed time!"

"Hey!" cried Fran indignantly, then after a moment's pause said, "Well okay, does anyone have a watch with an alarm they can lend me?"

Joe and Megan both laughed.

"Nope," said Joe, "but I bet we could borrow Katy's kitchen timer. I've heard that thing bleeping many times before—it's obnoxious enough for the museum officials to evict you if you ignore it."

"Oh great!" said Fran. "Way to be inconspicuous!"

Joe laughed again and left the room, only to reappear minutes later, the small kitchen timer in hand.

"Now, don't be late, or everyone will be looking at you!" he warned with mock ferocity.

Fran's expression as she looked down at the innocent object he'd placed in her hand was comical. Anyone would have thought it was a vicious scorpion with the power to kill, but somehow she put aside her loathing, and obediently put the offensive timer in her pocket.

***

Joe and Megan dropped Fran off outside the Museum of Fine Arts with two and a half hours set on the kitchen timer. She gave them a quick wave before hurrying up the steps to the entrance, not wanting to waste a precious minute of time. Megan rested her head against the back of the passenger seat, and relaxed as Joe pulled back out into the traffic and navigated the congested city streets of Boston with the ease of a long-time resident.

The sage green Audi was a far cry from the Renault Joe had driven in Wales. The plush leather seats added further luxury to the smooth ride afforded by the powerful engine and top-of-the-line suspension. Megan glanced over at Joe, and could see the concentration in his face as he maneuvered through a particularly busy intersection. He must have sensed her look because as soon as it was safe to do so, his eyes flickered her way, and he smiled.

"Not at all curious about where we're going?" he asked.

Megan smiled back. "No, I trust your judgement."

His smile broadened. "We've come a long way from our first stilted meeting at the Anchor Hotel," he said.

"Hmm, we have, haven't we," Megan agreed, and thinking back to that time less than two weeks before, it was hard to believe that all she'd experienced was real. Then Joe reached over and took her hand. He squeezed it gently and Megan felt her pulse quicken at his touch. She knew that whatever else came of this episode in her life, her feelings for Joe were very real indeed.

A few minutes later, Joe pulled into a small parking area. Cars zipped by on the busy road behind them, but ahead of them lay a wide expanse of green—grass, shrubs, and huge old trees.

"Where are we?" Megan asked.

"Colonial Park," Joe replied. "It's one of Boston's oldest public parks, and a favorite of mine."

He stepped out of the car and hurried around to Megan's side of the vehicle to open the door for her. A button on his key ring automatically locked the doors, and he held out his hand for hers. Megan slipped her hand into his, still marveling at how much his nearness and touch affected her. They walked in silence, Joe leading the way along a path winding between ancient oak, sycamore, and maple trees. Megan looked up at the shimmering leaves that were swaying softly in the light breeze and creating dancing shadows on the ground below.

"I bet this is beautiful in the fall, when the leaves start changing color," she said.

"Yes it is," Joe said simply, and drew her over to a wooden bench situated beneath one of the largest oak trees. "I hope you don't mind that I didn't take you to one of the many historical sites in town. I didn't want to travel too far from the museum, and I thought we'd have more opportunity to talk here."

"This is great," Megan said, and knew with shattering certainty that she really didn't care where she was, as long as she was with him.

They sat down together and Megan looked around her with delight. The tall trees formed a barricade between the outside world and Colonial Park. The park itself was carpeted with lush green grass. Meandering footpaths wove in and out of the trees and shrubs that appeared to be growing and thriving where nature intended, rather than in any logical pattern set out by a landscape designer. Birds in many varieties flew from tree to tree and branch to branch, filling the air with their songs.

A few other people walked the paths, but no one showed any particular interest in Joe and Megan. Two toddlers raced by, with their mother pushing a stroller closely in tow. The mother barely had time to exchange a brief hello with Joe before she sped up her stroller to narrow the space between herself and her rambunctious charges. Megan caught sight of a couple of young women sitting on another bench through the trees. They appeared to be eating sandwiches, and she guessed they were on a late lunch break together. An elderly man ambled by with a cocker spaniel on a leash by his side. The white hair around the dog's snout suggested that he was of the same ambling disposition as his master, and he didn't even bother to bark at them as he passed by.

Megan was so intent on absorbing the sights and sounds around her, that it was some time before she realized that Joe's eyes were upon her. She turned to face him, feeling her color mount as she did so.

"I have something I have to tell you," Joe said without preamble, and Megan could sense the urgency in his voice.

She kept her eyes on him, and felt her anxiety deepen as Joe looked away abruptly, as though bracing himself for what was to come.

He spoke again. "D'you remember when we were at the hospital in Bangor and I told you that the previous night, when you were kidnapped, was the worst night of my life?"

"Yes." Megan recalled it clearly.

"Well, it was," he said, "but I didn't have the guts to tell you the whole truth about my feelings that night." Joe's face was still averted, and Megan held her breath, wondering what was coming next.

"The whole night was a living hell," he said and ran a hand through his hair in agitation as the memories returned. "But the worst moment for me was when we had you on the deck of the lifeboat, and Fran shouted for Rob . . ." Joe took a deep breath and continued. "She asked him to give you a blessing. And I had to move back and let him through . . . to do something that I couldn't do for you."

Joe balled his fists, and Megan could see his pulse beating hard and fast in the hollow of his temple. He lowered his voice.

"For the first time ever, I wanted to lash out at Rob. I wanted to tell him to stay away from you, that you were my girl and I'd take care of you . . . but . . . but I couldn't! I knew that you needed a blessing, and he was the only one on that boat who could do it.

"I think I went through some sort of epiphany that night. As I held you in my arms on the lifeboat, I knew that every miraculous breath you took was quite possibly because you'd received a blessing. I took the time to reflect on my life—particularly my life since I met Rob and Katy, and realized what an idiot I've been. I've relied on their faith—well, on Rob's especially—instead of trying to develop my own.

"Rob and I have talked about religion many times, well into the night. It was easy for me to see the good in his LDS beliefs, but we always reached a point at which our academic discussions would grind to a halt. Rob's faith took over, and I wasn't willing or ready to take that step. It was a barrier that was always there, and as much as Rob tried, he couldn't get me to cross it.

"Maybe God knew that I needed a really big prod—and almost losing you . . . that was as big a prod as I ever want to have."

Joe looked back at Megan then. His dusky eyes met her green ones that were filled with unshed tears. "I had plenty of time to talk with Rob on the way home," he said. "I told him how I was feeling, and he's arranging to have the missionaries teach me at his home."

Megan couldn't contain her tears. She flung her arms around Joe's neck and sobbed into his shoulder. She wasn't sure whether she was crying out of empathy for the anguish he'd been through, or out of happiness for the course he'd decided to take. Either way, it was some time before she pulled away from his embrace—long after the tears had stopped, but not before he had kissed her tenderly.

He put his arm around her and drew her close beside him on the bench. "Megan, I wanted you to know about me taking the missionary discussions before you left, because I've been around Rob and Katy enough to know how much religious beliefs mean to Mormons. But I can't promise you that I'll be baptized. I will only make that commitment if I'm sure it's the right thing for me to do. You understand that, don't you?"

Megan nodded. "That's good. I'd hate to think that you were getting baptized just to please me. You'll need a much stronger foundation than any feelings you have for me if you want your faith and testimony to grow."

Joe squeezed her gently. "Actually my feelings for you are already pretty darn strong!" he said, and set out to prove it by kissing her so soundly that he sent her senses reeling.

***

They were almost late in picking up Fran. She was waiting on the bottom step of the museum entrance when they pulled up in the car.

It took her only a couple of seconds to jump in, and almost the entire journey back to the Jenkinses' home to tell Joe and Megan about all the wonderful things she'd seen. Only when Joe turned off the ignition outside the house did Fran pause long enough to ask where they'd been while she was at the museum.

"We went to a nearby park," was all Megan said. She would tell Fran about Joe's desire for the missionary discussions later. At that moment she wanted to nurture her precious little seedling of hope in secret—well, not quite in secret. Rob knew about Joe's decision she realized. He'd known when they'd talked together at breakfast time. No wonder he'd been so glad that she wanted to hold firm to her dreams. She drew strength from knowing that Rob's prayers, along with those of Katy and Fran, would join hers as Joe faced one of the most important choices of his life.

CHAPTER 17

Megan and Fran's deliverance from the hounding media came sooner than anyone had anticipated. The two women had joined Katy in the kitchen the next morning. It was Saturday, so they were enjoying the luxury of an unhurried breakfast when Rob entered the room carrying the morning paper, still folded in its thin plastic wrapper. As soon as he opened it up to the front page, he gave out a whoop that immediately drew the attention of all three women.

"Alright! That's what we wanted!" he cried.

"What is it?" asked Katy

"A senior senator has been caught having an extramarital affair," Rob said with great satisfaction. "They've got photos, tapes, and everything to prove it!"

"Honey, that's nothing to get excited about!" Katy said with consternation, embarrassed by her husband's reaction to such sordid news.

"I'm not excited about his behavior," Rob said with a roll of his eyes. "It's the news! The news that will blow a kidnapping, an IRA operation, and the arrest of Richard Garrett right out the door!"

Realization of what this meant for Megan and Fran dawned on each woman simultaneously, but before anyone could speak, Rob began thumbing through the newspaper, quickly scanning each page before turning to another.

"Ah ha!" he said eventually. "Megan, you've been relegated to the bottom of page nine. You're old news girl!" He looked up with a grin. "Want to try for Salt Lake City today?"

Stunned by the speed at which everything around her was happening, Megan could only stare at him. Then she found herself nodding, "Well, yes. If you think we can make it alright."

"Everyone in any line of news is going to be scrambling to get to Washington, D.C., today," Rob said with confidence. "The fact that it's Saturday is only going to make things harder for them—no offices will be open for interviews or information. Publishers and broadcasters will be pulling out all the stops to try and dig up more than their competitors. I think it would be a good idea to move while they're distracted.

"Now, it's quite possible that they'll try and contact you once you're home," Rob added by way of warning, "but hopefully you'll be able to deal with them one at a time—not en masse."

"D'you have a lawyer?" Katy asked.

"No," Megan admitted, "but I can get one if I have to. One of the counselors in our bishopric is a lawyer."

Rob looked pleased. "Good."

***

Eating breakfast suddenly sped up. Katy called the airline and booked Megan and Fran on a direct flight out of Boston and into Salt Lake City. Megan telephoned her parents to inform them of their intended arrival, and arranged to meet them at the airport. Her parents reported that the mob of reporters who had dogged their neighborhood for forty-eight hours had dispersed, with an occasional appearance by a local broadcast station newsman being the only current threat.

Fran and Megan repacked their cases. Thankfully this was not the ordeal for Fran that it had been in Anglesey, due largely to the fact that she'd had less than two days to disperse her belongings, and because she'd been sharing a room with Megan, who prevented her from wreaking too much chaos.

While the two women organized their bags, Rob called Joe and let him in on their plans. So, when Megan and Fran arrived at the airport less than two hours later, Joe was there to meet them. He, Rob, and Katy walked with them to the terminal and sat down to wait for the call to board the aircraft.

Megan found that she was unwilling to look anyone in the eye at the airport. She kept her face slightly lowered, and relied on her companions to block her from the view of the many passersby. Television monitors, suspended from the terminal ceiling, broadcast CNN updates on the investigation of the senator's private life. Megan's heart went out to his family. Not only were they dealing with a crushing blow to their unity and pride, but they also had to deal with all the unwanted attention directed their way. It was a double blow, and Megan had new empathy for what they were going through.

Fran and Katy chatted pleasantly as they waited. Rob joined in their conversation intermittently, but Joe and Megan said very little. They sat next to each other. Joe had his arm around the back of Megan's chair. She could feel his nearness, and it was all she could think about. As much as she wanted to go home and resume her normal activities, she did not want to leave Joe—especially now. His first missionary discussion was scheduled for that evening. She glanced at the clock on the wall beside the check-in desk. Anytime now they would begin boarding the aircraft.

"You will call and let me know how it goes tonight, won't you?" Megan broke the silence.

"Yes," he said.

He ran his fingers up and down her neck, sending a tremor coursing through her small frame. She closed her eyes, and for a few short seconds blocked out the world around her. But not for long. A noisy crackle from the PA system announced the first stages of the boarding of her flight, and the magical moment was gone. A tear escaped from beneath Megan's closed eyelids. She brushed it away and opened her eyes in time to see the emotion buried deep within Joe's dark eyes mirroring the torment she was experiencing.

Rob, Katy, and Fran were on their feet. Joe and Megan followed suit. Joe handed Megan her bag, carefully placing it over her right shoulder.

"Take care of your arm," he said.

Megan nodded, unable to trust her voice. Then he groaned and pulled her close, kissing her long and hard.

"Don't give up on me Megan! Rob and I are often sent out on assignment without much notice, for who knows how long, but I'll try to let you know before I go. Keep in touch, okay?"

"Okay," Megan whispered, tears running freely down her cheeks. "I'll be praying for you."

"I'll pray too," he said, and brought a smile to Megan's lips. Already, Joe had come a long way.

She turned and hugged Rob and then Katy, and with well-wishes ringing in her ears, she followed Fran over to the stewardess who was systematically gathering boarding passes. She looked back just once before entering the final walkway. The Jenkinses were waving, and Joe stood beside them. He smiled at her, and raised a hand in farewell salute. She returned the gesture, but was sure that her sorrow must have shown in her eyes.

Megan relied on Fran to find their assigned seats. Her eyes were too blurry. Mechanically, she stowed her bag beneath the seat in front of her and clicked the seat belt into place. Fran leaned over and touched her hand.

"You alright?" she asked.

Megan took a deep breath. "I will be, but it might take me a while."

Fran smiled and patted Megan's hand. "You know, he's wormed his way up to an 'A minus' in my book."

Megan couldn't help it. She gave a small laugh. "Only an 'A minus'?"

"Yes. He's an all-around good guy in an incredibly good body, but he hasn't finished his final project yet," Fran said with complete confidence.

"Oh, really?" Megan said, amusement and curiosity vying for control. "And what project is that exactly?"

"The missionary discussions," Fran said succinctly, then turned to her friend with an encouraging smile. "But I have this feeling that Joe Marks isn't going to stop until he has a straight 'A.' "

Megan's returning smile was a little less confident than Fran's had been. "I hope so. I really hope so," she said.

CHAPTER 18

Six weeks later Megan was back at school. She was adjusting to a new schedule and a new group of students. Her adventure in Wales and Boston seemed another world away, and it would have been easy for her to dismiss it all as a dream, had she not lived with the dull heartache of missing Joe ever since then.

Fran's and her arrival in Salt Lake City had been blissfully uneventful, and they had enjoyed a happy reunion with Megan's parents. The two women had returned to Jackson Hole the next day to find all well at their respective homes. Megan had spoken with Brother Moss, the first counselor in her bishopric, and he had been more than willing to help out with any legal difficulties, should they arise. She had already been approached by half a dozen representatives of various branches of the media, but had refused to speak with any of them, and they had backed off, at least temporarily, because Richard Garrett's court case was pending.

Joe had called frequently. He shared some of his experiences with the missionaries with her, but was not completely forthcoming with regard to his feelings, and Megan did not feel that it was her place to press him. They talked late into the night each time he called, and Megan had never felt closer to anyone. Katy had also been in touch, and gave Megan the benefit of her insights, telling her that Joe seemed to be responding well to the discussions. This revelation only made her separation from Joe even harder to bear.

Two weeks had passed since Megan had last heard from him. He had called to tell her that he and Rob were being sent out on assignment again. He was not at liberty to tell her where they were going, other than the fact that it was out of the country. Neither did she know when he would return. She just knew that her feeling of emptiness was more acute without regular contact with him, and that her prayers for his safety were even more fervent than they'd been before.

Megan missed Fran too. They saw each other every Sunday, and occasionally got together on a weeknight, but Fran was not part of her daily activity as she had been in the past. She was making the most of her sabbatical leave and was spending every minute painting. Many of the sights they had shared in Britain had come to life on Fran's canvas already, and Megan delighted in revisiting the British Isles through Fran's artwork.

So it came as a complete surprise to Megan to enter her classroom early on the second Friday of the new term and find Fran there. A few students were already walking the halls of the school, but as yet none had found their way into Megan's classroom.

"Fran, what are you doing here?" Megan asked, dropping a pile of textbooks that she had been carrying onto the desk.

"I'm your substitute for the day," she said.

"What are you talking about?" Megan's confusion was obvious, and Fran grinned at her, taking impish delight in her friend's discomfort.

"Well," Fran said with deliberation, "last night I had a phone call from a most officious FBI agent. He said he needed to spend time with you and would be arriving in Jackson Hole on Friday morning. I was to take care of getting a substitute teacher for you . . ."

Megan's knuckles whitened as her grip on the desk increased. "Joe . . . was it Joe?" she interrupted.

"How many officious FBI agents do you know?" Fran asked with a smile, and then as she saw Megan's expression, she relented. "He's waiting for you in the staff room."

With shaking hands Megan reached for her class planner, but Fran's hand found it first, and pushed it out of her reach. "Don't waste time going over class material with me. Your students are in for a day of art history. Now go! He's waited long enough—you both have!"

In a complete daze, Megan stumbled out of her classroom and began walking toward the staff room. Automatically she smoothed down her long denim skirt, and was glad that she had chosen to wear her favorite white shirt. She paused in front of one of the large windows that looked out over the track at the back of the school. The angle of the sun allowed her to view her own reflection in the glass pane. She ran her fingers through her hair, trying unsuccessfully to tame a willful curl back behind her ear. She gave up, and began walking more quickly, her anticipation mounting with every footstep, until she thought she must be radiating enough nervous energy to power the school.

Trying to appear normal, she purposely slowed her footsteps as the halls began to fill with students hurrying to classes and lockers. She greeted a few by name, and was amazed that not one of them seemed to notice her agitation. Bolstered by this unconscious praise of her acting ability, Megan paused only slightly when she reached the staff room door. She grasped the doorknob, turned it, opened the door, stepped in, and closed it immediately behind her, leaning back against it as she faced the almost-empty room.

He was the only one there, and he turned to face the door as she entered. For a split second Megan saw the same nervousness in his eyes that she was experiencing, but when he took a step toward her, Megan's hesitations fled. She ran into his open arms and felt as though she were going home.

It was several minutes before any words were necessary between them, but eventually Megan voiced the questions she'd harbored since Fran had made her startling appearance in Megan's classroom.

"When did you get back from assignment? What are you doing here?"

"We flew in yesterday. I went home long enough to do some laundry and call Fran, then headed out again. I . . ." he paused, a slow smile forming on his lips, "I came to issue you a formal invitation."

Megan looked up at him with surprise. "An invitation? To what?"

"To my baptism—next week."

His broad smile was now complete, but all Megan could do was stare at him. She tried to swallow the lump that had instantly formed in her throat, to no avail.

"You're really getting baptized?" she whispered.

"A week from Sunday at three o'clock. Will you come?"

"Yes," Megan sobbed, and threw her arms around his neck.

"Hey," he said, stroking her hair with his hand, "I didn't come all this way to make you cry. I thought you'd be happy."

Megan raised her head. "I've never been more happy in my life," she said brokenly as the tears ran freely down her face.

"Well, you sure have a funny way of showing it," Joe said with a smile.

Megan managed a laugh, then she leaned forward and kissed him. His arms tightened around her, and when they drew apart he said, a little unevenly, "Now that was more the response I was looking for!"

She led him over to a couple of plastic chairs in the corner of the room and indicated that he should sit. "Tell me about it. About the missionary discussions and how you made this decision," she said as she sat down beside him.

"I'm not sure that I want to admit what a blockhead I was," Joe said. "It took those poor missionaries three weeks to get through the first discussion. Every time they'd bring up a new point of doctrine, I'd start questioning and arguing around the issues.

"Finally Katy laid into me. She told me to keep my mouth shut until the missionaries had finished their discussion, and save my questions until the end."

"I love Katy," Megan said with a smile.

"Well, she's a hard one to go against," Joe admitted, "so I ended up listening to the missionaries for a change—really listening, and feeling . . . feeling in a way that I'd never done before.

"Then Rob and I were sent out again. I had a couple of long flights and a lot of waiting-around time, so I read. I read the Book of Mormon and I prayed." He reached for Megan's hand and grasped it tightly. "I really prayed, Megan—and for the first time ever, I felt something. I can't describe it exactly, but it was undeniable."

He sighed. "I know I've got a lot of catching up to do, but I think I'm finally headed in the right direction."

A sudden sound at the door diverted their attention, and they both rose to their feet as a man entered.

"Good morning, Mike," Megan greeted the man.

"Oh, hello Megan," he replied, looking over at Joe with curiosity.

Megan made the obligatory introductions. "Mike, this is Joe Marks, a friend from Boston. Joe, this is Mike Parkinson, one of our math teachers."

The two men shook hands, and after passing a few pleasantries, Mike Parkinson headed for the coffee machine, and Megan headed for the door, with Joe close behind her.

"Let's go," she said, when the door had closed behind them. "I don't want to risk another interruption."

A young girl passed by on the other side of the hall, and Megan recognized her as a former student.

"Cassie, would you take a note to Miss Brown for me?" she called over to her. "She's teaching in my classroom right now."

"Sure, Miss Harmer," the girl said, and approached the couple.

She stood patiently aside as Megan dug a small scrap of paper and a pen out of her purse. Joe watched with interest as Megan penned the few words:

Our summer student has earned an "A". Come over this evening.

Megan

She folded the note in two and handed it to Cassie, who promptly took off in the direction of Megan's classroom. Megan turned around to find Joe looking down at her, eyebrow raised, and a look of amusement on his face.

"What was that all about?"

Megan felt herself color, but she did not flinch. "I think I just admitted my feelings about you, in typical teacher fashion."

At her words, the amusement left Joe's dark eyes, to be replaced by another, deeper emotion. He took her hand and began propelling her toward the main doors.

"Where are we going?" Megan gasped, struggling to keep up with him.

"I don't know. Anywhere, as long as it's out of the school halls.

"But why?"

They had reached the parking lot, and a strip of tall pine trees stood between them and the building they had just exited.

"Because," Joe said, drawing Megan toward him, "I am about to tell the Jackson Hole High School history teacher that I love her, and when I've done that, I'm going to kiss her soundly—and since she's reluctant to be the subject of media attention, I'm going to spare her from being tomorrow's headline in the student newspaper.

"Oh, Joe . . ." she said, but it was the last thing she said for a very long time.

About the Author

Siân Ann Bessey was born in Cambridge, England, to Noel and Patricia Owen. After her father completed his doctoral work there, the family returned to their Welsh homeland. Siân grew up among the austere mountains and verdant hills of North Wales. At the age of ten she joined the Church along with her entire family. Siân left Wales to attend Brigham Young University and graduated with a bachelor's degree in communications.

She is the author of the novel *Forgotten Notes,* and several articles that have appeared in the *New Era, Ensign,* and *Liahona* magazines. Siân and her husband, Kent, are the parents of five children. They reside in Rexburg, Idaho.

Siân enjoys hearing from her readers. You may write to her c/o Covenant Communications Inc., P.O. Box 416, American Fork, Utah, 84003-0416.

Siân is the Welsh form of Jane, and is pronounced "Shawn."

RELENTLESS

A scream turned the girl's head. Two shots rang out in rapid succession. They were close, very loud, and extremely frightening. What she saw through the small group of pines edging the little roadside park where she had eaten her lunch made the eighteen-year-old girl's legs go weak. Everything seemed to slow down as she watched. One body was already on the ground, another crumpling from the shotgun blast.

The killer must have seen her move, or else he simply sensed her presence only a couple of hundred feet from where he had just committed the most heinous act known to man. That what she had seen was murder was somehow clear to her mind. She'd seen the two victims earlier. They were unfriendly and hadn't answered when she'd spoken to them as she walked by their van. Their greasy long hair, filthy clothes, and the flowers in their hair had drawn her attention. It was like they were from another age: the sixties look. But they hadn't deserved what had just happened to them. They hadn't been hurting anyone, just eating a cold lunch.

The second body hit the ground and lay still. The gunman, a young man of maybe twenty-one or twenty-two, was looking in her direction. His shotgun was swinging toward her! Panic clutched her chest. He meant for her to be next! She had started to turn when the weapon discharged again. Pain seared her cheek. She screamed and ran, the little grove of trees providing protection from the next blast of the deadly weapon.

The man who meant to take her life shouted, his voice full of laughter. "Run girl, run!" he called after her as her legs gained strength and propelled her toward her waiting Toyota. "You can't run fast enough to get away from me!" he threatened.

He was running. His footsteps pounded in her ears. She reached her car and grabbed for the door. Her purse lay on the seat where she'd left it when she first heard the argument across the park—the one that had caused her so foolishly to have a look. She grabbed the purse and rustled desperately through it in search of her keys, praying that she would find them in time. Her fingers felt the familiar softness of her key chain and she jerked it out, jabbing the key at the ignition.

As the engine turned over and she shoved the shifting lever into drive, she saw him approaching her, running hard. Expecting at any moment to hear another shot, or worse yet, to feel it, she gunned the engine and left the park in a spray of gravel. As her spinning tires hit the pavement and propelled her onto the highway, she heard him shout, "You can't ever run far enough to get away from me!"

She was alone on a trip to meet her grandparents, just outside of Denver. The girl had been in no hurry and had chosen a meandering but scenic route from her home in rural northeastern Utah. Her widowed mother had fussed about her—an attractive young lady—going alone, but she was an independent girl and confident of her ability to drive and take care of herself.

How she wished now for the comfort of her mother's arms!

She was speeding.

But she had to. She had seen that the killer had an old green pickup truck. Surely he would be coming after her. She was the only witness to his terrible deed. She had read books, seen movies, heard stories of things like this. Killers did not like witnesses.

His words rang in her head. "Run girl, run!" he had shouted in a voice full of hysterical laughter. And that was exactly what she was doing, as fast as her little Toyota would carry her from Pineview, Colorado. A small town in the Colorado Rockies, it had seemed like such a peaceful place as she had driven through. She had even stopped there and bought a few things to eat at the only convenience store in town. It was called the Quick Stop, and a man who looked like he was in his mid-sixties had waited on her. Sam, she had heard another customer call him. It had been busy in the little store, and he had scarcely looked at her as he rang up her purchases and handed her some change. Only as she turned to leave did he finally smile and say, "Have a nice day, young lady."

She'd smiled back. She liked the clean little store. It had been almost cozy.

Now she wanted nothing but to flee, to quickly get as far away as she could. She checked the mirror several times, and finally, after several minutes, she slowed down. The green pickup had never appeared. She hoped it never would. But she kept driving. Not for an hour or more did she even think about stopping. And then she only did so because a little warning light came on in her dash, cautioning that her gasoline tank was nearly empty.

As the gas pumped into her starving tank in another town, not as small, not as scenic, but a reasonable distance from Pineview, she tried to think rationally about her situation. The man with the shotgun had meant to kill her. Of that there was no doubt. She, a good girl, a Mormon girl who *usually* made the right choices in her life, had been the target of his rage. But she was away now. She could report what she saw and maybe the man would be caught.

And maybe he wouldn't!

In which case, she would always be in danger. He had seen her. He had seen her car. He might even have read her license plate number. He could learn who she was. He could hunt her down. He could . . .

"Hi, looks like it's full, miss," a friendly man with a cowboy hat and boots said with a chuckle. "Hey, are you okay? What's that on your cheek?"

She had been so terrified that she hadn't even remembered the spot on her cheek where she'd felt the searing pain as the killer's shotgun had blasted at her. She touched the spot just below her eye. It burned like fire.

"Looks like you've been burned or something," he said as he stepped toward her for a closer look.

"It's nothing," she said quickly as she grabbed for the nozzle.

"Looks bad," he cautioned. "I'd get some ointment on it."

"Sure, thanks," she mumbled as he turned away.

Conscious now of the pain on her cheek, and even more conscious of how it must look, she hurriedly paid for her gas and then entered the ladies' room. Examining her face in the mirror, she began to tremble as she realized how close she'd come to death. The mark on her cheek was small and very red, but it had only burned her. It wasn't serious, although she was sure it needed something on it.

Her trembling increased as the horrible scene replayed itself in her mind. Once more, she wondered if she should report it. But she was afraid to, and even as her conscience began to bother her a bitter memory interfered. The two hippie types deserved to have their killer caught. And she could identify him. But if he was caught, and if she had to testify . . .

The memory swam through her mind, and tears stung her eyes. Several years before, in junior high, she'd been a witness to a crime. Nothing like this today, but still a crime. She'd seen a young man steal a wallet from a locker. She had done the right thing and turned him in.

And suffered the consequences.

She was taunted, had threats painted on her locker door, even had her own purse taken. Oh, it was not that serious. No one had actually hurt her, and the young man had eventually been expelled. But it had been the cause of serious reflection, and she had resolved never to interfere again.

But this wasn't the same. It was not petty theft. It was murder!

And she could be the next victim.

She broke out in a sweat as she searched her heart for a way out of this dilemma. Finally, as she leaned upon the sink in the rest room, feeling very faint, a solution came to her. She could report what she had seen, but do it without revealing her identity to the authorities. She washed her face with cold water, then left the rest room. The more she thought about her idea, the better it seemed. She could remain unknown to the killer and yet help the police in bringing that horrible man to justice.

Resolved, she went to the pay phone she had seen earlier beside the station. Still trembling, she dialed 911. When a voice came on asking the nature of her emergency, she simply said, "I need to report a murder in Pineview."

The voice on the other end of the line was all business as it answered, "There has already been one reported. What exactly do you have to tell us?"

It occurred to the young lady that she was probably being taped and that they might be able to trace where she was calling from. She had to hurry. "I saw it," she said.

"Just a moment, I'll have an officer meet you. What is your location?"

"No!" she cried in alarm. "I can't let anyone know who I am. He'll kill me if he finds out."

"Now calm down," she was instructed. "It will be easier if you talk to an officer."

"Only on the phone," she insisted. "And not on this one. Give me the number of an officer and I'll call him," she said as her brain began functioning in overdrive.

"It would be—"

"Now, or I'll hang up," she insisted.

"Don't do that. Someone will talk to you. Just hold on."

Panicked, the young woman cut the connection. As she left town, she passed a speeding patrol car. She was positive it had been heading for the pay phone she'd called from. Later, in still another town, she went to another pay phone, but this time she did not dial 911. Instead she dialed the number listed in the telephone directory for the sheriff's department. Without stating her real business, she asked for the number of an officer in Pineview, any officer. It turned out that Pineview was in a different county, but they gave her the number of the sheriff's office near there. She dialed and repeated her request.

"That would be Sergeant Mike O'Connor, but he's not available right now. There's been a murder and—"

"I know," she cut in. "I saw it happen. But I'll only talk to one person."

"Just a moment," the dispatcher said, and her call was put on hold.

She hung up again, waited five minutes and called back. "He'll take your call," the dispatcher told her this time, and she was given the number of a cell phone.

"This is Sergeant O'Connor," the phone was answered, "to whom am I speaking?"

"I can't say," she said through trembling lips. "But I saw the man who killed those two hippies."

"Who was it?" the sergeant asked quickly, as if afraid she'd hang up. She was getting a reputation it seemed.

"I don't know, but he had short brown hair and was driving an old green pickup." She then repeated the license number which she had memorized.

"Thank you, young lady," the voice on the cell phone said. "You and I need to get together. This is a serious matter, and you might be of a lot more help."

"I know how serious it is. He shot at me too," she said as desperation and fear drove her to get this over very quickly.

"Are you—" he began

"He just nicked my face. But he said he'd hunt me down."

"Okay, okay, calm down. Tell me more. What did he look like? How old was he?" the officer asked. "And what time was it?"

She answered his questions, and within five minutes she was off the phone and on her way to her grandparents' house. She'd done all she could, she told herself. Now it was up to the police. They would never know who she was, and she would never mention it again—not to anyone. She had to live with the fear, maybe for the rest of her life, but her identity in connection with what she'd seen must forever remain a secret.

And would haunt her for years to come.